WUNDOR

A CELESTIAL SPHERES EPISTOLARY NOVEL

LISA BORNE GRAVES

AUTHORS 4 AUTHORS PUBLISHING
Marysville, WA, USA

Published by Authors 4 Authors Publishing
1214 6th St
Marysville, WA 98270
www.authors4authorspublishing.com

LCCN: 2023939141

E-book ISBN: 978-1-64477-172-3
Paperback ISBN: 978-1-64477-173-0
Audiobook ISBN: 978-1-64477-174-7

Edited by Rebecca Mikkelson
Copyedited by Brandi Spencer

Cover design ©2023 Practically Perfect Covers. All rights reserved.
Interior design by Brandi Spencer
Scene break icon by Lisa Borne Graves

Authors 4 Authors Publishing branding is set in Bavire. Titles and headers are set in Mr Darcy. Mary's handwriting set in Vintage Handmade. Henry's handwriting set in Jim Nightshade. Emily's handwriting set in Gothic Ultra. Mary's handwriting set in Vintage Handmade. Cobalt's handwriting is set in Alister. Newpaper articles set in UglyQua. *Courtly Cuckolds & Cads* title set in Relic Island. All other text is set in Garamond.

~~Joan~~

Wunder

LISA BORNE GRAVES

AUTHORS 4 AUTHORS CONTENT RATING

This title has been rated 17+, for older teens and adults, and contains:

- Brief sex
- Moderate negative alcohol use
- Moderate language
- Childbirth death
- Parent death

Please, keep the following in mind when using our rating system:

1. A content rating is not a measure of quality.

Great stories can be found for every audience. One book with many content warnings and another with none at all may be of equal depth and sophistication. Our ratings can work both ways: to avoid content or to find it.

2. Ratings are merely a tool.

For our young adult (YA) and children's titles, age ratings are generalized suggestions. For parents, our descriptive ratings can help you make informed decisions, but at the end of the day, only you know what kinds of content are appropriate for your individual child. This is why we provide details in addition to the general age rating.

For more information on our rating system, please, visit our Content Guide at: www.authors4authorspublishing.com/books/ratings

DEDICATION

To my readers, young or young at heart, continue to
always learn about, believe in, and love yourself.

That's the real magic.

Works by Lisa Borne Graves

Celestial Spheres

Fyr
Draca
Bladesung

Wundor
Lyft (February 2025)

The Immortal Transcripts

Quiver
Fever
Shudder
Glimmer (February 2024)

Stand-Alone Titles

Apidae
"Dare"

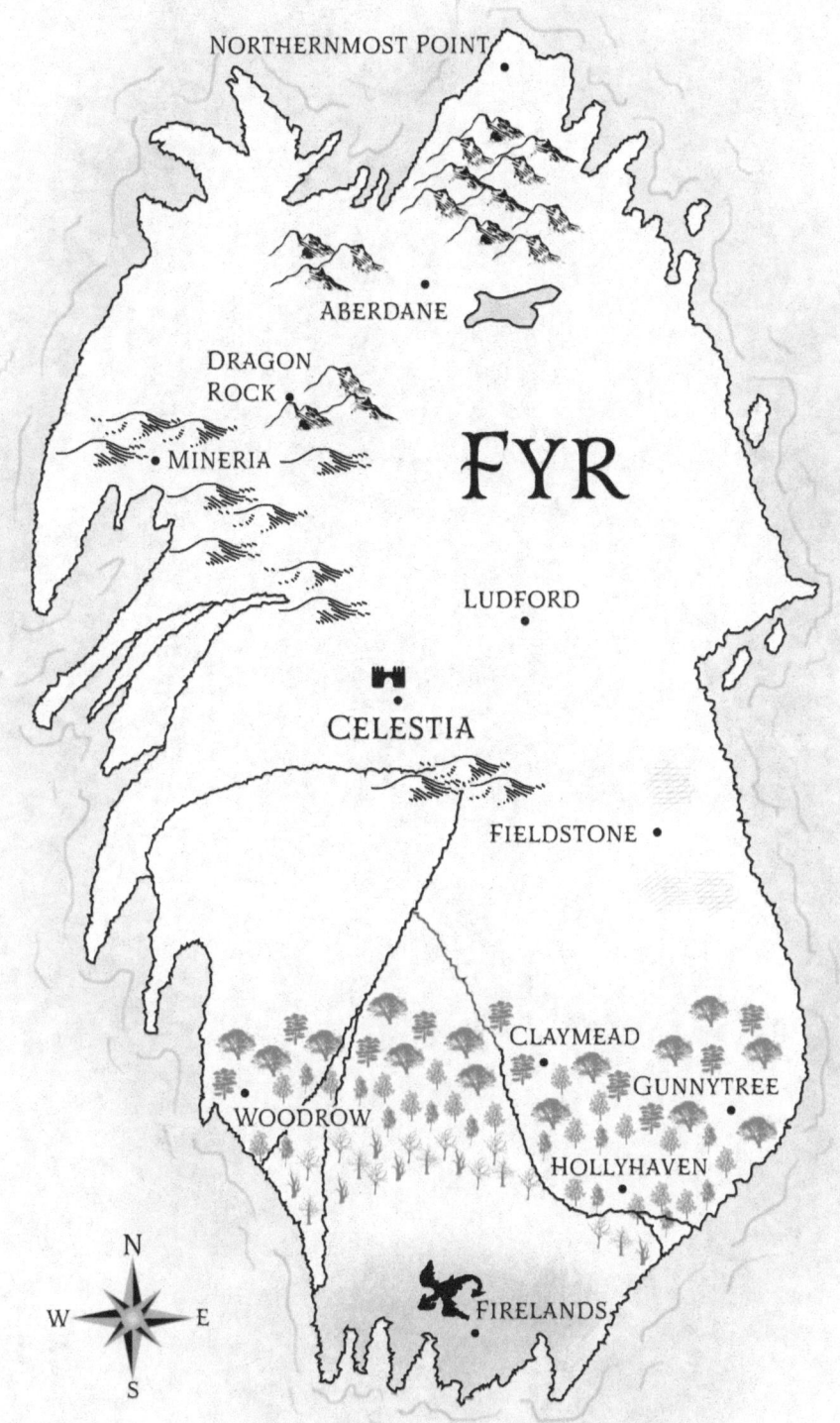

TABLE OF CONTENTS

September

Dear journal,

Hmm, maybe I should give you a name. "Journal" sounds so insincere when I'm supposed to reveal to you the inner workings of my soul. Or something of that nature. I'm not sure how to go about all this journal-writing business, but Alex—my brother—gave you to me as a birthday gift. I turned thirteen today, and Alex told me, "All ladies write in journals."

His calling me a lady made me feel radiant, to be honest. Only my brother has ever given me the benefit of the doubt that I am way more of an adult than a child. When I asked him if he had a journal, he laughed at me. Then, I didn't want to write in you after that, but Alex always reads my moods well. He explained they're great places for visions to be written down and secrets to be kept, since telling friends could be dangerous for me. Ladies of the court do tend to gossip, so he was right, but I wasn't dumb enough to tell anyone my secrets.

Poor Alex. He's naïve if he thinks I have any friends to share secrets with. Not being "out" in society is limiting for girls, but boys don't suffer that fate—nor would Alex, despite his gender. He is the heir to the throne of Fyr.

In the end, I thought to write in you and see if it is worthwhile. This is a trial, so don't get excited, Journal. I'm not sure if this will last. I really don't know what to say. I wrote at the top who am I—the only princess in the entire sphere of Fyr; My brother, Alex, is the only prince. In case you want to know what it feels like, it puts you on this pedestal that you can never live up to while separating you from everyone else. Alone, with too many expectations weighing you down.

What a dismal first entry. I apologize, but I think Alex knows—or maybe feels the same—and he's giving me a place to vent my woes. Hopefully, I'll have many good things to record and look back on with happiness. Yeah, I'm not sure I believe my false optimism either, Journal. We shall see.

Dear Joan the journal,

There. I've given you a name. This feels better because I am about to get personal today.

Alex said to write visions down to help me cope with them. I've had one in the flames that greatly troubles me. It was of Stephen Cobalt and me. I've had them before about him, but this was the first one of us actually kissing. We looked older, and my boobs were much bigger—thank the god and goddess for that—and oh, I don't know how to feel about it right now.

I don't think of boys like that—especially Cobalt—which is one of the many reasons I don't have friends and don't get along with the court girls. All they want to do is talk about lords, all day long, like they have no interest in anything else. Plus, half of them make fun of me, while the other half are so fake and obviously want something from me. I'm pretty sure that "something" is direct access to my brother since he is now of marriageable age.

Fifteen, to me, is way too young, and the way Alex argued with Mother and Father, I don't think he's at all excited about finding his lifemate. I'm never getting married. The flames did show me I'd marry Cobalt, but they are subject to change often based on decisions. Maybe I'll let Cobalt kiss me, but I am not marrying him or any other man.

The idea of being told what to do, to live for a man—never. I am Princess Mary Elizabeth Sapphirian. No one could tell me what to do.

Joan,

I'm starting to understand why ladies write in journals. I just talked to this girl, and everything she said was so cuttingly cruel, but backhandedly veiled where adults wouldn't intercede. It's like a secret language of being brutal, and the parents forget that it had happened to them long ago. Here's what happened. "Lady" Justine Citrine gave me a compliment on my new blue dress, telling me it "makes your stunning Sapphirian eyes more vibrant."

I honestly thought for a moment having a girl two years my senior compliment me meant we could become friends. She is nobility, and her dad is Father's best friend, so it was flattering to have her attention turned away from Alex to compliment me. It was a ladies' luncheon—if you could call them that. Ever since Alex was cursed during infancy, Father lets very few courtiers visit. The Citrines are among the few loyal, but after what Justine did to me, I question that.

I'll hold you no longer in suspense, Joan. After her nice compliment, she turned to the two other girls standing with us and said, "However, blue looks more divine on Prince Alexander. Too bad his good looks didn't extend to all his family."

Insufferable brat! She literally called me the ugly sibling! If my brother is attractive, I don't see it, not even subjectively. He is brooding, sad, and worried all the time. Rarely is he smiling or happy, even when I try to make him laugh. It is the curse. These silly girls see the curse as this dark, forbidding, and dangerous trait and, worse, even see it as attractive. They make him into whatever they want him to be. They don't really know him; only I do.

I'm sad to say, Joan, that I did not combat Justine and her horde of friends. I couldn't come up with quips to put them in their place in that pleasant way my mother is able to pull off with equally false statements of insincerity. I cannot be fake, and yet I could not be bold enough to put them in their place.

Instead, I excused myself. They laughed at me, while I fled from the room, crying. I should've transported out of there—to remind them of my power—but I was too upset to think straight. I ran right into someone, my tears blinding my path. I looked up to see my cousin Henry.

"What is this?" he chastised me with a concerned tone.

Lately married, I was surprised to see him back at the castle. Being six years my elder, we have never known each other well. Being a male, he gets to do all men's things that are fun that I'm not allowed to do like learning swordplay. It really sucks being a girl, Joan. I should've made you a boy, but that would be weird to share my thoughts with one of them.

Henry calmed me down and led me outside. We hiked to the pond, while I regaled him with what had happened.

He touched my shoulder gently. "Women fight with tongues sharper than men's knives. Some of the ladies of the court are more devious than the most conniving man. They are forced to be more secretive in their attacks. Ladies wear masks, see? They are one person among those they trust, and they're sweet and false to others."

"But I don't do that."

"I'm afraid you'll have to learn to, Mary. Otherwise, you'll never survive the court. Think about it. If you show them who you really are and they attack you, it leads to tears and insecurity. If you present a persona to them and they attack, it doesn't cut deep. You've duped them."

"I don't know how to create a fake me."

3

"Not a fake you, just one that wears a shield of confidence, authority, aloofness. Tell you what. I'll bring Lady Emily to see you. She is gifted at playing roles." He lowered his voice. "She is extremely intelligent, educated far more than even us under the best tutors. She understands politics enough to rule this country. Among the court, she is demure and weak, but behind that façade, she is an extraordinarily crafty, clever, and confident woman."

Henry sounded so in love, which is good, being married to her and all, unlike Mother and Father. My parents are sweet at times, but never speak of each other like this nor show much affection. This is another reason I don't want to marry and why I worry about my brother being forced to marry one of these nasty girls. Each of us deserves to love our lifemate or, at a minimum, respect them.

I hope Lady Emily can at least teach me how to deal with these girls. I hate them! I'll never have a real friend like Alex has in Cobalt. Girls are the worst!

A very uneventful day, but Mother not only came to my room as she always does at night, but she also forced Alex to join. Mother used to sneak back into the nursery when we were young to kiss, hug, and read stories to us. It made me realize I was loved. Father didn't permit an ounce of affection publicly, but even in the palace, alone, he'd chastise us for any abundant show of emotion in front of servants. To him, feelings are weaknesses to be used to exploit and usurp you. What does that say about me, Joan, when all I do is feel everything and burn through emotions so acutely?

Mother forced Alex into the room by prodding his back. He rolled his eyes and made a gruff noise, but he winked at me. He was telling me Mother needed this more than we did, yet I knew I needed it too. Alex wasn't angry; he just felt too grown up for mother's storytelling and affection.

Mother kissed my cheeks and called me her princess. Then she dared to do it to Alex, calling him her prince. And he let her! I withheld my laughter since neither of them would appreciate it.

Alex sighed and took a seat. "Mother, these games need to come to an end."

When Alex had moved into his quarters at eight, she still snuck in to see us, sneaking Alex into my quarters to continue the tradition. When we became too old for these "games," as Alex called them, it gave way to just her saying goodnight and giving us hugs. It had been almost a year since Alex joined her in my quarters to say goodnight, and her visits were few and far between as if she sensed I was much too old to be babied.

"Games?" she said. "These are not games, Alex. Love is the most important thing in the world. Both of you listen to me right now. Love is the strongest magic, the best magic to combat anything. It is pure, created of your soul, and not conjurable. Your hearts need to be open."

Alex rolled his eyes at her. I looked away because he was about to make me burst into a fit of giggles that would anger Mother—or worse, upset her.

"One day—hopefully soon—you will fall in love, Alex, and you'll know exactly what I'm talking about."

I highly doubted that, and so did he from his dismissive expression. He didn't dare argue with Mother, though. She was too gentle and sweet. If he was smart, he'd take advantage of that, but he was a big softie like Mother. He took pains to hide it from everyone, Father especially.

"You never outgrow the need for love," Mother chastised him. "It simply evolves."

"I'll take your word for it," Alex said.

"Alex." Mother sighed, taking his hand. "I sure hope you fall in love and not end up in a marriage of convenience. Just start thinking about it, okay?"

Alex didn't answer, staring at the floor. Poor Alex, as the heir to the throne, he'd have to marry soon. How could they make him? He still looks way more like a boy than a man, and I know firsthand what he thinks about the "ladies" of the court. His words to me in private about them are not polite enough to grace these pages, Joan.

"I like these meetings." I changed the subject to save him—well, and because Mother would move on to me next. I'm supposed to be learning to be a lady rather than running around in fields and climbing dracaberry trees. There are way more important things in life than etiquette. Mother would disagree, of course.

Alex didn't stay long. I think discussing marriage ruined his night. I don't blame him.

Mother and I talked for a while until she realized how late it was and left. It was a much-needed night. These moments were sacred and secret. They were everything.

October

Joan,

I swore I'd never fall in love or get married, but the craziest thing just happened. I was climbing in the orchard, having lots of trouble in my dreadful slippers. I usually climb barefoot, but Mother caught me and sent me back to my quarters for "proper attire." The "walking" shoes had poor grip, so of course, I slipped trying to climb a tree. Luckily, I caught myself on one of the branches. I tried pulling myself up, but the dress was so restrictive over my shoulders, and my arms were too weak for me to pull myself back up. Looking down, I gauged a fall from that height would turn or break an ankle—or two.

A whistle blew behind me, but I couldn't turn around to see who was there.

"I don't see beetles, and I don't see ants, but I definitely see Princess Mary's underpants," Cobalt sang. He could not see up my dress, the liar, but it was not the time for me to argue with him.

"A little help here."

"It's going to cost you."

"Are you serious? I can't hold on much longer." I'd thought he was going to let me get hurt for some silly game.

"I'll catch you for a slice of cake."

"Cake?" I had no idea what he was thinking or why he couldn't simply get cake himself from the kitchens, but my hands were slipping.

"Cook slaps my hands with a wooden spoon when I try to steal it. She never denies you anything."

"I'll get you a cake. Now catch me."

"Okay. Let go."

It was hard to trust Cobalt, but I let go, closing my eyes as I fell. Instantly, two arms caught me. I opened my eyes, finding myself in Cobalt's arms. He immediately put me on my own two feet. His face was much too close to mine, even though he was a head taller than me.

He backed up, those vibrantly blue eyes twinkling. "Better stop climbing trees, Mary. You're almost all grown up now and harder to catch."

At first, I wanted to give him a good punch, thinking he was calling me fat, but then I realized he was seeing me as perhaps a lady and not a little girl. Then my stomach flopped, and I felt like I'd throw up. Is that what love feels like, Joan? An illness?

He walked back inside, whistling. I got him the cake, and then he rushed off late to his training session. He'd regret eating cake before sword fighting. He probably would vomit.

So, I guess I'm in love. All afternoon, all I could do was think about Cobalt and analyze everything he said and what it could mean. Did he love me too? I don't want that, though. He'd marry me and then dictate my life, and I'd have to have a lot of kids. It's infuriating to have your future known before you even know what you want.

I went to the library for some research and was heavily disappointed. Joan, there is no magic or stones with the power to prevent or lessen the effects of love. I'm doomed. Here it is in writing, for the future lovesick, pathetic Mary to read and wish she could've stopped the feeling back when she was thirteen.

Father is absolutely right. Love is a weakness. It has made me lose my mind. I'm inventing excuses to see Cobalt. I brought him cake today, hoping he'd want to spend time with me, but Alex stole him away. In retaliation, I spied on them. They were boring to watch most of the day: passing their secret-coded notes during tutor lessons, sparring in the courtyard, horseback riding, and telling each other stories of some sort that must be funny because they were laughing. I lost them when they raced away. I'm not a very good spy, Joan. Lucy does not help. Now that I'm a lady, I have to have a waiting maid-bodyguard. Lucy lectured me a lot. She is only sixteen, so her matronly scolding about my behavior rubbed me the wrong way. Lucy was annoyed by my "immature" spying attempt, but at least she played along.

I found them again down by the pond. I hid in the bushes as they stripped down to their pantaloons to go swimming. I looked first at Alex, not bold enough to look at Cobalt. Alex is tall and strong but lean; he no longer is a lanky boy with big hands and feet, like a puppy. He is looking more like a man, which is a stark reminder we are growing up. I was afraid of that. Everything is changing and that isn't fair. Was Mother right? Will he find a lifemate soon? Will I like her, or will she be the Justine Citrine type? The thought saddens me. No matter who she is, she'll take my brother away from me in some sense.

I took a deep breath and found the courage to look at Cobalt. Nothing. I didn't go dizzy, and my heart didn't race like these court girls say when they look at men. I didn't swoon at the sight of his bare chest as they professed they do when they see cunning folk men stripped down to the waist on warmer days. I wasn't like other girls, or they were simply copying the older ones who gaggled around Alex all the time.

Cobalt is strong. He is a couple inches shorter than Alex, but he has bigger muscles. He looks manly in comparison to my brother, older too, although he is only by a few months. I'm a bit disappointed. Maybe this isn't love. If I'm supposed to kiss him like my vision showed, I should feel something, shouldn't I? Mother wanted me to marry in a couple of years. How could I if I don't really like anyone like that?

I came out of my hiding spot since they were busy splashing about, mocking each other as men tend to do. Lucy said something, but I ignored her. I was making my way down to the water's edge when Alex noticed me. His smile fell, and his eyes narrowed. Cobalt's eyes went wide, and he ducked his shoulders under the water so only his head could be seen.

"Mary, you shouldn't be here." Alex's tone was quiet but firm, sounding like a softer version of Father when he lectures me about something I did wrong. I wasn't sure why Alex would say that. It was weird because he and I went swimming together often, just weeks ago.

"This is my property too and my pond. I have equal claim on it as you." I crossed my arms, showing him I was not one of his lowly subjects. He would not command me just because he was in line for the throne one spot above me.

"Cobalt's here," Alex stated the obvious, nodding in Cobalt's direction as if I were blind.

Cobalt stared awkwardly at the water, his cheeks pink.

"So?" I scoffed. "It is warm out, and I want to go for a dip." I took my slippers off.

"You can't!" Alex barked at me. He glared as I futilely tried to undo my laces on my back.

I looked to Lucy, and she cringed but came closer to assist me. I was doing something wrong, apparently. David, Alex's equivalent servant to my Lucy, came over to us and spoke some hurried whispers to her.

She let go of my laces. "Your Highness, let us go back and get the right attire. You're a lady now. Ladies cannot swim with gentlemen, not in your undergarments," she whispered to me.

"It's only Alex and Cobalt," I scoffed.

"Mary!" Alex scolded. He reminded me of our father with that dark anger pulsating. I can always tell when the curse tries to rise up in him. His eyes go cold, his face slack; plus, Cobalt's staring at him with concern always tips me off. Cobalt can feel and manipulate others' emotions, so he sensed the massive rage boiling in Alex. My brother was scaring me. Rarely would this darkness be directed at me. He teased, yes, and I could tell I was a tagalong sometimes that he put up with, but never had he ever raised his voice at me like this. "Go back and put proper swimwear on, and we shall let you have the pond to yourself."

How dare he. "Because I'm a girl? This is ridiculous!"

"You're a *lady*, Mary. Ladies can't swim with gentlemen," Alex said.

"Well...well, being a lady is the worst thing ever!" I shouted at him to show him two could play this power game.

Alex was wide-eyed but said nothing more.

I stormed off, Lucy trotting behind me. "Don't you dare lecture me."

"I would never dream of it, Your Highness, but being a child is much easier than being a woman. This will be a hard transition."

"Be quiet, Lucy, unless you can actually help me."

She didn't dare respond.

I expected Mother to come give me a lecture on etiquette. She didn't. Even when I saw Alex at dinner, he acted no differently than usual, said nothing. I expected him to regale my parents with the tale to make me look bad so Father would get off his back. But, no, he took Father's insults, as did I. It was what we had to do.

I never want to admit the thought aloud, but I can tell you, Joan—and not be judged for the thought—but I don't find that my father living a long life is ideal. It's horrid to admit, but my childhood comprised of watching the brute attack and belittle others, doing whatever he wanted, and emotionally hurting Mother all the time. I hate him for that. I hate what he did to Alex, too, and I hate more than anything how he scolds me for being myself. Perhaps Henry was right about the need for a fake persona. I should try it out on Father, act more demure and idiotic. I bet he'd love that, call me a "real" lady.

At the end of the meal, Father invited us back to the king's quarters for a family nightcap. Prior, this was something I had never been privy to, but apparently, I am a lady now.

"Father, before we bring Mary into the fold, could I have one more night with my not-so-little sister? Mary, will you join me in the prince's room? Tomorrow, we'll join Mother and Father as adults. Let us have one more night for you to be a kid, Mary." He didn't give our father time to protest or demand obedience but offered his arm.

I nodded and looped my arm in his. Father's jaw clenched as he stared Alex down, but he snapped out of it when Mother said his name sweetly. I needed to study Alex's and Mother's varying methods of how to control Father more keenly.

He transported us outside the doorway, then extended his hand for me to enter first.

"Women aren't allowed in here," I said, looking around.

It was not an impressive room, but that fit Alex. It was the same size as my princess salon, where I could entertain friends. My salon went unused most of the time because I had no friends, but often I went there to read with the door closed so no one would bother me.

"You're my sister. There are rules about non-married women entering a prince's room; that is all."

"Why?"

"Because people assume princes will be naughty with them." He sighed. "I don't understand why I have to be the one to have this conversation with you; frankly, it is awkward, but it is a duty I'd rather do now than have the worst happen to you."

I had no clue what he was talking about.

"Mary, it is wrong that they put a label on thirteen as when we become a man or woman, but it is tradition. You cannot be around other men in a swimsuit or without being fully covered. You cannot act like a little girl anymore. It is a drastic change, I know."

"But you can?"

"Not really. There are rules, and I know your tutor has been drilling them into your head. Propriety is everything now."

"I don't understand why, though."

"Because men are... Men don't control their...lust as well as women can." He blushed.

I snorted.

"I am not that way, Mary, but other men are. Some prey upon innocent girls. And *the* princess? So many would love to take advantage of that for power...and other reasons."

His face was so red, I could hardly take him seriously. However, the message did come through. My tutor explained the ways of the world, and I understood; if I act improperly, some lord might take advantage and make me with child, where I'd be forced to marry him.

"I understand." I had to stop him before he felt compelled to tell me exactly how babies got into bellies.

He took up my hands. "If I could, Mary, I'd give you two more years. They weren't granted to me either."

"It's just...sometimes I forget Cobalt isn't family. I'll do my best to behave in front of men."

Now I wondered about Cobalt's behavior that day he caught me from the tree. Jokes about my undergarments and telling me I'm grown up? That was breaking rules of propriety too. Instead, I'll watch Alex's behavior around ladies and use it as a guide.

I'm not going to lie, Joan. Being a princess is the worst! How much of my life will be spent hiding who I am and curbing what I want to do? Growing up scares me to death too. Love seems even worse. My brother, though, is the best, not that I'd ever tell him that.

November

Dear Joan,

A light has entered my life. Henry came back with his lifemate, Lady Emily Sapphirian—formerly of the Topaz family. I absolutely love her. She is the most intriguing person I have ever met. She put on this docile demeanor of elegance and refinement among the rest of the party, and then, once we entered the princess salon, she dismissed Henry with a peck on the lips, a look only newly married people give each other, and a flick of her wrist. She had him under her command.

Once he was gone, Lady Emily closed the door, smiled at me, and then slumped onto the couch, asking her bodyguard to get me some firespice whiskey.

"I don't like that stuff."

"You'll learn to." She measured me with her eyes.

"Where is yours?" I asked.

Emily's eyes lit up, and she couldn't help but grin. "Do not say a word, because Henry has not wanted it announced quite yet, but I'm with

11

child. The stones have confirmed, but there is a time when things are delicate in the beginning."

"That's so amazing!" Hang propriety, I hugged her tightly.

She squeezed me back. A baby Sapphirian? It is so exciting. There are hardly any of us Sapphirians left. Henry, Ruby, Alex, and I are the only ones in our generation. A baby would be welcomed news.

"Yes, but tell no one. Just one more month to be sure everything is fine."

I put my hand to my heart. "I swear it."

Emily laughed and gave me a look as if to say I was cute, but immaturely so. "Today is not about me. Henry said you needed me to help you with the court ladies. Your mother will tell you some things, but she is only seeking your good behavior for a fabulous match. I can teach you so much of what mothers will never tell you—most of all, how to deal with those wretched and brutal sycophants."

"They hate me."

Lady Emily gave me a teasing glare. "Some act as though they love me so much that I want to vomit at their fake feet, and not from my with-child sickness. These girls want a path to your brother, to be a queen one day. That's all they care about, and they're likely willing to kill each other for it. Never trust them."

I laughed at that. "I never do."

"Smart girl. The other half, of course, envy you, and if they see your weaknesses, they'll tear you down."

"My weaknesses?"

"Your innocence, gentleness, kindness. You're not a natural leader. Not that we women should be, but we can be. Behind closed doors, a woman can convince a lord of anything—to put it delicately. So, you need to learn strength and knowledge behind closed doors because, one day, you will be in the same place as I am. You will be able to control a man, but he will seek to equally control you. Suitors will also want your brother's ear and a position. Beware of those who care more for him than for you."

This is already happening with the ladies trying to get to Alex, but men would too? Just great. What of love and romance? Then I thought of Cobalt. He already has Alex's ear, so he wouldn't need a reason to use me in this way.

"I'll be direct with you, Mary. Observe me. Learn the subtleties of fighting women with demure words and small actions that others do not notice. Learn to bend a man to your will. With your status, it should be quite easy. Your brother will rule the kingdom one day. You will rule his court...with his lifemate as well, one day. Before that day comes, you could lead it. You could even choose his wife for him through influence."

"I won't find his wife. They'll meet by happenstance."

Her eyes went wide, and she went rigid, her hands clenched. "You've seen it! Who is she?"

I felt a chill. Her husband can see the future like Alex and I, but he has never excelled at firebranding. Still, it felt like she was prying too far, and I was hesitant about why she would want that information. Well, I wouldn't tell her. If I couldn't even share this vision of an unknown woman with my dear brother, why should I tell my cousin's wife, who most likely ran the court now? Then again, making an enemy of Lady Emily sounded worse.

"I just haven't met her yet, but my acquaintance is limited. I don't know her name."

"Of course, you wouldn't." She laughed. "Flames don't speak words, just images."

Interesting, because Alex and I sometimes hear words. Perhaps Henry cannot. I've never asked him. Henry holds the information about his powers closely to his chest, but Alex has told me it is because the power he has is not as great as ours.

Lady Emily smiled, her shining brown eyes full of intelligence and wit. "I shouldn't push anyway. Henry always tells me that these visions change so often. That does remind me that we should remedy the issue of your lack of acquaintance. Why don't you and your mother set up a ladies' picnic or luncheon so we can introduce you to more people, gain you some real friends?"

It was a great idea, but I didn't know what to make of this woman. She is everything I wished I could be one day and only six years older than me.

"Cheers. Take a swig." She held her glass of water up, and I clinked mine with hers.

The drink looked darker than I was used to.

I took a sip and coughed at its harshness. "Ugh!" I put it down. "I'm not a fan."

"Funny that. Henry said you were. Maybe I'm confusing the present with the future. Perhaps you will become a fan of it. Best not drink it again then. You are a bit young to pick up such habits." She winked at me.

I wasn't sure what to make of that comment. All I was sure of was I liked her, but I was kind of in awe of her too.

I had the worst night ever.

Sorry if there are smudges on your pages. I just can't stop crying. I'm inept, idiotic, and spineless. Father banishing the court after Alex was cursed put me at a huge disadvantage, because I don't know how these girls truly operate. Well, I learned how vile they can be today at a "ladies" picnic. How did Alex plaster on his fake face, straight posture, and play his role? It must be exhausting, because I was over it minutes after I entered the great hall, merely to meet my guests for tea before we took a walk into the orchards, where the blankets and baskets of food were being set up. There were too many ladies invited to fit comfortably into my salon. My confidence didn't last long. I had never seen so many ladies at one time, particularly in honor of me.

Mother had decorated the great hall with lace and flowers, cloths over the tables brightening the room with a feminine touch. Mother was so good at these things. I would never live up to her reputation, so hopefully, Alex would marry someone who could run a household well. Or maybe Mother would live a long time. I've seen her old and wrinkled in the flames. At least, I think it was her. Father, I haven't. I'm still torn about that. He isn't a caring man you could get close to, but he *is* my father.

Sorry, Joan, I got side-tracked. Back to the tea.

I was announced and had to walk the room with Mother and Lady Emily Sapphirian. Mother would whisper who we were about to greet, while Henry's wife would whisper "avoid," "okay," or "yes," about each lady and sometimes added gossipy tidbits. I was enjoying myself until we were seated. I noticed Justine was at our table. Just great. I hate her. She is obsessed with my brother, and after she realized from our first meeting that I would not help her snag Alex, she has snubbed me and insulted me whenever she can.

Once we were seated, Lady Emily on one side and some girl—Lady Pearl, I think—on my other, I felt alone despite being at a table for ten. It was Mother's absence. She had to sit with and entertain the other mothers. The room was full of about forty women altogether. It was suddenly intimidating because they were there for me.

"Princess Mary, it is such an honor to be invited to your first luncheon," Justine cooed. I could not ignore the sarcasm or contempt, whatever it was, in her tone, which showed me she was far from genuine.

Her face was plastered into a smile as false as her painted face and vibrantly canary-yellow dyed hair.

The first response that had shot into my head was "Liar," but I couldn't say that. I floundered for a moment. "The honor is all mine," would've been ludicrous. I hated her, and she knew that. "You're welcome," was what officially came out. My tone had been a bit clipped, and a couple girls dropped their mouths in shock. Great.

"Yes, welcome, Lady Justine. You are all welcome," Lady Emily said graciously with that twinkle in her eyes, smoothing out my statement, making it mean I was literally welcoming them.

Everyone started chatting as if my slight on Justine had never happened, except Justine. Her jaw was tight, and her eyes were full of rage, but she kept herself in line. For only a moment. "Is this your luncheon then, Lady Sapphirian? I had believed the princess had invited me."

"Princess Mary is one of my newest but best friends, and we are cousins—family. I might be presumptuous, but a tiny piece of this luncheon is mine as well, but we really are here celebrating my cousin joining us ladies in society." Emily was good! I could never spin the words she could, but my mind was taking notes.

There was a shift in tone at the table. Ladies started to ask me questions and make conversation in kind and neutral tones. They were giving me a chance. Lady Emily's influence saved me. And as the conversation continued, Justine and her two friends who flanked her became increasingly sullen.

Finally, the question I had expected came from Lady Opal: "Will your brother be stopping in?"

"No, Alex is busy," I replied.

The lady in question kept her smile plastered on her face, but her eyes showed her disappointment. "A shame, but it is still great to be in the palace." She seemed genuine, but she still was after Alex. All these girls were.

"Why would the future king have time for his baby sister?" Justine scoffed. "He has way more important things to do, I'm sure."

It hit me hard, even though it was a lie. "Baby?" I challenged.

Emily gripped my hand under the table and squeezed it gently. She was telling me to back down.

How could I? "You know nothing of my brother or me."

"I simply call it as I see it. He never dotes upon you as my brothers spoil me."

Because Alex did things in private! But saying how gentle and caring Alex was would've made half these girls swoon and the other half—the Justines of the world—would've learned my brother was vulnerable. A future king could not be seen that way. There was no right answer to this. I was amazed by how crafty Justine was. She was a force to be reckoned with. I was no match for this. My lack of response opened more room for attack, but I was frozen, unable to use my fiery temper to defend myself or Alex. I doubted my magic would've worked at that moment if I'd wanted it to.

"Plus, no offense, Princess Mary, I don't see a woman across from me." She let her eyes traverse to my bosom—or lack thereof. Others' eyes followed her gaze.

My eyes stung, and my ears burned. I had to hold it together.

"I admit, 'baby' was cruel. Please forgive me."

What was she about? Why say one thing and then take it back?

"I see a girl. It's okay, I'm sure you'll develop one day. After all, I am older than you." Justine's hands swept across her chest. It was only impressive because her too-tight corset pressed them up so high, almost nothing was hidden, and there probably was stuffing underneath too. It was a desperate attempt to make her chest look much fuller than it was.

There was a long pause, ladies all looking at each other, shocked, not sure whether to defend me or join in Justine's courtly insults. I was about to transport out of the room for fear I would burst out crying in front of them.

"Princes Mary is not much younger than you, *Justine*," Emily stressed her name with a hiss to make others note the lack of distinction of "lady."

The ladies inhaled in unison at the insult. Justine's features sharpened, and she turned red—embarrassment and fury combined.

"Mary simply believes in being natural with her beauty. Look at that milky white skin without the use of the paints and powders you have caked on your face. In fact," —Emily paused, leaning in— "it looks like it is cracking in the creases of your nose. Not to mention, we all know that vibrant of yellow hair is absolutely unnatural. The fact there is no bosom *in* your dress tells me you are not nearly as developed as you make out to be. Just look at the tone of Mary's natural hair, ladies, her vibrant eyes, and her adorable nose. She'll be a catch one day, when she is ready, that is."

Wow. Emily took me from tears to triumph and feeling truly beautiful. Emily was right. I was by no means ugly. I was just young and still a bit awkward. And Justine? In all honesty, she could be beautiful if she didn't try so hard to exaggerate the court's beauty standards, thinking it was somehow better. She had unique golden eyes and a pleasant face...if you ignored the scowls and what lay underneath; inside, she was hideous through and through.

Lady Pearl discretely wiped off her overuse of rouge. And, surely enough, girls were looking into backs of spoons to make themselves a tad more natural. Justine looked around, floundering.

Emily sighed. "I'm sorry, Lady Justine. I'm protective of my loved ones, and I truly believe natural beauty outweighs falsity." Emily spoke the truth. Her own look was natural and beautiful. Her rich dark eyes, pale skin, and vibrant brown hair complimented each other to make her far superior to most of these girls. "Plus, Lady Justine, Mary is no baby, nor a child. Therefore, your insults could land you in heaps of trouble. Haven't your parents taught you that it is treason to insult royalty?"

Justine stood, looking as if she'd dare to say more. Instead, she excused herself and stormed off toward the mothers' tables. I felt elated for a moment until I realized, due to the silence of the table, that I was not the victor. Emily was. The ladies appeared disturbed by it, not cheering for the defeat of Justine. I'm not sure if Emily's defense made things better or worse for me. I felt adrift, not understanding my surroundings.

So here I am now, crying about all the things I should've said and done that came to me hours later. You are my only friend, Joan. How sad is that? All I can do is bleed my heart onto your pages, hoping things will get better, that I will find a friend, that I can master court life.

When will I be strong enough to be my own champion? I fear it will never happen, and yet, there is something in me that screams as loud as these draca roars I've heard of, telling me there is something so much greater that is to come.

I take back the melodrama I wrote about the other day. Girls aren't the biggest issue to contend with. Boys are so much worse.

I was leaving the nightcap with the family—after father made me drink firespice whiskey until I stopped making a face when I swallowed—and headed back to my quarters. When I turned the corner, right by the servant's closet where they stored their cleaning supplies, the first thing I saw were men's boots covered by trousers. Scanning up, I saw a man's bottom and a lady's stockinged leg wrapped around it. I froze, not sure what I was seeing. How could I get by these servants without being noticed? For once, I longed for Lucy to take the lead. She stood frozen, her mouth agape—not in confusion like mine, but pure shock.

The man grunted, and the woman moaned. He was moving in a weird, rapid way.

"Turn away, Your Highness," Lucy finally pulled herself together to command me. "Let us transport." Before I could use my magic to make us reappear in my quarters, I noticed something too familiar with the man's blond hair and stature: Cobalt. With a woman. What they were up to finally clicked. I only understood procreating progeny in simple terms, but I was seeing it firsthand. Fifteen! At fifteen, he was already doing this?

I stood frozen. If I moved, I might've thrown up. How could he? I could never marry a scoundrel. I have always believed people go into marriage pure because of the way they insisted us ladies must be chaste. Men do not have to have their virtue measured in power stones, though. You know my sentiments by now, Joan; being a woman in this sphere sucks. And this was another hit.

I wanted to stop them, scream at him, kill him, but what could I say? He is not engaged to me, nor could be until I am fifteen. Now, I never want it to happen.

In a cowardly fashion, I backed up, trying to get far away enough that they would not hear or see my fire magic when I transported. Lucy hadn't been ready for my sudden retreat, and I stepped on her toes. She didn't make a sound, but our steps were enough to spark Cobalt's military training. He looked over his shoulder, meeting my gaze with frightened wide eyes. He was still in the woman's embrace. I closed my eyes, disgusted by him in every way.

Transporting to my room seemed to be the easiest thing to do, but my disgust morphed into rage. I wanted him to be embarrassed, scared, reprimanded. I ignored the sounds of his fumbling and her complaints of lack of satisfaction.

I opened my eyes and marched right past them, shaking my head as I passed. The girl gasped, seeing it was me, and raced down the hall, still trying to fix her bodice. Her job was in my hands. I kept walking, not sure what I would do, but I knew she could no longer be my chambermaid if she was seducing gentlemen right by my quarters.

"Mary!" Cobalt called.

His shaky tone made me stop. I was only ten steps from my chamber door.

I turned to look at him properly clad—well properly dressed, but disheveled—his face full of fright. "Please don't tell anyone. I'm sorry that you had to see that. I...she was flirting, and before I knew what was happening—"

"Stop. I don't want to know, and I won't be silent. This is *my* hallway, and you desecrated it like a disgusting animal!"

"Mary," he pleaded, but I felt no remorse.

I will tell Alex and Mother and make sure his own father, who believes in values and honor, would hear. Cobalt deserves a flogging.

"Fifteen and this depraved? God and goddess help you find the right way."

He mumbled as he stared at his boots, "It was the first time." His face turned scarlet.

"Even worse you chose *my* chambermaid." I shook my head. "She'll have to be let go. You know my mother's standards."

He swallowed hard and bowed to me. "Princess Mary, I truly regret disrupting your night with my rash mistake. I hope you can forgive me." It was so formal, I wonder if he meant the apology at all. If he dares to be mad at me for telling truths...

Forget him, Joan. I would tell on any gentleman who did the same.

He took off out of embarrassment, shame, or anger—it matters not. My entire future and heart just pulled a huge turn. I could never marry a man like him if, as a boy, he does things like this. Cobalt is a pig, worse than a pig. There are not enough insults to hurl at him. And not just because I thought I loved him or would in the future, but how he left all reason and did something with such a lack of propriety out in the open where I had to witness it! These things should be done out of love, to create children, not lust with whatever random flirty person who comes along.

Everything I have ever known is under question, thanks to Cobalt.

I was too embarrassed to bring Cobalt's indiscretion up to others, so I asked Lucy to pass the message on to mother's maid. Sure enough, the whole staff found out, the girl was fired, and Cobalt was reprimanded by his family. He was missing from lessons for a day, and when he returned, he gingerly sat himself down. He had been whipped on his behind: a clear reminder his parents were calling his actions out as childish, an insult that he was no man or gentleman. I had to agree and inwardly smirked. Yes, I know, Joan, it was an unkind thought, but I'm learning as I grow up that many are unkind in this world.

After lessons, I sat with mother to have tea with women who gossiped about nonsense I couldn't care less about. After the company left, I was scolded for not partaking in the conversation. How could I? I rarely get to leave the castle, Joan. How can I even gossip if I don't know many ladies personally? Maybe Lucy could prepare me for the next social engagement by finding me gossip. Is this how trite my life will be? Gossip, tea, marriage, and kids? Mindless duty, no happiness? How can Mother endure it? Aside from Alex and me, is this all my mother is? Gossip in a pretty dress? I wish something would happen to change this course set for me. I cannot abide by my future being like Mother's life.

I apologized to my mother and then fled. I could not bear these melancholy thoughts, hoping riding would distract me. I found Alex there, saddling up with Cobalt. I wanted to run away. Would Cobalt be mad I told? Did he hate me? Did I care that he might? I was still angry but also disappointed in him. When I entered, Cobalt was not saddling up. He was mucking out the stall. The stable boy had a mocking grin on his face, but Alex's was stoic and saddened. His eyes met mine, and I could tell his friend's behavior had disappointed him. Alex was a gentleman, and his friend was disregarding Alex's chivalric code. I wondered how long he would let him get away with it before he might cut him loose. I was happy Alex wasn't mad at me for tattling. I doubted he would be. Alex had values. But I had been worried he might've thought it should've been settled by him rather than adults.

I asked Alex, "Going out for a ride?"

Cobalt's back stiffened when he heard my voice, and he paused shoveling the horse manure. He did not dare turn to look at me.

Great. Things would be weird between us for ages now.

"Yes," Alex said.

"Mind if I join you?"

Alex sighed. "I intended to get out some of my energy and anger by galloping. That's dangerous for you sidesaddled. Next time, Mary, I promise."

His flippant disregard of me stung. My brother and I used to do everything together, but now he was acting all grown up and unable to condescend to spend time with me. I thought then that perhaps he was mad at me for telling.

That night, Alex said nothing during our family nightcap. Father was in good spirits. He and Lord Citrine were whispering and laughing. Mother was rigid in the corner, her eyes on the floor. I was over everyone and everything. There was too much disappointment in my heart, so I let Father ply me with a strong firewhiskey. The burn hurt, but it numbed my dying heart.

I heard little pieces of conversation that made me pour a second. "Little piece on the side...remember that one lady with that *talent*?" Eww. Father and his buddy were talking about women they bedded? I prayed to the god and goddess it was before their marriage. No wonder poor Mother was so sad. I wished I could do something for her.

"That young buck Cobalt will beat our records at this rate," Lord Citrine jested.

After that one, Alex draped his arm around me, glaring at Father, who was red-faced and into his cups. "Come, Mary, I think Mother needs a distraction as much as we do."

"So, you're not mad at me?"

"Mad at you?" Alex squared my shoulders. "Why on Fyr would I be mad at you, dear sister?"

"Because I told."

Alex sighed and looked down. Then his eyes met mine, identical in color and shape, but the soul behind them is much different than mine. "Mary." He shook his head and pulled me into a hug. "Never you. I was livid with Cobalt. When you showed up at the stable, the curse made my fury almost unmanageable. I had to get away, and I would've been the worst company. All I could think about was how he not only disappointed me and his family but also how he subjected my innocent sister to such things. You'll hear more about these things soon enough. The courtly girls love their gossip, but thirteen? You did not deserve such a rude awakening into adulthood."

"I wasn't good company either. You should've let me come along. Sometimes I need to get my anger out too, Alex."

He held me tighter and whispered in my ear, not wanting our parents to hear, "This curse...it scares me, Mary. If I feel angry, it almost feels like it can overtake me."

He let me go. His words worried me. Does he really think he would lose control of himself?

"No," I insisted. "You are only feeling this way because Cobalt lost control of himself in another way. He never was disciplined in anything. You are."

He smiled, but I could tell he did not believe me. We went over to distract our poor mother. Thankfully, Lord Citrine left not long later, and Father dozed. By the time we left, Mother was happy, like a plant watered. All she needed was love. Isn't that the essential ingredient for life?

The Sapphirian Emerald Fort
Ludford

Dearest Cousin, Princess Mary,

  I have meant to write to you for ages. My Father has been working me to death. I also am caring for my dear wife. Emily is not feeling well, and I feel I must be by her side at all times. I hope you are well and that you are keeping those catty ladies in their places. Emily wishes she could help. Please write and distract her. She needs a friend like you, but I know you cannot leave the palace, and she is too unwell to leave here. Please let me know how you are.
       Kind Regards,
       Your Cousin Henry

The Sapphirian Palace
Celestia

Henry and Emily,
  I have given up publicly caring what those girls think. They still mock me, but I don't engage with it. It has made them stop doing it in front of my face. Privately, it cuts deep. They create rumors that reach me, and it upsets me more than I should let it. I just want friends, but they make me distrust everyone. There's also a lot of things going on here that have disrupted my life, but I'm rather embarrassed to talk about them. I hope you feel better, Emily. let the healers ease your suffering as much as possible. It must be so tiring growing a life. I long to see you, so please take care of yourself.

Your Cousin,
Princess Mary

The Sapphirian Emerald Fort
Ludford

I write to you privately, Mary, because some things are not problems men can solve. Bless Henry's kind heart. He wants to help, but I know I can do much better. You must find yourself one influential girl who is kind or ambitious—dare I hope there is one who is both? Just one lady is all you need to turn the tide and gather some friends. They follow like the mindless sheep some ladies are taught to be. You and I are of another mold completely. While searching for this friend, find something that keeps you busy. I find that drives all melancholy away. I've taken to knitting baby clothes since Henry will not let me lift a finger or be off the settee for more than a moment. He is overbearing, but it is because he cares so deeply. I feel better and hope to see you soon. I wish you could come see me, but your father would deny me such a privilege—for your safety of course. Please tell me your troubles. I long to help. What do you think of being godmother to our child? I cannot think of anyone else I would prefer, and it would be the highest honor to our child.

Your friend,

Emily

PS–I think it is time now that you are a lady, you are introduced to the gossip rags. Here are a couple clippings I thought you'd find interesting. They're from Courtly Cuckolds and Cads. Your servant should be able to get them for you discretely. I'm sure your mother would not approve, but any lady who wants an edge in society reads them. You should know what they say to protect yourself always and know what to expect from ladies. Study their weaknesses.

I unfolded the little newspaper clippings, squinting at the tiny print. There were two that Emily had cut from a larger page. I had seen these in the teahouses and among ladies we visited the rare moments we left the house. The mothers always seemed to slip them away when us young girls were about. I was a lady now, according to society's rules, so I felt no guilt in devouring the words, a thrill of excitement making me read quickly.

PRINCESS OUT OR OUT OF LEADING STRINGS?

The princess is out so they say, but those close to the royal family say hardly out of her leading strings.

My stomach dropped. It was about me. Calling me hardly more than a toddler. I suddenly knew who influenced this article and fed the information to them: Justine Citrine. I didn't want to, but I read on.

There was a lack of bosom, but what is one to expect in a thirteen-year-old debutante with a thin frame? According to our insider, she likely will not ripen into a fruit many suitors will want to pluck. Then again, it is our opinion at *Courtly Cuckolds & Cads* that many a men will vie for her hand once the newest royal out decides to entertain suitors. The position in society could not be better, and frankly, those who proclaim her plain perhaps should stop applying so much paint to their faces, colors to their hair, and padding to the upper regions of their corsets. Whatever our princess will be, she will be respected and elegant, like our dear queen.

I sighed. Thankfully, they turned on Justine or whoever else supplied the horrid description. It wasn't as bad as it started off. I doubt they would be allowed to really talk poorly about me and get away with it, so the hidden snub—via someone else, so they said—left me uneasy. They were pushing the line as far as possible without crossing it.

I dropped it onto the table and read the other one.

NEW CAD IN THE CASTLE

Society has been in need of some new cads to gossip about, and this latest tidbit is about a fresh young buck who is already making his mark—on the world of women it seems. Rumors from the palace tell us a young lord, we shall not name, has been consorting with the maid staff on more than the topic of cleaning. Caught red-handed, he is now redbuttocked from the whipping rumored to have happened by his more-than-proper family, who had an untarnished past for two generations—that we know of. Could lust in such a young man be passed down secretly? One wonders what secrets rattle around in sorcerers' manors. Readers, I know you are salivating to know of whom we speak. All you need to do is visit the palace and see which blue-eyed gent has a tender backside. We assure you it is not our noble prince, who deprives us of stories with his righteous morals. No, ladies, cast your eyes away from the castle. The young guilty buck will not be able to sit, or do more, for some time to come.

I put the article down. I wanted to burn them. They were horribly cutting words in such a self-righteous tone, reminding me of those like Justine, but older, the mothers of the court. They lived for nothing but gossip and scandal, gloating over others' misfortunes and savoring every juicy morsel of information that could get them higher up the ranks. They spread news to feel important.

At the same time, I felt that their attack on Cobalt was right. He needed this chiding, these warnings. Everything in it was right. He besmirched his family's name, sullied it. He deserved it. However, I didn't. I'm glad no one connected us. I will be sure to hide my emotions around others when it comes to him.

Great, now I have more to worry about. The rag sheets. I know Emily was trying to help me, and this was something I needed to know about that mother would never tell me, but it is overwhelming.

I'm going to paste these into my diary instead of burning them. I feel like I need to read them again later, when I am way more accustomed to reading them. I think I might need Lucy to get me them. It would've been better to dabble in this kind of gossip about other people, those not close to me, not about myself either.

Emily was right, not about sending me the rags—I still wonder her real motivation—but about being allowed to see her. Father would not let me go. At least I was bold enough to ask. On the way back to my quarters, I saw my new chambermaid coming out. She was pretty, with a striking figure and beautiful blonde hair that peaked out of her snood. Instantly, I thought of her being with Cobalt. All the anger and disappointment came back. The gossip, how everyone knew how much of a cad he was—everyone.

Lucy tsked me as I poured a firewhiskey to write this, but how could I not? How can I deal with knowing so much and seeing so much, then being burned by betrayal? Cobalt doesn't even know, but I'm too chicken to tell him. I have no one to turn to but a book that cannot comfort me. The whiskey takes the edge off my pain, these feelings that have no outlet. It is only one drink after all; that's what I said to Lucy, but she was irritated because it was not yet evening when she thinks a drink is more acceptable.

I think I will write to Emily. Tell her about Cobalt. Maybe she might have sound advice. How could I not? She called me "friend" and asked me to be godmother. It was so exciting!

The Sapphirian Palace
Celestia

It would be such an honor to be godmother to the next Sapphirian. I'm so excited. I cannot believe you chose me. likely, you chose me because I will spoil that little princess or prince. I tried to cheat and see the gender. But the flames did not wish to speak to me today. I'm sure Henry knows already and is keeping it secret.

Not to be a pessimist after such a great start to a letter. But I have a problem and no one to talk to. It's about a boy. It's not that I have a crush on him or anything. But I saw some things in the flames that had led me to believe he might be a future suitor. if not the one. But he has done something so awful that I have lost respect for him completely. I cannot resign myself to a future with him. yet I feel it as if it is a loss or breakup. even though nothing ever romantic occurred between us. He doesn't even know I have seen anything about our future. I'm not sure what I'm asking except. how do I come to terms with the turn in events?

Your Cousin.
Princess Mary

The Sapphirian Emerald Fort
Ludford

 Boys! They are always a problem. There are a few precious stones among the rocks, but they are hard to find. Take this advice, and use it wisely: a woman can create her perfect man. Like a loveable pet, women can bend men to their wills if they play the game right. You're too young to understand now, but one day, you will understand the power we hold over them, to bend them to our will and mold them toward the man we want them to be. Lust is a powerful weapon. I'm guessing from the description in your last letter, the boy's failing was exactly that? If so, he will be malleable indeed, unless he grows up to mistrust women as some brokenhearted men are oft to do. As a woman, you must use every weapon possible to win over a man. Not that you'll need that. Your station alone will bring in a slew of suitors. Choose wisely. Someone you can manage who in turn can protect you. That is the perfect relationship, one like Henry's and mine.

Your loyal friend,
Emily

Emily's idea of a relationship seems pretty progressive and very cutthroat. I almost feel bad for Henry because she seems so calculating. But anyone who has seen their courtship knows there is love on both sides. It just seems strange that I should want to control a man rather than work together. Often, my world expects women to listen to men—always. To say I should do the opposite seems like a big jump. I always had imagined that Cobalt and I would be a team, with me automatically in charge due to my station. If I have to choose another lifemate, I would not want someone who would take my power, but wasn't taking someone else's power from them just as bad?

 I have time to ruminate the kind of man I want to marry and how our relationship should be. I will ignore Emily's flippant comment. She is, after all, my only friend.

 Lucy surprisingly got me the weekly rag sheet without complaint. She even went as far as to say I should know rumors to educate myself, but warned the writing style was mocking. I already sensed that but did not chide her for pointing out the obvious. It was a rare moment we agreed.

The gossip paper this week was about a lord left by a lady who dashed away her great match to marry a magician. They really made her sound a fool, but I have a feeling that love is a type of magic beyond rationalism. How else would I end up with someone like Cobalt?

December

Joan,

Henry came to the palace, apologizing that Emily couldn't join him. Apparently, she was still ill. She had written me more letters that were perky and trite, probably because I did not share any news with her, not having any news to give; she had even less news to give me, being on bedrest. She still sent some clippings until I told her I now had the rag sheets delivered. I fear this lessened what we could talk about.

When Mother became concerned about Emily during tea, Henry admitted she was with child, so I no longer have to withhold the secret. Another Sapphirian after so long; it was exciting for Mother, and Henry was beaming with pride. We need more Fyrians who could conjure fire. And unlike Cobalt, my dear cousin doesn't seem to stray from his lifemate to make baseborns.

When I left for my lessons, it was lucky that I had decided to walk to prolong the agony of learning stately matters and economics.

"Mary," Henry called out, running to catch up to me. "You and Emily are close. She writes to you almost daily. Aren't you happy about being godmother?"

"I'm ecstatic! A baby Sapphirian. There hasn't been one since me. It is great news."

"But something is wrong? I have concerns too. Shall we go for a walk? Orchards? Do you still like climbing trees?"

"No." I laughed, although the idea was tempting. "I'm too old for that. A walk to the pond?"

Lucy cleared her throat. "Your lesson, Your Highness." She was always out to spoil my fun.

Henry winked at me. "I'll get you out of it."

After he talked to Mister Tutor, Henry had only gotten me a rescheduled lesson for after supper when Henry would leave for home. At least then I could drink some firewhiskey with my meal, enough to drift listlessly through the lesson, I hoped.

We headed to the lake, and we spoke of trivial things. Finally, I said, "Have you foreseen the baby? Will it be a boy or a girl?"

Henry's jaw tightened. Something was wrong. "Ladies first, Cousin. Something is dampening your spirits."

I sighed. Who else could I talk to about Cobalt? Alex? Yeah, that would be a fun conversation. Emily hadn't told him about my boy troubles. It was good to know I could trust her with secrets.

"I saw Cobalt getting intimate with my chambermaid right by my door," I blurted, feeling my face burn red.

Henry laughed loudly and then apologized when he saw my glare. He cleared his throat. "Sorry. He's always been a wild one, and I heard about it and his flogging. Not much stays secret in our world, Cousin Mary." His smile did not last, and his brow furrowed. "Why do you care?"

"No reason."

"Oh no, the flames told you, you'd end up with him?"

"No!" It came out so fast that he'd never believe me.

Those visions are private and mine, and maybe Cobalt could change. Maybe he really did make a mistake. I cannot admit that I thought Cobalt was my lifemate, not to my cousin, not even Alex or Mother. "It's a stupid crush, okay, and now it is dead."

"Ah." He nodded knowingly. "We all go through this. Mine was the now Lady Diamond."

"She's old."

"Is not. She's only in her late thirties. Plus, I was your age, and she was beautiful to me. But crushes we admire for looks or other surface traits, they're not love. You'll know when you're in love. It's an overwhelming crushing feeling that you could never walk away from, painful but so exquisite." He was thinking of Emily, but he seemed sad for some reason.

Could I walk away from Cobalt? Right now, yes. So maybe it was just a crush. Henry did have a much healthier description of love than his lifemate's.

"Mary?" Henry's shoulders were firm, and his face was scrunched up almost like he was wounded. "Have you firebranded lately?"

Nope. I didn't want to see the swine Cobalt with me in visions. "No, why?"

"Could you try for me? Fixate on Emily. You're the best firebrander in the family."

29

I was, but he must've seen something of concern to ask me. "Henry, you're distressed. What is it?"

"Do not tell anyone, not even Emily." Whoa, it was serious. "I searched the flames to see my child. I don't see it or Emily. I'm not the best at it—not like Alex or Ruby, and nothing like you—but it concerns me. It is already a difficult pregnancy for her a few months in. The healers have her on bedrest and whisper to each other."

Oh no. My heart sank. I had to tell him something to bolster him. "Order them to reveal what they gossip about."

"I have. They are concerned about her swelling feet and hands and her headaches. That's it, but those things seem normal for being with child, so why the bedrest?"

"Maybe they're just being cautious. I will try my best to search the flames."

He squeezed my hand. "Thank you, Mary."

"I can't promise anything. You know how this works."

"I know, but you can see better than me. If you see her and my child, then I'm needlessly worrying."

"I'll look."

Henry hugged me, but the hug felt as if I was holding him up. My poor cousin. He has always been there to talk to me when Alex has no time for me. I had to be there for him. I was now growing concerned about what bedrest meant for a woman about halfway through her pregnancy.

Of course, I went straight to my rooms and conjured the fire, trying to find Emily. What I saw was horrific, and I couldn't bear to watch more. She would die of convulsions with the baby inside her. They would cut the baby out of her, but it would be too early, and the baby would pass away. How can I tell Henry that? I can't, but maybe I could find a way to save her, suggest the best midwife and healers? It is a hopeless case. I can't fight against nature. There is no understanding of how or when convulsions come, and they don't always kill. But there is no stone or magic that could prevent them.

Between Cobalt's betrayal and learning my only friend would die, most likely within the next few months, I couldn't handle it. I went to the bottle of firewhiskey in the princess room and poured myself a small glass. Hating the flavor but not the end result too much, I downed it. The liquid burned so badly, I thought I might be sick. I poured another. Downed it.

Lucy started to speak, and I told her to shut up. I drank another. After that, I don't remember much, especially how I ended up in my room in my nightgown. Lucy took care of me, I'm sure. My head was throbbing violently, and my mouth was dry. I had missed my makeup lesson and dinner.

On top of that, I'm not getting up today. I am never going to drink again.

COURTLY CUCKOLDS & CADS

CAD COLLUSION?

One has to question our future leader, the prince, for the easy forgiveness of his friend's sinful deeds and blasé treatment of the fairer sex. Will our prince now sow his oats as many princes have before, influenced by his friend? Some say the sickness should be cut out of the castle, but then we must question all past deeds. We tell the people truths, but even this writer is not bold enough to regal the tales of the king and his brothers' deeds. There were high hopes our prince would be of a different mold from his father, but perhaps the curse can cause many faults we are not yet aware about. Only time will tell.

I feel like I'm dying, like the fire is eating me from inside. Cobalt has broken me. I started liking him because of these ridiculous visions. Then I was mad, apathetic, and now I'm torn up again. A future with him, as the way he is now, would be dealing with a cad who seems to want to do "it" with anyone who will offer. I would never let a lifemate of mine have a mistress. Never. I was so mean to him. I don't regret it, Joan, but what I regret most is his reaction to my hatred. He is slightly uncomfortable if I bring up seeing the incident, but more so, he doesn't seem to care. He doesn't realize I'm angry that he's jeopardizing our future. And how can I tell him that? The way he is, the terrible flirt who has no care for the women themselves but only for his own needs, makes me want to be sick. If I tell him something, if I say he must stop because he'll ruin the best part of his future, will he even care or listen? Let's say he does. How many questions will it take to get the truth out of me?

Alex forgave his friend more easily, even though he was still disappointed in Cobalt. My brother has principles. I know he would never treat a woman the way Cobalt did, no matter what the paper said. I have always held Alex up as a standard to other boys, because he is a good person. I could never compare lords to Father. He'd probably clap Cobalt on the back and tell him to create more powerful baseborns to override the cunning folk. It was a conversation I heard often enough when he was into his cups and loud when he entertained lords. It all made me sick.

Alex didn't care about the papers, or perhaps he was smart enough not to read them. I wish Emily had never told me about them. I want to live in a bubble again, be a little girl and be ignorant of the world. That's the thing though, knowledge—once you have it, it can't be taken away. I'm on the path to becoming a lady, and everything I learn will bring me closer to that end result. But there are things in my future I might be able to control if I cannot control growing up.

How will I—in the future—love a man like Cobalt? Impossible. The flames must have lied to me. The visions trapped me and made me care. They have to be wrong for once, or my future will be utterly bleak. This gift of foresight is a curse. Alex has never seen as well as me, probably the curse's fault, but I see too much. I should just throw the same burden onto him about the woman I saw who will steal his heart.

No. Never. Alex could not handle that burden on top of everything he'll inherit and the dark curse. Nothing good comes from meddling with the future, as my ancestors proclaimed. I love Alex. He is a great brother. I have to let it all happen in its own time, but I wish visions were more measurable. When and where this girl will come from is unknown to me. I don't know her name and have never seen a girl like her before. Maybe she has a parent from Lyft or an ancestor from Water sphere. What if telling him would ruin not just his life but Fyr's future? What if me telling Cobalt about us would do that? Firebranding is my burden to carry. I feel an affinity to Alex in this respect. We both have our curses, and I now understand him more than ever. Yet I could never share that fact with him. I would never burden him with my inner pain.

Just like that, Joan, writing these words, I feel as if I have grown up years.

I have learned to withhold my anger and pain from Cobalt and others. No one would understand. Well, Alex and Henry would but that would take me admitting I had a huge crush on Cobalt and that I saw we were together in the future. That might make Alex harder on Cobalt. My brother was great but overprotective at times. When it came to Father's wrath, I did not mind Alex protecting me. Afterwards, I would always feel guilty. Either Alex took the brunt of our father's anger, or I was weak, making Alex step up because I could not voice my strength. God and goddess, I have the best brother a girl could ask for. He would know exactly what to say—if only I could tell him.

The Sapphirian Emerald Fort
Ludford

Cousin Mary,
Please write to Emily soon. Her spirits are low. She is tired, and her head hurts terribly. I feel awful for putting her in this situation. If this is what having a child does, this must be our only child. I cannot watch her suffer like this. Please, write. Take her mind off things. Tell me, Mary. Tell me that you have been firebranding and have seen something. Anything to assure me, to assure her. She now worries too.
Cousin Henry

I have to tell Henry something, but what? His letter was so desperate. I have tried firebranding several times and keep seeing similar scenarios. That only happens when a path is unchangeable. Otherwise, the future is usually in flux, just like the flames. Emily won't make it, and the baby won't either.

The papers were worse. They made up rumors about her, from Henry abusing her and holding her prisoner to her faking she has been with child so is hiding from society now. You'd think they'd have the intelligence to realize something is wrong and to ease off, but I'm learning the gossip rag is utterly powerful.

I delayed writing for a day, but that made me feel more guilty.

The Sapphirian Palace
Celestia

I am sorry, dear cousin, the flames fluctuate. I don't know what to say, what to tell you. I've seen many varying things. How does Emily fare? Is she well? I will try to persuade Father to let me visit. I will keep firebranding.

Your cousin

Mary

The Sapphirian Emerald Fort
Ludford

Mary,
    You must know. I have seen some things that alarmed me, and you see the best of all. Ruby will not give me answers. Your silence will confirm my worst fears. Please tell me Emily will live. Anything but her death. I cannot bear a world without my lifemate.

Henry

Not knowing what else to do, I have decided to ask Alex, the only person who would understand.

I have done it. Talked to Alex. Let me backtrack. Alex was hiding from his tutor. He had snuck away into the library, demanding David find him books on the rebel wars. Lucy and I were reading in the window seat with the drape partially drawn.

I poked my head out. "Hiding, Brother?"

He jumped, having not seen. "Mary." He bowed his head slightly, ever so formal.

I wish I remembered propriety as he does. I've never taken yet to the rules of society.

"I am. I have an exam today, and I swore Mister Tutor had said it would be two days from now, and I didn't study." He looked sheepish and sad. "What are you reading?" he asked, walking closer.

I closed the book and tried to hide it in the cushion. He stopped and laughed. "A romance, then?" He raised his brows and laughed.

I'm sure my face turned red in admission.

Alex didn't gloat long. His face became serious. "You know those books are fantasy, right, that men and women fall in love more naturally. At least, I would think. Damsels in distress. Heroes saving the day. It's all a bit over-the-top. Just entertainment."

"Still fun to dream. Sometimes you need to read the fantastical to escape the mundane, or even the drama of real life."

"What drama could you possibly have?"

The question rankled me. Fiery rage boiled up in me. Normally, I'm the one in control of my temper when it comes to Alex and me, but his question was so condescendingly rude.

I glared at him, but Alex's mirth had already flagged.

"Is something wrong, Mary?"

"I'm fine." I was too curt, unable to hide my emotions as Alex expertly did. I couldn't leave it at that. "I don't like when people downplay my feelings or knowledge simply because I am younger. Seeing the future is taxing. It matures you. I'm the best seer in our family for a long time. It weighs upon me."

"I know," Alex said quietly. I gazed up ready to see understanding of my plight in his eyes, but he was looking out the window as if seeing something just as heavy. His hands clasped the golden chain of his prince's medallion, and I knew then he was equivocating my foresight to his hefty role of sovereign one day. I'm sure it's equal. Alex will have a hard life. I will too, but mine will be more of a breeding mare, while Alex will have an entire sphere to run while also spawning more Sapphirians. None of it is fair. I remember a time when my brother wanted to be a sculptor of glass. Father squashed that quickly, even as a hobby, just as he squashed my hope of ever having a dream of being anything. He reminds me all too often that my purpose is to create more of our race.

"Mary, if there are any gentlemen wronging you in any way, even if inadvertently, you can let me know. I can be discreet and get rid of the problem."

He understood but didn't. He thought I was upset at some sad flirts who dared to wink at a girl freshly out in society and not marriage ready.

"Thank you, Alex. It's not that."

He waited patiently, even after David had the books Alex needed to cram for his exam he was supposed to be taking now.

I had to open up, but I had to be careful. "I am not getting into particulars. I saw *the one* for me in the flames."

"You saw that when we were little, or so you said. What has changed?"

"My vision was of a man. At six years old, how would I know who that was? He is a man now, and I have recognized him. Before you ask, I will not tell you whom he is."

Alex was pensive for a moment. "Then, why are you upset? Does knowing feel liberating or confining?" He was trying so hard to understand.

"I don't like the man. Who he is and what he represents repulses me."

Alex's eyes met mine. His were full of anguish for me. I had to look away.

"Mary, listen to me." Alex's voice was rough with unfettered anger. "You will never marry anyone you don't want to. The edicts protect us. If Father tries to force you, I will intercede. I promise you this."

It was so touching to know my brother loved me this much and would help me. I had no will to explain to him the complexity of the problem nor turn him against his only true friend. "Thank you, Alex. Maybe he will change. I know my mind, and I will not marry unless I can respect and one day love the man."

"I can't imagine a man worthy of you, Mary, but one day, I'll have to resign myself to your choice. Make sure he is good for you."

"It doesn't matter. As you always say, 'Time changes as much as the flame flickers.'"

"Yes." There was nothing else he could say.

Regardless, his conviction to be on my side, to fight for what would be best for me, was a comfort. I love my mother because she is everything that is good in the sphere, but she has no power. Alex does. With him in my corner, I fear father's future plans for me less.

"I didn't realize it had been about a boy. I had thought..."

"It's that too," I said when he was too lost in his thoughts to continue.

His eyes darted to meet mine. "Lady Emily?"

I nodded, looking away, tears forming.

Alex sighed. "Did Henry write you too?"

"He writes frequently about it. Lady Emily's letters to me stopped. We were becoming friends. I don't have any." All my problems spilled out of my mouth.

"Oh, Mary." He pulled me in, and I buried my face in his shoulder. His hug filled me with strength. "I'm so sorry. I didn't see how the child will fare in my visions, but I saw Emily won't make it."

I pulled away, wiping the tears away. "What do we tell him? I'm afraid he'll come here if I do not answer. I wish I could go. Talk to Emily."

"Then go." Alex shrugged as if it were that easy.

"Father won't let me."

"Since when has that stopped the pair of us from transporting?" He smirked, but it was halfhearted. He was weighed down by the truth too.

"And what do I tell Henry?"

"Be vague. I wrote and told him I could not help, but that I would have Father send the head court healer. Father sent him today. I hope the healer will tell Henry the news. Surely, it'll be obvious to that talented of a healer."

I nodded. I could be vague and promise to visit. I penned Henry that night to expect me the next morning.

A couple weights were momentarily lifted off my shoulders.

I longed to see Emily because it could be the last time. I also dreaded it because I wasn't sure I could lie to Henry's face, and I feared the state of Emily.

It was worse than I thought. Henry was deep into his cups, unshaven, and unwashed. He was a mess. You'd think he had just lost his wife and was mad with grief. Perhaps he had seen it and was grieving beforehand. I could not imagine how anyone could mentally grapple watching their loved one deteriorate, and perhaps foreseeing it with the knowledge he could not stop it.

"Emily will be so happy to see you. Her body is weary, but her mind is still pretty sharp. She hates being on bedrest."

I nodded as he led me to their quarters in the fort.

"The healer told me. I know. And I understand why you, Ruby, and Alex did not tell me. You didn't want me to give up hope."

"*I* didn't want to give up hope, Henry. I wanted to see another thread."

He grunted, not turning around. "Did you come because—"

"No. I don't think so. Your letters led me to believe it could be. It's impossible to know when through visions."

At the door, he stopped and turned. "She doesn't know. It's important for the baby's health that she stays positive and doesn't lose hope."

I nodded, trying to hold all my emotions in. When I entered, she was sitting on the settee, knitting a baby blanket. I hardly recognized her. Her hands looked swollen, her face puffy, and her nose was twice the size it had been. Her stomach bulged slightly, making it obvious she was with child, but not full term. She placed the knitting down as Henry announced me with a slur. She smiled widely at me, and her eyes sparkled with excitement.

I wanted to run from the room and bawl my eyes out. How could I bear to watch a soon-dead woman make clothes for her soon-dead baby?

I took a deep breath and plastered a fake smile onto my face, focusing on how I was glad to finally see my friend again.

"Sit, Princess Mary. You don't know how happy I am to see you." Her face beamed with genuine happiness as she patted the chair adjacent to the settee. It was obvious she didn't leave the settee, except perhaps to sleep. There were books, the knitting, a drink, and an empty plate strewn around her. I peered down at her feet. They were swollen beyond belief; her ankles were not even discernable, nor her feet. The only way I could tell there was a foot in the puffy flesh was from the toes.

Henry pulled a blanket over her feet and up to her waist.

"I'm warm enough," Emily playfully chastised him. "You keep the fire burning incessantly."

"It could help to stay warm."

Emily gave him a loving look and smile. "Perhaps you are right. I feel a bit better being snug."

Henry gave her a grin, but the pain in his eyes was apparent. He took up her hand and kissed it.

She squeezed his hand back. "Do you mind leaving us, darling? Girl talk." Emily winked.

Henry laughed lightly. "I have always wondered what the fairer sex talks about, but I must admit it frightens me. Therefore, I retreat and allow you ladies your time together. Ring the bell if—"

"Yes, darling. If I need anything I will ring."

Henry transported.

Instantly, Emily slouched on the settee and rested her head back. "Take this blanket off me, will you?"

I did it immediately. "Are you all right, Lady Emily?"

"Define all right?" It was a snarky comment.

I backed up.

"Sorry. I'm sorry." She pinched the bridge of her nose. "I'm dying."

"You don't—"

"I do. I play dumb, perky, and hopeful for Henry's sake. Every day becomes more difficult in multiple ways. My body has betrayed me and my child. I know deep down that we will not make it. I just wish someone would put me out of my misery. This is the worst way to die. Imagine slowly deteriorating while the life inside you struggles for more of you and you have nothing to give."

I started bawling.

"I'm sorry, Mary." She reached her swollen hand out and grasped my own. "I should not put this emotional burden on someone so young. I just have no one to talk to. No one else knows the truth of what will happen to me, save Henry. He doesn't know I know. I have read it in his eyes, in his face, in his overbearing desperation to do something. It all proves he knows he cannot. And the healer's faces. They're doing a routine to ease some suffering, but I can see the pity in their eyes. I need to talk to someone."

I bolstered myself, wiped my tears away, and squeezed her hand gently. "I am here. I'm listening."

"I just pray and hope with all my heart the baby will make it, but I can't imagine I will live long enough to protect him or her. Henry can't see. I thought...maybe you...?"

I shook my head. How could she ask this? What to say? I thought about my conversation with Alex. I could sort of lie. This lie would be what is best for my godchild. Maybe my lie would change the future, let the baby live. If she had hope...

"The flames change—"

"Please don't patronize me. I thought at least you would give me the truth."

"The flames do change—not for you, but for the child, your son, they do."

She stroked her belly and a laugh-cry combo bubbled out of her. "A boy?"

I swallowed the lump in my throat and nodded.

She smiled.

"You know the longer you can hold on, the better for him. You cannot give up mentally. If you can make it long enough, he could live." They were not lies. I was diplomatically slipping in the truth and insinuating they had been visions.

"I want him," she touched her belly, "Emery, to live. I'm envious you might see him, and I will never. It is hard to be a martyr, Mary. I suggest never trying it."

I wasn't sure if she was joking, but if she was, it wasn't funny.

"Emery?"

"We agreed to name the baby Henry if it is a boy, Emily if it is a girl. Then, when I wasn't doing well, we came up with a combination name to name the baby regardless of the gender. Henry will not bear this well. Promise me you'll watch after my baby. When I die, it will break Henry. If you must, take your godchild to the palace and have him raised there."

"I couldn't."

"I'm not expecting you to do it. Your mother." Emily closed her eyes. "She will love that child more than any Emerald could."

I wasn't sure what she meant by that, but I didn't want to bother her. "Will Henry agree?"

"He knows my thoughts. He knows what is best."

"I will." I felt bad about agreeing, knowing the child's survival was unlikely. I still hoped Emery would live. I searched the flames in the fireplace in front of me, focusing on a name, but nothing came. It didn't mean he might not exist. At times, the flames were fickle.

"Thank you." She sighed. "I tire easily. I wish I could help you with your problems. It would be a good diversion. I am too tired. Write them to me, will you? I'll help you."

"I will." I stood. This was a dismissal. "Take care. I'm not sure if Father will let me visit often." I started for the door.

"I'd rather you remember me before, not like this, not how bad I will become."

I could not speak but nodded. She couldn't see me, but I believed she knew.

"Mary?"

I turned.

"If the baby dies, I don't know what Henry will do." She didn't elaborate, so I went to leave. "Watch..."

I think she fell asleep, so I left the room and then transported home, not wanting to see Henry again. It was all too much to deal with.

January

After my visit, the weight came back full force. I was anxious, upset, and turning to firewhiskey at dinner to block out my father, who was the icing on the cake of devastation I felt inside. I lost time and did not write.

Again, my brother helped. I feel better. If you haven't noticed, I write in you more when I'm upset. When I'm beyond upset, unable to reach for a shred of hope, I stop writing.

After Alex asked questions about my mood, I asked him to come to the princess salon after the family nightcap of firewhiskey. I felt emboldened and loose-tongued. It was good because I needed to talk about it, and I had no one to talk to.

Alex seemed happy to be alone with me. With his political studies and training, and my failing etiquette lessons, we hardly saw each other in the day outside of our common history lesson with Cobalt and Ruby.

"Mary," he began, and I was glad for it. How could I start this conversation when I had to be so careful with my words? "You seem troubled. Is it Emily or the future you saw for yourself? You know you can tell me anything, but I hope it's not something new."

"Not new, why?"

"It's just...the flames." He was distracted by his own thoughts. "I see all sorts of unclear things, and a lot of them are..."

"Foreboding." I gave him the word he was searching for. I wanted to spill it all, for I have always been better than the others, differentiating which ones are more likely to occur, but withheld. "Emily's agonizing death bothers me tremendously, but also visions of my lifemate again and maybe yours and the future and—it is too much to bear."

"Stop." He starting pacing.

That's when I knew he was as distressed as me about the future. I wasn't sure what was worse: me seeing and knowing more, or his unclear snippets that likely contradicted each other.

"I won't tell you anything, but Alex, you bear a curse, and so do I. This is so hard. I feel like my entire life is mapped out for me, and I have no say in it."

"We cannot reveal what we see. Our ancestors—"

"I know. It either never affected their destinies or destroyed them by altering things into terrible outcomes."

"I can't help you if I don't know, yet I probably shouldn't hear it. Be careful with your words, Mary."

That meant I must be vague. "I want to sort out the future now, change it really. I should not fight it, I know, but it is hard to accept."

Alex stopped pacing and gave me a smirk. "You've always been impatient. You need to let what you've seen go. If you saw your mate—or mine—that's not happening anytime soon. I promise. The edicts say no one can force us into a marriage. I'm Mother and Father's concern as the heir. You have time. Just forget what you saw, and find another pastime."

"Like what?"

Alex laughed. "Yes, you never liked ladylike hobbies such as embroidery, dancing, or art." Then he got thoughtful. "I will have to marry one day, though. Maybe you could help me out a bit by becoming a lady—in public, I mean—condescending to visit other ladies. You could let me know who to avoid and who could be suitable. You hate these courtier ladies, so who else but you could find a gem in the rubble?"

God and goddess, he is too good of a speaker. He convinced me of what mother had begged me to become for years now, couching it as helping him. He knew I'd never deny him assistance. He'll make a great king one day, making Father's speeches and diplomacy seem like the written-for-him and rehearsed rubbish they were.

"Justine Citrine is out. She insulted me while simultaneously complimenting you."

"See? You're a natural. I agree. She is the falsest girl I think I've ever met. She insults my sister? Never."

I withheld my tongue about one of the premonitions I saw. I hope he never ends up with Justine. The other woman is the one for him, the darker-skinned girl—wish I could foresee her name. For some reason, my fire power told me then and there to fixate on her. She is Alex's path. I just had a feeling. Just one image was all it took, the look in their eyes as they stared at each other was enough to show me what true love looked like.

I wish I could assure him he would be happy one day, but he asked me not to. Knowing his feelings on matrimony, he'd likely run from her the more he fell for her if I prepared him. If anyone is scared of marrying as much as me, it's Alex. "I love you, Brother."

"Mary, we have a hard life, but behind closed doors—without Father around—we need to be *us*. Let us never let go of that. My kingdom one day will not be like his." He pulled me into a hug and kissed the top of my head. He rarely expressed his feelings in words, but he was telling me he loved me too.

"Agreed." I bid him goodnight because I was starting to tear up. I'm sure he knew it but made no indication of it; he knew it would embarrass me.

Alex is my rock. He has made me feel so empowered and in control; who knew by giving me a purpose that I would find my footing?

Concentrating on helping him gives me something to do. Learning to be a proper lady couldn't hurt if I help Alex weed out the Justines of the sphere. Maybe I can pick up a friend or two along the way.

March

I cannot write words to express how I feel at the moment. I don't even want to write about it, yet I must. Lady Emily Sapphirian passed away of the swelling disease. Baby Emery only breathed for half a day before he passed away, too tiny and fragile for the world. Henry's loss is so incredibly much more than mine. He is a broken grieving man who swears to never remarry. Father has given him leave and then is sending him and his father on a military mission. Father thinks a busy mind staves off the grief and heals. I would just think it puts it off, and it could return full force. Father never listens to me—the little spare princess. I just can't say more. Words cannot show how I feel, and I cannot give it justice on pages. I will have a drink to Emily and another for her baby. Maybe it will take my pain away. I'm not dumb—I know nothing will, but at least feeling nothing for a while will alleviate it.

Well, I had more than two and woke up with a terrible headache and dry mouth. Lucy took care of me and scolded me. When she finally got me out of bed, bathed, and dressed, I went down to lunch, where I barely ate. Mother wrote it off as grieving. I let her believe that. Of course, it was grief in a roundabout way, but I felt too sick to care about anything, including myself. I just wanted to curl up in a ball in my bed and never leave it.

That was what I did. I waited to feel better. But the bad head and queasy stomach shifted to an aching heart, a tight throat, and lots of tears. Why did she have to die? The only person who showed me kindness and friendship, the only person whom my cousin would love? Why did good people die and terrible people live? If religion were still practiced, I would curse the god of fire and goddess of light. How would they condone such horrible things? And the innocent young baby. Henry had to watch the healers try to keep the baby warm, but he couldn't breathe well enough in his fragile tiny form. I had foreseen it, and the image was burned into my memory forever. Such an innocent life taken because his mother's passing forced his early arrival. My godchild's funeral pyre was today; he left Fyr in his mother's arms. We all attended, although Father seemed nervous about transporting out of the castle, even if it was just the Emerald Fort. I thought saying goodbye at the pyre would give me closure. That's what they say. I can tell you, Joan, it does not. Death leaves a gaping hole in your heart that can never be healed.

I made the mistake of reading the papers. I have given them up. They lapped up Henry's grief and portrayed it as romantic, making every single woman in Fyr likely to try to ensnare him. What about love and grief? What about letting him have time to get over this and think of a lifemate much later down the line? They are called lifemates for a reason. I cannot see him marrying again. I don't need flames to know that.

May

I have not written in a while. I didn't have much to say. I am over Emily's death as much as one idle girl can be, meaning my thoughts drift to her often, and I get melancholy. Henry is out of my life too, on some secret mission where he cannot write to me nor me him. Aside from having Alex, I feel alone. Well, Ruby was around for schooling, but with everyone gone from the fort, she returned frequently to care for her mother. Not that she has ever been particularly kind to me. She treats me like a childish pest, although she is only two years older–when she isn't completely ignoring me.

I try my best in my etiquette lessons. I am improving. I realized not to fight my nature but put on an act, like my brother does. He acts aloof and almost arrogant when, inside, he's all mushy and full of kindness. Sometimes, I think the curse makes him somber and angry too, and I don't think he would be that way without it. It is not his true nature.

I still don't have the guts to visit other ladies and am too scared to invite a pack of them here to attack me. Lucy thinks the problem with my self-esteem is Justine. I think I have to admit Lucy is right for once. Justine is always about, tagging along with her father as an excuse to see my brother. Alex always hides when she is here. He invented a method of escape as well. He has David hand him a missive that is blank, and Alex says he must attend business. Ingenious really. For me, Mother does not let me escape. And let's just say Justine can slice you down with compliments that ring false, and her eyes and smirk judge you with such power, you'd swear that was her stone magic trait.

I have to find a way into society around her. I have to find a friend to help me.

October

Joan,

It's been a while. There hasn't been much to say. I now can pretend to be a lady in public and pass even the most judgmental mothers' scrutiny. My own mother is pleased with me—for the most part. She is not pleased I drink a firewhiskey and water before these outings. I hate to admit it, but it makes me relax. Gives me the confidence to put on the act of being aloof, untouchable, and to feign the confidence I don't actually possess.

I look into the flames and see the person I will become: intelligent, powerful, and confident. It is hard to come to terms with that image and what a useless, weak girl I am now. I would never utter this aloud—not even to Lucy—but I don't like myself. I wish I were someone else. Not the princess on the periphery, the spare no one thinks of twice. Don't get me wrong—I love my brother, and I have no wish to rule and be responsible for the entire sphere. I want to be the heroine in my own story, rule my own destiny. Instead, I feel great anxiety about the lack of control I have over things. The flames tell me what will be. People in my life—Father, Mother, Lucy, my tutors—tell me what to be now. I look back to the past and realize I've never had control over my life. It's depressing and distressing to think about.

I still can't come to terms with the whole Cobalt-and-me thing. Do you know what happened today? In lessons, we had to partner up. Of course, with only a few of us actually being schooled in the palace, there was an uneven number. I thought Ruby would be kind and be my partner, or Alex would be there for me, but no. The three of them were giggling over Ruby burning the boys' secretly coded notes to prevent them from getting in trouble. Cobalt suggested they be a group of three since the class consisted of seven of us of various ages. The tutor agreed, which was so unfair. The other three kids, my cousins on my mother's side, ranged from five to nine. I was paired with Geoffrey, the nine-year-old. And I was supposedly a lady. Fourteen years old.

The slight didn't just end there. I hurried out of classes, asking Alex what he was up to.

He stopped. "I'm headed to the stables with Cobalt and Ruby."

"Can I join you?" It was a desperate plea.

Alex immediately opened his mouth to respond, likely to say yes, because my brother rarely denied me his attention and included me when I asked.

But Cobalt cut in, "Mary, you can't ride as fast as we do. You'd hold us up."

"I can too," I fired back.

"Not safely, dear cousin," Ruby said. She and Cobalt exchanged a conspirative look. I wonder if they talked about me behind my back. I wondered how much of the future she saw; maybe she knew about Cobalt and me and had told him. I insecurely backed away.

Alex gave me a look that begged forgiveness. He would make it up to me somehow, but if he had been insistent on my company at that moment, Cobalt and Ruby would follow him. He is the future of Fyr. Everyone would listen. Even he let me down.

I turned away from them as Ruby and Cobalt shared a secret and giggled. Then I transported to my rooms, not letting them see my tears. Firebranding depressed me even more. I don't have the energy to even share what I saw, not even with you, Joan. I have no friends. I have no one.

The firebranding is driving me crazy. Lucy has told me to stop, and I must agree it has become an obsession. I keep seeing Cobalt and me together. I'm resigned to not think of men or marriage, in hopes he grows up into someone more worthy. I refuse to say any more on the subject for now and will only write in here when I have something to say—unrelated to that cad of a boy.

November

I'm getting better at etiquette by watching my brother. Alex does this funny thing right before he enters a room. His smile drops, his shoulders stiffen into a perfect posture, and his eyes dim. He has perfected the aloof look that I could never master, but I'm close. It is so fake, but it is safe, and the lords give him some respect, and it makes the ladies vie even more for his attention. Interesting. I think I learn more from watching him than in my etiquette lessons. Performing the reserved act myself has helped me see why Alex does it. It is a shield. No one can hurt you if you show no weakness, no emotion.

You'd think this would help me make friends? Nope. All ladies stink. They are falser than any act Alex or I could perform. Fake. All of them. Not one of them is real. Like Alex plays his role, they all do it too. As a future king, he must play a role, or they could see him as weak, see the curse as making him unfit; they could revolt or usurp his throne. Ladies though? Their only agenda is to marry well. How will their lifemates feel when they realize they have been duped? When the docile sweetheart turns into a shrew, isn't it obvious that she was a liar?

Sigh, the truth is, Joan, they are so mean. I don't understand their nasty games. Lucy never warns me. Not that that is part of a bodyguard-waiting maid, but it should be. Isn't protecting my mind as important as my body? The truth is, I don't think Lucy actually knows, because she's a cunning folk, and they tend to be real and direct with each other.

Anyway, the girls set me up, then tear me to shreds. I hate them all. The only consolation I have is I give Alex a weekly update on who to avoid for his future "happiness." Unfortunately, it is most ladies I've met with. The ones who pass as tolerable and somewhat kind don't seem right for him. I hope this girl I envisioned is much different than them, because, from what I have seen, poor Alex has no good choices with what Celestia has to offer. I'm not sure what he will do. If it comes to it, I'll tell him to keep delaying until he meets the one. But where is she? What family does she belong to? What town is she in? I've been studying families and crests to remember all the noble families and have not encountered many with tan skin. We Fyrians are a pale race. Perhaps she has heritage from Lyft or Water?

I'm impatient for this girl to cross our paths. I don't think our parents will let Alex pass eighteen without marrying. He only has a couple years.

I'm at a low point. I drank too much firewhiskey again last night. Lucy is lecturing me about my drinking "problem," but I told her it wasn't one. So what? I like to overindulge when I'm feeling bad. It keeps me numb for a while. I don't know how to attend these events or to face Cobalt daily without it.

Okay, yeah, writing it down is showing me that I'm lying through my teeth. I have a problem. I just don't know how to or want to solve it. Not yet. If I had a real friend—no offense, Joan—who could listen to me, I think I could easily stop. I thought I was going to have that with Lady Emily, but even she was taken away. Alex is slipping away, and Cobalt is a lost cause. I'm over him—done with him. I don't care about the flames, because what I heard today proves I'm a terrible firebrander.

In short, Cobalt has gotten a lady with child. A *lady*, one of my peers, ergo he must do the honorable thing and marry her. He could, of course, choose to make her his mistress instead, but I think I would hate him more if he disrespected any woman that much, even the loose Lady Anabel Diamond. She is two years older than Cobalt, and if rumors are to be believed, he is the fourth nobleman she has gone to bed with, not counting cunning folk servants leaving her rooms late at night. I wondered why no one would marry her. And why did she think this was the best way to trap a man? Getting with child to snag a lifemate was a dangerous game to play, since all men are not gentlemen. So, as you see, Cobalt is gone to me, no matter what he chooses. They are called lifemates for a reason. He will be tied to her for life. I'd hate to say losing a future with Cobalt has left a faint feeling of grief. I hate the cad, but part of me had loved him.

January

Well, I take back what I said two months ago. Cobalt called off the wedding. "Lady" Anabel was not with child; she lied. The Cobalt family became suspicious when there was insistence on marrying right away. After all, the child is only born on the wrong side of the blanket if the parents don't marry before the birth. Many marriages end up with the woman marrying and showing right away. Not that I would ever be one of them. Royals and royals-to-be—only the women, ugh—had to be pure when they entered marriage, and even my asinine ancestors figured out the stone to measure our purity or what they saw as women's "worth."

I digress. Cobalt is free, but I have realized something profound: I don't want him. I got over that grief I felt in my previous entry days later. I had closure. Regardless, the event helped me get over this silly crush, and I can put the idea of marriage behind me. At least until mother gets on my case about it. She's nagging Alex in earnest. Sixteen feels awfully young, but he is the heir. This might become amusing to watch. Mother and Father cannot force Alex to marry, but they sure can pressure and nag him until he'll do it to be left alone.

I have been miserable lately. Cobalt and Ruby had always chatted after lessons. Then, since they recently completed their education, I've been left with the younger kids, ignored and alone. Ruby comes to the palace almost daily just to see Cobalt. I thought I didn't care much, but Cobalt and Ruby have been talking *a lot*. It never looks like two lovers, but friends. So, I was deeply surprised when I heard he had put his name on her suitor list. I thought it was a joke, so I cornered Ruby in the library.

"You and Cobalt are going to marry?"

"Likely." She perused a bookshelf, without any emotion about marriage. One should be excited, lovestruck—something. Ruby didn't even look up from the book she was flipping through. She put it back and picked up another, obviously searching for something.

"You don't seem excited."

She put the book back. "I'm not. I'm about as thrilled to get married as Alex is, to be honest. I'm sure you know your brother's sentiment on the topic."

"Then why are you marrying?"

She looked up at me, her Sapphirian blue eyes locking on mine. She was shocked at my question; then her face fell into a sympathetic one. "Let me guess. You naively believe you'll never be forced to marry? We are Sapphirians, a dwindling race, the race that continues to keep the fire on this planet going. We *must* marry and have children. I want out of my father's house, to take my mother with me to a new home. I knew I'd never marry for love, so I'm marrying my best friend."

"Does Cobalt know you don't love him?"

"Yes."

"And he still wants to marry you?" It didn't make sense. Cobalt was in no need of social connections or money, two reasons for arranged marriages.

"Of course. He agreed because I will allow him mistresses."

I could not believe this, Joan, so I lost it. "What about the sanctity of marriage? What about love? He should marry someone he loves, someone he wants to be faithful to, not someone who urges him to be with others!"

Ruby scrutinized me in that way that always made me feel ignorant, like I was missing something. "Mary, you're naïve. If I can't marry for love, I can marry someone I respect, who will treat me well, and I can allow him to love others."

"Why can't you find someone you love? I know it must be hard, but there is someone for everyone."

She put a book away quite roughly. I had struck a nerve. All I wanted to do was shake her and tell her that the someone he would love would be me, and if he married her, it could never be. A future with Cobalt was better than this loveless marriage with some other man I might have. And it would be unfair on both Ruby and Cobalt to enter into the arrangement.

She did not answer but stared at me, willing me to understand something I was missing.

I didn't know why she could not love someone, so I switched my motive. "Why Cobalt?"

"He is my best friend, as I've said. Look, Mary, I'm trying to find something important, and you're distracting me with your questions. Can we talk about this later?"

"What are you looking for?"

"I need to figure out magic against a necromancer."

"But they are long gone, aren't they?"

"Yes. But I saw one, Mary—in the flames," she added hastily.

My spine prickled at the thought she might've seen one in person.

"And my future has dwindled. I cannot see much farther." She met my gaze and then looked away.

We both knew what that meant. Ruby could die soon if the flames did not show her more.

"Go to Tobias Firebrand. He has all the contraband and archaic books. He's bound to know more about necromancers than anyone else in Fyr."

Tobias had been Alex and my tutor for our firebranding, but he rarely came anymore. Alex had graduated, and I could see beyond Tobias's abilities by the time I was twelve. Alex still visited him now and then.

For the first time since I entered the room, Ruby smiled. "Thank you, Cousin. How could I forget about him?" She squeezed my shoulders lovingly. "We'll talk about Cobalt later. I feel like there's something you're not telling me."

We didn't talk. When Ruby returned, she seemed nervous. She stuffed away something into her pocket. I decided to leave her alone about Cobalt and not bring it up. Ruby had more to worry about than my petty jealousy. I feel like it was a very adult thing to do. Maybe I could be a lady after all. Maybe I didn't need Lady Emily to be my champion. Maybe I could be my own.

March

I think this is goodbye for now—in a good way.

Ruby spends most of her time at Fort Emerald, which alleviated any lingering jealousy. I'm tired of writing about my problems only in here. If you were a human friend, you'd have ditched me by now due to my whining. This story is a happy ending to my journal-writing days. I have decided to become my own champion, step by step. First, I will continue using Alex's aloof act, but throw in some sass. Being unapproachable and above the ladies will at least protect me from censure. Lucy tries to tell me to find the nice ladies and pull them in as friends, and by my very name they'll become the most influential. As always, I dislike her advice. The Justines of the world will always rule because the cruel prey upon the nice, and they usually win. I will get her one day, but I will plan it out strategically. I made my first move: to hold my own. Pretend I was too good for her and cling to Alex when I could to protect both of us. I noticed he prefers my company when ladies are around. He talks to me, so he doesn't have to talk to them.

I talk of my brother because he has become much dearer to me—or more so, after a selfish period, has returned to caring about and respecting me. Let me give the tale justice.

We had a family session where father was drilling Alex about state affairs, telling him he needed to know everything before he even let him join in meetings so he wouldn't embarrass himself. That meant Father didn't want to be embarrassed for having a son who wasn't perfect. I couldn't handle that pressure. I could've never succeeded as firstborn and heir. Alex seemed exhausted, floundered over his answer, and Father started to yell at him.

I opened my mouth to help Alex, to give my input, and it backfired. First, Father said I needed to know my place as a woman. Second, he threatened to make me heir if Alex couldn't handle it.

When we left, Alex asked me to meet him early the next morning by the stables. I had thought he wanted to discuss father's threat; maybe he didn't want the throne, but I sure didn't either.

However, it was nothing like that. It was something so much better.

We met at the stables, and he told me we were going riding. He obviously needed to talk. Any time with my brother is better than being alone. He was trying to make time for me, so I appreciated that. He bears the weight of the kingdom on his shoulders, and Father is already pushing his studies to be more hands-on training. Something very odd since, in the past, most royalty allowed their heirs to marry and secure an heir before they had to dabble in politics. My stomach dropped. I could only think of one reason Father would prepare him early, and it aligned with me not being able to foresee him in his old age. Sadly, I felt for Alex more than Father. Such a sweet soul will be crushed by the pressures and problems he would inherit.

"Are you worried about ruling one day?" I asked.

"Huh? No." He was distracted, checking over his shoulder to see how far back Lucy and David were. He was up to something.

"What are you up to?"

"A surprise, but we have to lose the bodyguards. Mary, hold on tight." He winked. I barely had a tight hold on the reigns when Alex slapped my horse's flank hard. She whinnied and took off, me bumping up and down from the annoying sidesaddle. I knew how to soothe her, but allowed her to run off her fright, for this was part of his plan.

Alex called out my name, his voice tight with feigned fright. I heard his horse galloping behind me and gave my mare a nudge to speed up. As his horse overtook mine, Alex reached out his hand, and I took it, knowing he'd transport us somewhere away from our babysitters. I trusted my brother.

We appeared in a one-room shack in a warm place. I heard strange noises outside.

"Alex. Are we in the Firelands?"

"Yes. Mary, Father and I fought recently. I'm sure you've sensed the tension between us."

"About you taking on more responsibility or you getting married?"

"No, well, yes, that is normal. He and I fought about you."

"Me?"

"You are of age, and you hopefully will never have to rule, but you *are* the spare. It is only right you meet the draca. Each Sapphirian came here at the age of ten, but Father did not give you that. I don't know why, Mary. He says he is not well enough to do it, that he cannot leave the castle as the ruler. Father forbade me to take you. Don't look so upset, Mary. It's because the heir and the spare outside the palace together without soldiers..."

"Could not Ruby? Or Henry?" They were the only other Sapphirians—excluding my crazy aunt—so they could take me.

"I don't know why neither took you. This is not the first time Father and I have fought about it. And I asked our cousins before. Henry was always busy with studies and training, then courting, and now he's on some special assignment. Ruby, on the other hand, has not been helpful in the past and more so now. She has some trail of information she is following, as she always does, but refuses to tell me or Cobalt about it. Now, we can continue to waste time chatting, or you can meet some draca. I'm going to get into a lot of trouble. Let us make sure it is worth it."

Alex opened the door of the little hut and stepped out onto the porch. A loud shrieking sound made me jump. My overly observant brother turned back with a reassuring smile and offered me his hand. I took it, and he gallantly ignored the fact my hand shook with fright. I had only seen dragons in picture books and never knew how they sounded.

I could see the heat rippling in waves off the ground rather than feel it. No normal person could withstand such heat, which was why we had to leave the bodyguards behind, but us Sapphirians could. I gathered strength from the pride for who and what I am: a princess, a descendant of the god of fire who had been born of the draca's flames.

Alex was quiet for a moment. Then he said, "I communicated with my thoughts. Told them 'I, Alexander Rowland Sapphirian, have come to visit. I have brought my sister, as is custom, to meet the draca and be recognized.'"

Was it that easy? Thinking would communicate with them?

"The older ones do understand human words pretty well, but they have their own language too. It is more respectful to speak in tandem, in thoughts, a language our united blood can innately understand. Think the words, but try to project them."

"Why can't we communicate to each other this way?"

"I don't know. I think because they are so much stronger than us, they listen and they speak back, but it is as if they make the link to us. It's more of their magic, not fully ours. But we have to be able to listen to them. Be prepared: Henry can't think-speak to them, and Ruby can't hear them. Father and I can do both."

He was preparing me in case it didn't work, but realizing my father had taken my cousins to this monumental life milestone, and not me, stung acutely.

As if he sensed it, Alex squeezed my hand. "Mother, you, and I must love each other more fully since we cannot have his. I think he has been ill for some time, Mary, which coincides with why he couldn't take you."

It was an excuse. Father was able to take Ruby only two years before I turned ten, and he could have ordered Henry to take me.

Alex's hand in mine, his reassuring blue eyes made me realize I never needed Father. I had Alex as a brother, mentor, and father-figure if I needed that type of advice.

His eyes twinkled with excitement as the first few draca flew and landed either to pay their respects or out of curiosity. "Are you ready?"

As about five of them walked closer, I could hear a mixture of their voices. I squeezed Alex's hand.

"Can you hear them?"

I nodded, speechless.

A bearn came up to me and nuzzled my hand. *HI!* The bearn's voice rang in my head, full of youthful exuberance. I ran my hand along his glassy-hided snout, and he moved to make my hand run down his back spines, which made him purr.

"Bearn Draca P. You memorize them off their coloring. Outside of the Sapphirian draca, they go by Dame, Lord, and Bearns." Alex told me. I was half listening. I was hearing the thoughts of the draca around us.

Never saw this one before.

A female one. Is that two of each left?

Of bearns, I think.

She's pretty for a human.

You think humans pretty? Eww.

They're nice to look at, like a toy.

I didn't like the sound of that. I imagined draca pulling off my legs like a child might do to her dolls if too rough.

I'm not a toy, but the princess. I pushed my thoughts out, hoping they would hear me.

Princess, one thought back, *A lord, a lady, a prince, and now a princess. Are there more?*

No, that is all. I told them.

Sad, a large one thought. *Used to be so many of you. Had visitors weekly. There will be more. The flames say so. Many more. After Bladesung comes.*

"I take from the silence you are communicating back and forth fine?" Alex asked.

"You can't hear us?"

"No, like I said, they are sharing their thoughts with us one-on-one. I've been chatting with this Draca J over here, the blue, the prince, the Sapphirian draca." He nodded to a draca to our left, who bowed his head at me and fed me the thought, *Princess.*

Prince, I thought back and bowed my head as well out of respect.

We lingered for only a few more minutes as I was bombarded by questions about my name, my age, and other such qualities. Then Alex urged us to go. The dragons complained. He explained that we snuck out so I could meet them. They called us rebels and did snorting sounds that I took as laughs.

All too soon, we said goodbye, and Alex transported us back to the stables, where a livid David and cringing Lucy warned us we had been found out, and we were in trouble.

As soon as we entered the castle, the summons to Father's study came. He shouted, paced and raged, his face turning so red, it began to turn purple. My knees shook from fright under my gown. Alex sensed my unease, or perhaps he was terrified under the cool exterior he had mastered to hide his emotions. My brother took up my hand in his, squeezing it. It reassured me. Alex will always be there for me. Father was just someone who ruled over us, and we must play our parts for him. Alex tried to take the blame, and I protested, saying I deserved to go and that Father denying me my right was a slight all would see to make me inferior.

Unable to deny any of that, instead he shouted for us to, "Stop holding hands like children!" Alex let go of my hand, and I felt instantly vulnerable.

"You will be punished! Both of you." Father rubbed his brow, weary, and plopped into his chair, seemingly exhausted.

Alex's jaw clenched. "How do you think you can punish us? You cannot keep us in quarters with the transporting, and you can barely stand up. You are ill, and you let your anger eat away at your energy."

I was shocked at his response, and Father was equally so. "What did you say, boy?"

They were shouting such horrid things to each other that my shock has made me forget the exact words, Joan. There were curses and raised voices, and I wanted it to stop.

I touched Alex's shoulder. His arm went rigid under my touch. He shirked it off, his gaze cold and dull when it met mine. Oh no.

"Father, please, stop. You triggered the curse. It's causing the anger."

Father glared at me. Alex squeezed his eyes shut and clenched his fists. I had seen him do this often enough to know he was pushing the curse back, overpowering it.

"One wonders how you fight it," Father spat. "And it makes me think you're ill-equipped to rule."

I did not understand his comment. Why did he wonder about Alex's combatting the curse? He always had. Alex was so strong and full of goodness. He wore amulets to keep him grounded as well. He hid them, but I had seen them. I never asked, but guessed they were black tourmaline to weaken the dark curse.

"Glad you took your sister, then. She might have to rule after all. That is, if she stops drinking. I've heard about your love for the bottle, girl. I'm disappointed in both of you."

"I can see why," Alex retorted. "Because you refuse to see the good in anyone, and the flaws in yourself."

"Alex!" I shouted.

Alex turned from the room and stormed out as Father shouted out multiple punishments.

"Go away," Father moaned.

"If you just were a touch kinder," I dared to say, "you would not evoke the curse."

"He cannot rule if he cannot control it." Father was still livid, and I was the brunt of his anger.

"He never loses his temper until you scream at him. Just talk to him. He's not a child."

He glared at me. "Go."

It was an intense day, Joan, but I would not let Father's tantrum bother me. I met draca. My brother proved to me that I mattered most. I stood up against Father, even after Alex left.

When I found Alex, he was having a firewhiskey with Cobalt in the Prince's Room. He let me enter, and Cobalt poured me one. Alex was already in a better mood, and I felt Cobalt's magic permeating the room. I was feeling great and poured another one for us all. Alex stopped after a couple, but I challenged Cobalt to a drinking contest. Alex didn't find it funny and cut us off after a couple more drinks, kicking us out of the room. After Cobalt offered to walk me to my quarters, Alex insisted on transporting me to my room himself. I don't remember much after that, sadly. I think Alex and Lucy helped me to bed and I slept.

In the morning, I had a tinge of a headache, and regretted overimbibing because it lessened my triumph over Father. The second thing that I did was hear my punishment. I'll fill you in when I'm done.

Father made us muck out the stable stalls, a metaphor likely for how he felt about us. It was so awful in the beginning, and part of me remembered and pitied Cobalt. He deserved it for what he did—and continued to do. I simply saw draca. Soon, the hired help was so disturbed by us actually doing it, they chipped in and helped. It was hard work, and my arms and back instantly ached, but Alex and I talked the entire time. First, we relived my trip with the draca and exchanged what the draca said to each of us. Then I turned the conversation to Father.

"It wasn't just the curse, you know, Mary. The more I learn about Father's principles and way of ruling, the more I plan on changing all of it as soon as I can. He is ill. I don't want him to die, despite what he is, but this sphere might be better for it."

I gasped. "Alex, that's treason."

"You have seen the flames. Do you see him as an old man?"

I shook my head. Still angry at Father, the absence of him would be relief—a sigh after such a long-held breath. Guilt overtook me for the thought. I had thought Alex feared ruling, and I felt bad he would have to do it young, but here he was embracing his destiny, looking forward to it.

"You feel the same way too, I'm sure, Mary. How can we love those who hurt us so much?"

Little did Alex know that another man in my life did the same to me. I cast Cobalt from my mind.

"But Mary, please. Don't drink your problems away. I'm sure they come right back afterwards."

I sighed. There was nothing to say, because he was right. I have to get a grip on it. The feeling of not caring or worrying about anything is exhilarating, though it always comes back, twice as badly.

We stopped speaking after that, both of us lost in our thoughts. The stablemaster insisted we were finished after about two full hours. My body was. I knew he was being kind, because it was not done. I told Lucy to send out a small feast of pheasant, potatoes, and ale to the stable servants in thanks. I saw pride in the girl's eyes for once in her life. I guess I could be nicer to her and other servants.

Alex and I walked, neither one of us wanting to transport back.

"A swim? Get this muck off us?" Alex asked.

"I thought I wasn't allowed to."

"With Cobalt, Mary, or any other man not related to you, without proper bathing attire and a chaperone like Mother to watch the men. We won't venture deep, so the clothes won't weigh us down. We should at least get a bit of stink off. It'll annoy Father if we walk in clean."

I scoffed. "Father is too busy to care what we do."

"You need to be more observant about your surroundings, Mary. I saw a couple of his spies checking on us from afar. I saw the reflection of the sun glancing off a telescope, and a 'message' for the stableboy when no horse was prepared to ride. I'm no good at these parlor tricks either, but I'm learning what Father is truly like in front of others. Everything is a façade. I will never be that way, especially with you."

"A swim then." I nodded. "Come back clean."

He laughed, and like kids we ran to the pond, all the way into the water.

Hate to say, but the clothes only became so clean. They proved heavy climbing out, but we used our powers to steam them dry. We still smelled, and our clothes were likely ruined, but the unsatisfied look on our father's face was worth it. We were not dirty enough for his liking.

Lucy bathed me and sent my laundry down to be cleaned. I felt strong, despite the soreness already spreading through my body. This conquering over Father was silly and small, but I feel triumphant. And I have my brother back. Despite Cobalt and Ruby, he was there for me when needed. He is the best brother ever. Add Mother into the mix, and there is no better family in Fyr. I'm just suddenly at peace and so happy. I am looking forward to my future and hope I won't need to write for a long time. A boring but happy existence is not worth the ink to put it down, so I'll be satisfied if I don't need to write to you for a long time, Joan. Please take no offense. There's always Cobalt to stir the pot.

See you again one day!

Mary Elizabeth Sapphirian
Her Royal Highness, Princess of Fyr
(the one and only)
aged 15 years

September

Joan,

Since I stopped writing for a while, you can safely assume all was well with me, and pretty dull. I was longing for something exciting to happen, but had I known it would be this, I would love tedium again. Ruby is missing. Father's men scoured the land to find her and return her to the castle. After all, maybe she was just trying to run away from home. That was my suggestion because she had told me she'd marry just to get away from the fort. I don't know why. My uncle was kind, although old-fashioned. The only thing I could not figure out was why she left her mother behind if she fled.

Alex and I tried to piece things together. We knew there was more to it. I remember her necromancer research and telling her to see Tobias. Alex sent the man a missive asking about it. This is horrible. I resented her so much for wanting to take Cobalt away from me through a loveless marriage, but now I want her back and safe. The guilt is overwhelming. I have a terrible feeling her disappearance is a start of something bigger, something cataclysmic and dangerous. All the visions I had of strife and horror, are they going to happen soon? The flames flickered and became unstable to read. They weren't telling me much. Ruby's and Alex's decisions seemed to shift everything around.

Mother and Father are pressuring Alex to choose a bride. Of course, Father suggested Justine. It is a daily occurrence during nightcaps.

Tonight, I had enough. "Stop! Leave him alone. I have seen his lifemate in the flames. He will marry, and from what I can tell, it's not that far into the future."

Alex's head darted in my direction so fast, I wondered how he didn't get a twinge in his neck.

"I haven't met her yet, but it is not Justine Citrine. So please, just let him be, and he'll marry on his own."

Father scrutinized me; then he looked at Alex. "Have you seen her?"

Alex shook his head.

Father made a disapproving grunt. "She sees better than you, and she's not cursed. Perhaps she should be studying politics, and you become my spare."

Alex's jaw clenched.

"No thank you," I said. I knew it would make my father attack me, but Alex protects me so often that I felt I owed him in the moment.

"I didn't ask you, *girl*," Father condescendingly said, his face snarling at my gender.

Oh, how I loathe him sometimes. I am beginning to understand him. Jealousy. Of what, who knows? Likely my firebranding abilities and Alex's youth and ability to overcome everything thrown his way, including a curse. Father is the angriest about how he is weakening, and we are growing up and becoming stronger. I wanted to tell him he'd die soon, but looking at Mother dote on him, I could not hurt her.

"Well, you should. I see much more than you'll ever know." It was coded. His glare and shaky hand as he went for his drink told me I had hit home. He knew I meant his death. "Alex will marry, and she will be great for our sphere."

Alex fidgeted, clearly not liking the topic. I'm sure he was also itching to ask me questions yet debating if he wanted to know the answers. I know my brother's character well enough that I will have to pretend I don't know her when he meets this girl in my visions. He needs to be with her, so I decided then I'd never tell him she was the one. I'll give him that gift of falling in love without it being ruined for him. It is what I wish I could have with Cobalt: a blind path into courtship and love.

Father dismissed us. I could've transported Lucy and me to my quarters, but I knew Alex would want to talk. I left on foot, and he followed.

Once in the hall and away from Father's hearing range, I broke our silence. "I won't tell you. You deserve to fall in love and not have the flames dictate it."

"No, I'd never ask. I just want to know if I will love her and not simply resign on the least awful girl."

"You will love her beyond what I have seen love to be, and she will equal that love. I don't know how things will go or how you will end up with her. I truly don't know who she is. That wasn't a lie, but I promise I won't tell you."

Alex sighed. "It's so difficult wanting to know but not."

"You shouldn't know. I know what you're like. You'll spoil it."

Alex sighed. "Will you tell me who your lifemate is?"

I shook my head. "I don't want you to judge him. He's immature, but I hope he'll grow up. I don't want you holding that against him."

"Understood. Thank you, Mary." He squeezed my hand, let go, and transported to his room, likely to brood and firebrand as he is oft to do these days.

Mother is going to ship me off to finishing school. Madam Mage's. I'm devastated. I can't say I don't deserve it. Mother had one of her tedious luncheons, and the girls were so insipid, I turned to the firewhiskey just to get through the event. I admit, I was a bit tipsy, and I did something she was not proud of, but I am proud of myself. Lady Emily would secretly cheer for my triumph—if she were still with us.

Justine and her little pack of wolves were chattering, while I was trying to avoid most ladies in the room, making small talk with ladies who were real—well, less fake. I wasn't watching, and Justine and her entourage cornered me while talking to Lady Julia Garnet.

"Nice dress, Princess Mary," Justine purred in her saccharine breathy falsetto.

I thanked her, awaiting the barb that would follow. I'm tired of her cruelty, falseness, and persistent ambition to marry my brother. Thankfully, she is likely to be the last girl in Fyr he'd marry.

"Would look better if you had some curves to actually fill it out." There it was. She grinned. The audacity she had. Insulting royalty was a punishable offense.

I have never had the courage to tattle on her, but I was tempted to this time. Instead, emboldened by the firewhiskey, I said, "Well, not all of us want to mislead men as you do, Justine, with a padded corset. In fact—" I paused to scan her up and down "—I feel bad for your future lifemate when he wakes up the day after your wedding. He won't recognize you after all the paint, powder, and padding are gone."

Justine's eyes bugged out. Her friends' mouths dropped, but a couple bit their lips to not laugh. Then Justine's eyes cut sharp, narrowing on me. Pure hatred emanated from her. Her fists clenched, and her shoulders went rigid. She would not dare to hit me and end up in prison, but for a moment, I had thought she might.

"Your brother loves a woman's natural beauty, so I think he'll be fine waking up in my bed."

Her friends gasped. I tried not to react. To insinuate she would either marry, or maybe just even bed, my brother was tactless and bold.

"You're right, Justine. My brother does love natural beauty in a woman, which is why he'll *never* marry you. You see, the beauty my brother seeks is in the inside as well as the outside. Inside, you're rotten to the core."

Justine's hands were still balled, and she twitched. I held firm, although my knees were shaking. I hate confrontation, but I'm also tired of her bullying me and insinuating I am lesser than her. There should be no one in the land who esteems herself my better.

Silence and tension followed. "I read the flames. You are not his lifemate. Only I know who is."

Then Justine surprised me. She started crying, straight up wailing. She fled from the room, a couple of her shocked friends running after her.

Mother was livid. I was in deep trouble with her. After I got over the initial shock of the punishment—go to finishing school to become a better lady and find a lifemate—I realized I hadn't beaten Justine. She wanted so badly to hit me but could not. Instead, she feigned crying, knowing I'd get in trouble, knowing my mother likely spoke to her mother about finishing school. I might've gotten her to stop bullying me, I hope, but she has won the round since I'm packing up my things. If she thinks getting me out of the way will help her get Alex, she is so wrong. Without a young lady at the castle, she'll have less excuses to force an interview with Alex.

Still no news about Ruby. Father's soldiers cannot find her. There's a reward for her safe return. Alex thinks the worst. I feel guilty, but I think the guilt only comes from the thought of Cobalt being free from a marriage of convenience. It is a horrible thought. Aside from that, I have no issue with Ruby, and I have never been cruel to her. My only negative thoughts toward her involve her and Cobalt and her purposely leaving me out of things. I cannot help that I am human and fallible—not a god as my ancestors professed we were.

My freedom is dwindling. I have to endure the Citrine Centennial Ball before I am shipped off. Mother is making Alex go, likely to keep me out of trouble. More like I will need to protect him from Justine. Mother said I'm not to speak to her, which is fine with me. Let's hope the ball goes well. Maybe, if I behave, Mother will decide not to send me away. I'm not afraid of leaving home or being in the boarding school. I'm afraid what will happen when I leave it. Women leave the school engaged or with a list of suitors. I'm not ready at all to even think about marriage. Every time I do, I think of Cobalt and the kind of man he still is. Rumors say he learned nothing after his scare into an almost-marriage.

Lady Citrine and the dreaded Justine visited today, again. I had the task of making my brother go downstairs to greet them. Mother wouldn't take no for an answer. She didn't tell us who was there in her note, so I was unpleasantly surprised to see them. The little battle between Justine and me was not mentioned, and the Citrines were dripping with their fake charm. It was a bit fun, I admit, watching Justine fish for compliments and Alex laying his bored aloof persona on thick. He had to, but it still didn't work with this girl. Justine is determined to snag him, even if Alex hated her. His tone shifted to being rude, and Mother was becoming vexed. I joined in being sarcastic, but Mother's glare told me to cease and desist. Alex extracted us when a note came. Tobias had news about Ruby. Strange he didn't respond right away when she went missing—and suspicious. I hope she is alive.

Ruby is dead.

Alex and Tobias saw it in the flames. Her body is on Earth. How they could see into another sphere was confounding, but Tobias is gifted and my brother powerful. My father won't risk sending anyone to retrieve her body. She can't even have a proper pyre. I'd rather her be alive and take Cobalt from me. How selfish were my thoughts in previous entries?

At first, I was too upset to ask for more details, but when I did, Alex shut me out. I know there was more to her disappearance, and perhaps he suspects who killed her, but he kept telling me not to get involved or we'd end up like her. That was enough to shut me up. Asking too many questions might just get us killed because Ruby had been researching necromancers. The thought of them being alive still gave me chills.

For once, you'll enjoy this story. No Cobalt nonsense and whining about finishing school. No more grieving for my poor cousin. Oh no. I have a gem of a story, one I cannot share with anyone, for my brother deserves privacy, and the court girls would lose their fake hair at the idea of what occurred.

So here is how it played out: Alex and I knew we had to go to the Citrine Centennial Ball. I hate the girl, and their celebration of being nobles for a hundred years is a pathetic claim. It simply means that they bought their way into it and came from cunning folk originally. Money secured marriages to real nobles, which finally enhanced powers enough to be accepted as a sorcerer. Anyway, I wanted a new dress, and Mother had been excruciatingly controlling and emotional when she took me to get my "women's apparel" on my birthday. I begged my brother to take me so I could order a new dress. The ballgowns mother had picked out were adequate, but I wanted something less modest. I wanted to look like a woman for my first major ball, being now of "marriageable" age. I wanted everyone to see me as a young woman and not a child—especially Justine.

When we entered, I rushed to the proprietor to tell her not to do that embarrassing thing they did for us in every place: shut them down and kick customers out to cater for me alone. The place had about a dozen people inside, so losing those sales for my one order would be ridiculous. I would point out what I wanted, a worker would take me into the back and measure me, then it would be made and sent to the palace tomorrow, where our seamstress could make any slight alteration if there were tiny areas to take in to be perfect.

As always, when we entered, it went silent. Except, this time, two people continued talking. I ignored them and told the proprietor my wishes. When I heard my brother's voice and whispers among other patrons, I glanced over to see him standing near the dressing rooms, talking to a girl. God and goddess, I almost dropped the book of dress designs on the floor. It was the tanned girl from my visions. His future lifemate!

I held onto the book and flipped through it, hardly looking at the pictures. Alex was so engrossed with the girl—one might say lovestruck—that it was as if none of us were even in the room. She insulted him. I held my breath, fearing his reaction. I wondered why she would dare insult him. Was she a shrew? My brother could not have a fishwife. Of all the silly reasons for my brother to become starry-eyed. Calling him an ogler. Was that how people fell in love? Weird.

When Alex went as far as to suggest the girl was right about her bosom showing too much, and the dress could use some lace, I almost burst out laughing. The only thing that stifled my humor was my jealousy. She has a chest I would kill for: not too big, but not flat-chested like me. The fact her waist is thin, and she is taller than I am, with thin arms, and probably legs, it makes her chest look bigger than it would on an average girl. She is what I long to be.

I pointed out the dress I had my eye on in the book. I examined my brother's future lifemate—if visions could be trusted—and noted that although I found her very pretty and my brother was marking an obvious interest when he never had before of any young lady, she was not court material. Her manners made mine look great, and her skin and hair were not the favorably courtly pale and light. She was taller and thinner than was the current fashion. Was that why he found her attractive? Like me, my brother hated the falsity of court. Was this a rebellion thing? Oh, I would so support it—visions or not—because the less enforcement of court social law, the more I could just be myself one day. The girl looked naturally pretty, not done up with paints like some of the ladies. I liked that.

When Alex left her and came back to me, I gave him a look.

His expression asked why I was smug, but then he shifted back to his aloof role with, "Well, that was entertaining."

"I think it was for everyone." I slipped into the back to be measured quickly.

When I came back out, Alex was handing over more Sapphirians than necessary for my dress. What was he up to?

Oh, Joan, I got it out of him on the carriage ride home. Can you believe he bought the lady a dress? I laughed so hard, but then pulled myself together to ask him his intentions. He said it was to show her she wasn't in trouble, and I had to inform him it would be misconstrued by her and everyone as him courting her. I can't wait for the rumors to spread and see Alex squirm. I think he's stuck now. I should tell him it was destined, but I really want to be a spectator and see this unfold.

I've done it. After giving up the rag papers, I finally asked Lucy to resume buying them. With wicked excitement, she brought it to me. I was stronger now, older. I could handle gossip. I got one because I had to see the rumors unfold about Alex. There was no way his actions would go unnoticed. Of course, it was the largest article at the top of the sheet:

COURTLY CUCKOLDS & CADS

A BESOTTED PRINCE

The latest news to hit this sphere is our suddenly besotted prince by a dark beauty, some would venture to call her. He was seen at Celestia's Mage Modiste with his sister, likely to buy attire for the Citrine Centennial Ball. Lo and behold, a patron revealed to us that a strange girl with dark features and a strange uncouth accent insulted the prince, but he merely made conversation and condescended to flirt with her. Our prince! The very young man who never has time for girls' simpers and winks, never has looked at a woman for more than a disinterested moment, seems awestruck by this stranger.

We have done our research, readers, and we have uncovered the girl's lineage. She was with Lady Edwina Hematite, so one must assume from her coloring she belongs to Aschen Hematite and Angelica Tourmaline. Is she theirs? Is she baseborn? Or had they married in secret? Does the prince know of that scandal? One must wonder and quake at what the king will do when he finds out his son might be besotted by a Hematite.

For those interested, the prince and princess both made purchases. We are sure their simplistic but fine taste will create a spark at the upcoming ball.

I'm fairly confused. There are no rumors about the dress. None. This girl is either some strange creature who doesn't gossip or has no friends to gossip with. And the aunt. The paper left the purchase vague. Someone saw Alex hand over money, but no one knew about the dress. At least he was safe in that. They'd assume he'd come attired in rich clothing to please the Citrines, and then confusion would ensue when he did not.

I have to go. I leave for Madam Mage's school, Alex volunteering to go with me to save me from Mother's emotions. Something tells me that his willingness to enter a vipers' den of over a hundred gaggling girls wasn't only to help me out; he wanted to see Lady Tourmaline Hematite again. I had asked the worker measuring me her name. She also happens to be on the school's registrar list, and Alex asked me to become her friend. Not having any of my own, I will give her a chance. Well, I don't need to. What Alex doesn't know, nor could he handle knowing, is that I saw her in the flames as my friend anyway. Kind of fun just watching him play out what I have foreseen, like a moth flying to the flame.

Oh, before I go, the Citrine Ball was a bore. I got drunk to pass the time and to deal with the annoying men two or three times my age who asked me to dance. It was a huge letdown. This Lady Tourmaline was not present, so Alex was a disappointed and distracted bore too. Now, I will have to suffer many suitor balls with this school, where lords only come in search of a lifemate, or if Lucy's rumor is true, they might also be looking for mistresses. What a scandalous thought!

October

I'm back. The first day of school was quite eventful. I'm loving it. Lady Tourmaline—or Toury to me now—and my brother have caused more gossip than I have heard in ages. I had to pull him away from her because he gave her too much distinction way too fast. He'll be engaged in a week if he continues in this fashion. Maybe he should be? I'm not sure. I sent him away and saw Toury alone and befriended her. I really like her, Joan. No airs about her; in fact, she's a sweet lost girl who seems to have this inner strength and resilience. I think we'll be fast friends.

I'll help her, and maybe she could help me. I truly think I have made my first real friend. I am overwhelmed with this amazing gift in a girl like me, one who is *real*. Many stopped believing in the god and goddess, including myself, but this seems like some divine intervention after losing the only friend I had in Emily and with Henry gone. I don't think I understood friendship until now.

Inversely to being real to all, I continue an Alex-like persona at the school. Aloof, quiet, austere, as if I have no time for anyone beneath me. It will keep most girls away. I've decided Toury is enough for me when it comes to friendship. Most of these girls hate me because all the ambitious suitors will vie for me first; unfortunately, I'm the most eligible lady in Fyr in rank and finances. The other girls have their eyes on Alex and are false sycophants trying to cozy up to me. Lady Emily warned me of this very situation.

My brother has it right, fake it like they do. Maybe if I fake being much stronger than I really am, I'll start believing it.

School is exactly the boring and useless nonsense I knew it would be. "School" is the wrong word for it. Producing vapid lifemates for noblemen is their real business. I went to the headmistress before my first class of etiquette. I was not about to make a fool of myself or deal with these horrid girls. I insisted I didn't need them. Miss Headmistress was insistent, likely on Mother's orders. I pushed back. She hesitated, but I gave her my death stare and threatened to make a fiery fuss. I have never asserted myself in that fashion, but I could not stand a class like that.

"Perhaps, we have a private tutor discretely attend to you in your room for 'political' lessons? This would please both your parents' requests and your own. Is that amenable?" One-on-one etiquette lessons that none of the other girls know about is a decent compromise.

"Thank you, headmistress. That will do."

I do not like that she knows my weakness but am equally happy to escape a class with girls who would've used each of my mistakes against me. Toury was not at all pleased, and they relentlessly pick on her, exactly how I thought they would've done to me. She is far from court material. It makes me curious about her upbringing and her strange accent. I know better than to ask questions. We will be best friends from what the flames tell me. I must be patient. I hoped my influence would help her, but it seems Alex's attention to her marks her as competition. I have kept my aloof attitude with the other girls and soon I did feel impenetrable. The only way they can get to me is through Alex or Toury. I am defensive of those I love. I feel a need to protect Toury already.

Watching Toury and my brother try not to fall in love with each other is amusing, but also inspiring. I want to feel the same as Toury does about someone. I want that interest returned adamantly as my brother admires her. Just mentioning my brother perks Toury up. Today, she was sad he did not come to see her since we arrived because he said he would. I honestly had no idea what would keep him, but I made excuses about stately business. He was up to something about the Ruby business, and I'm sure Toury had something to do with it. Asking Alex outright would yield no answers, and Toury is pretty private about her life before school. From her skin tone, accent, and lack of Fyrian knowledge, it is clear she is not of this sphere and likely belongs to these Hematites. If only I could figure out what they did and why father would dislike them as the paper hinted. I wouldn't ever know, though, rotting away in this school. Papers are banned. I had really wanted to keep up with what was said about my brother and Toury so I could help her, and I was hoping for more information about the past. It must wait.

I also have to admit, it is also kind of fun watching them without the gossip papers sullying things. Toury tries to hide her feelings, but as soon as Alex arrives, she grows nervous. He waited a week. I bet it killed him to do so. It stung a little that he did not want to see us both. He could have then taken her privately away on a walk if needed. To exclude his sister marked Toury as being more important—not just to me, but to everyone else. I'm losing my brother to Toury, but I cannot resent her for it. She will be my friend, always. I just have to share her with my brother and him with her.

Justine Citrine arrived this new session of school. I should've foreseen it. Without me at the palace and rumors of Alex courting Toury, Mother would not force him to entertain any of the young ladies who visited with their mothers. No ladies could use the excuse to call upon me to try to see Alex either. To make things worse, Toury has changed. Not any worse, but suddenly, she knows things and her powers are stronger. She no longer wears her brooch as she constantly did before. I sense more than ever this has to do with something larger than just a romance between Alex and Toury. They do like each other a lot, but there is a piece I'm missing. Something happened after his visit.

She told me little about it but that she was now going to learn to control her powers. Having no other friends or anything to do—and frankly already tired of Justine's annoying rumors—I joined Toury and her servant in the dungeons. When we returned to our rooms next to each other,

Toury's door was open, and her gown for our first suitors' ball was torn to shreds. She said she would not go. If she didn't, Alex would be disappointed. My brother had written to me that he would attend on my behalf. Liar.

Something had to be done, because if Alex found out what happened, he would be livid. It was too late to have one made. We went through my ballgowns and her wardrobe.

Of course, mine did not fit her bust. I am slighter than her, but it's my lack of a bosom and height that are the problem. I tried not to be jealous, and she gallantly pointed out she was older, and I was not done filling out. It's true because I have seen a bigger-chested me in my visions...kissing Cobalt. Would he be there? He and Alex are usually together at a ball, and Cobalt has attended them for his elder sister... I have to forget him, Joan, let things happen in good time. Maybe I'll meet someone at the ball to distract me.

Anyway, I had the brilliant idea to use the dress my brother had bought her, where her new bodyguard-waiting maid Madge could spruce it up to be more elegant. I cannot wait to see his face. This will crack his aloof exterior, and all of Fyr will see how much he admires Toury. I just can't wait.

Today, I went to Ms. Headmistress to formally complain about Justine's actions in destroying Toury's dress.

She told me I cannot accuse people, even after I told her the nasty rumors Justine is making up about my brother and how obsessed she is to become his princess. I was told, "Every girl here wants to become the next princess. I'm sure you are used to this by now. I will talk to Lady Tourmaline about the dress and get her door repaired, but I do not accuse ladies unless they are directly seen doing wrong."

In short, she is no help, and I'm kind of worried how psycho these girls might become. I will write an update after the ball tonight.

Well, Joan, that was interesting. I guess that is the word for it. My first suitors' ball. At first, I thought Alex had abandoned me. Toury was a bundle of nerves, and the girls were getting chatty, their whispers a mix of disappointment he was not there and gossiping about Toury not being in his favor anymore. But Alex had promised Mother and I he'd attend.

"Relax, Toury," I told her. "My brother is trying to avoid the attention of watching us all walk in and stealing my due attention for my first introduction at a suitor ball."

"Did he say that?"

"I know my brother."

Of course, he arrived right before the first dance started. Everyone looked at him when he entered. He hated that as much as I did. Then he saw me, and his eyes darted to Toury beside me. He hurried to us, his eyes never leaving her as he crossed the room.

For a split second, he diverted his stare to glance at me. He gave me a peck and mumbled how I looked pretty in blue, but he was distracted by Toury, who was smiling at him as she bowed her head. He was beaming back. The aloof façade was gone, likely with Alex's heart as well. At least he remembered to give me the proper distinction and claimed my first dance. During our dance, I caught him watching Toury talk and dance with a man, the fire of jealousy clear in his eyes. I tried to get him talking to get him to relax, but it was hopeless.

Next, I had to dance with a creepy old man, Lord Geode, whose hands I had to move up as they kept slipping down to my rear end while he told me I reminded him of his daughter. I wanted to vomit. As I was spun around, I saw *him* across the room, talking to Alex: Cobalt.

My heart started beating madly. He was not there for me. I had to remind myself of that several times.

I was not able to greet him because man after man came up to me for a dance. Some were old, and some young—most groveled, though a few were too forward for my liking. Thankfully, no one was as bad as Lord Geode. He would be an immediate cut if he signed my suitor list. Finally, I begged off a dance to rest my feet by the sitting and refreshment area. A drink was held up in front of me. I peered up to see that adorable smirk looking down upon me. Cobalt looked divine, his rich blue doublet making his eyes sing.

"You look fetching tonight, Princess Mary."

I took the glass. "Thank you. You shine up well when you try."

He grinned and shrugged. I was hoping he'd ask me to dance.

"Where's my brother?"

Cobalt looked around. "He stepped outside. I have a feeling he was about to sign a suitor list. He is a ball of nerves tonight."

"And terribly jealous of every man dancing with the darling of the ball."

"*You* are the darling of the ball, Princess."

I scoffed.

"Bet your suitor list will be a mile long."

"For my status, not for me."

Cobalt frowned and drank his beverage. "A man would be stupid not to see your merits, the real you, Ma—Princess." Cobalt flared up red. He had almost slipped up. Forgetting my title in the castle is a norm since he is practically family. He cannot do that in public, though.

"Watch yourself, Lord Cobalt, or you might find yourself forced onto my list."

If one uses a name without the honorific, well, it means you are intimate. To do that to a royal? My guess is it would lead to an engagement or ruination.

His eyes met mine and darted away muttering, "Few men are deserving of being on your list. I am not one of them." Then he walked off. I cannot imagine what he meant or why he got so strange about my teasing joke. His words were insulting himself, but somehow, I felt rejected.

The rest of the night was a blur of dancing. Alex danced with me several times, since he was only allowed to dance with ladies once and had already danced with Toury. I couldn't recall seeing him dance with anyone else.

For the last dance, Cobalt took up my hand and led me out to the floor. "Am I worthy of at least a dance?"

I gazed up into his eyes, cocking my head slightly. "Why would you not be?"

As we started dancing, he said quietly, "I'm afraid I have a reputation that you might be aware of. I'd hate to tarnish yours inadvertently."

Two years had passed since I'd become aware of his continuously bad reputation. It was a poorly made joke. Yet, he was blushing and refusing to meet my gaze. Ashamed. Good.

"Well, you seem more well-behaved than Lord Geode while dancing. He has no conscious control over his wandering hands."

Cobalt's eyes darted to mine, and he broke into a smile, his laughter booming. "How I have missed your candor, Princess Mary. Nothing has been the same with us since that day. I want to be friends again."

Funny thing for him to say since I thought we had eventually put that day behind us. Then again, he is always with Alex, not me.

I noticed Cobalt looking over at Toury and Alex, who were talking by the refreshments. "Then again, Lord Geode kept his eyes on me while dancing and not on other women."

Cobalt's gaze met mine. "I was looking at your brother. He worries me, suddenly so fascinated with this lady. Not like him. I signed her suitor list—"

"What?" He will break my heart and my brother's simultaneously.

He was the one studying me now, his brow wrinkled. "Why do you..." Something clicked in his expression, and he shook his head. "You misunderstand. I did it to unnerve him, make him act, create some gossip. I did not expect it to work. Is she truly right one for him, to make him happy? I know so little of that family or her in general."

I let out the breath I had been holding. He signed her suitor list as a joke. Such a foolish and dangerous act, typical of Cobalt. He is safe.

"Don't kid yourself, Cobalt. Alex and Toury are already in love. You simply sped it up, but I wish you wouldn't meddle. She is a bit lost and needs to find her footing before she should marry my brother."

"I will tease him, but I will stop meddling. For you, my Princess." *His* princess. I kind of like the sound of that, even though I'm reading way too far into it.

"She is the one for him though, so rest easy."

His grip tightened on me. "You've seen it? In the flames?"

"Of course. I've seen my lifemate as well. You know I'm a great firebrander."

The song finished. He still held onto me.

"If you tell my brother she's his lifemate, I'll chop off that very part of you that has sullied your reputation."

His eyes went wide at my comment, and he let go of me.

"Thank you for the dance, Lord Cobalt." I started to walk away.

"Who is he?" Cobalt asked.

I pretended not to hear and walked away. I was spineless. What would've happened if I told him he was my lifemate? Would he sign my list and try to court me? Or would he be weird around me and stop talking to me? Rejection from ladies stings enough. Rejection from Cobalt? That would kill me.

I hardly slept that night in anticipation of my suitor's list.

Cobalt did not sign my list. But that is here nor there, and I hardly care. My mind is fixated on poor Toury. She was poisoned this morning. We can guess who did it, but the headmistress, per usual, is not helpful. Alex came to the school, demanding to see her, raving like a lunatic until Toury and I went to the headmistress's office. I've never seen Alex this distraught. He was holding her, hugging her—too intimate. Toury wasn't ready, and I wanted to warn him. He cut me off and told me to firebrand. Foolish boy. I knew what would happen, and of course, she denied his proposal. When I asked, Toury told me it was not in the least romantic. I wanted to tell her Alex was in love with her and perhaps he just couldn't find the words, but she wasn't ready to hear it. I have to let them work it out on their own.

I no longer regret not telling Cobalt he is the one for me. He is far from ready for marriage, Joan—neither am I.

November

I cried myself to sleep. I've never been so mad at Alex in my life! To trap Toury, who has become my best friend, and then to steal her away from me? I'm not being selfish as Lucy tries to proclaim about the situation. It's the way my brother acted that is reprehensible. I thought Toury and I had time together to solidify our friendship, that we would leave school together, and she could help me figure out how to maneuver—more like stall—choosing a lifemate. But she is gone to me now. That means I have to deal with the sycophants and, worse, the Justines of the school on my own. Toury had been my only champion; she thought I had helped her, but the power she has that she is unaware of for being my brother's choice makes her even more influential than me.

Now I'm alone. The glimpse of having someone to bond with has been dashed away. Just as it was with Lady Emily, just as her death took Henry away. Not only was it cruel of Alex to do that to me, but what he did to Toury? It was stupid. Whether she wants to admit it or not—well, her denying his proposals said she wasn't about to admit it—she loves him, and he loves her. I mean, as much love as can happen while being chaperoned. I've seen way too many marriages with less attraction or regard between the couple. This should've been a love match, and my brother mucked it up.

Should I have told him she was the one? No, something told me he'd run into it even more foolheartedly. Love makes people rash and outright stupid.

Toury will hate him for this. He might've thrown away his chances with her, thrown the future into some unknown path the flames have not told me yet. It was unlike my brother, and yet I have never seen him infatuated as he is now. The aloof prince who never gave a girl a second glance was rendered powerless by an uncourtly new girl. The back of my mind knows that something else must be going on. Alex could not wait for her to become acclimated. He needs her by his side, and as soon as I get home, I will try to find out. If only I could go home too. I wrote to Mother, but I know she will not let me return.

Toury and Alex will marry, and I'll have to marry, and we'll never be the same as we are in this short spell of time. Another thought. She *has* to marry Alex. We will be in the castle together once I spring from this hellish finishing school. No matter how much time he'll suck up of her life, surely, I will get some time with my friend. Alex will have duties that don't involve her. I can steal some time with Toury...if only I can get home. I need to figure out a way.

The day after Toury left, Justine was smug. I am starting to feel the full force of Toury's absence. Girls are vying to sit with me at luncheon, and Justine's crew snubs me in every way possible. Most girls avoid her gang and me because they aren't sure which side of the battle is safest. I would stay out of it too—if I could. A few girls are nice, but none are real. All fake to their vibrantly-colored hair and stuffed-bosom cores.

I had thought Justine addlebrained, since Alex has made it obvious who his choice is. He entered an engagement. But Justine is the queen of lies and can spin a tale. According to Justine, it is too late, and Toury is to be his mistress. I have to admit, after seeing firsthand Cobalt give in to lust, I have no doubt many men do. It seems a stretch to think Alex could be so ungentlemanly, and yet there is the way he looks at Toury, the regard he cannot hide from all. There is also everyone who witnessed her intimate use of his name, the way he kissed her—even I sadly could believe Justine for a split second.

But I could not outwardly ignore it, and instantly combatted it with, "My brother is honorable, and if word got back to the palace about your accusation, it could be construed as treason against the princess-to-be." It's true, to be sure, that now engaged, Toury is considered royalty.

This did not kill the rumors but made Justine more careful about how I overheard them. The rumors are growing worse. Now Justine has half the girls here convinced Toury thinks she is princess-to-be, but Justine and Alex have secretly engaged first and he despoiled Toury to be his mistress. Even after Lady Delphine Opal pointed out Justine would be second best to his mistress, Justine said all men had to get it out of their system and all that mattered is she would be queen one day. I think a lot of girls right then saw what she really wanted—the notoriety of the throne.

The rumors are worse, and girls believe her. Apparently, Justine has been getting gifts, signed by "Your Admirer, A." She says it's Alex. There are gaudy jewels, scarves, and even a dress as if he'd do the same for her as he impulsively had for Toury. I wrote to Alex about this, then burned it. The rumors will not spread far from this school, but when girls got home, what will happen? That's for Alex to control. School is my battle. The least I can do is squash it here for my brother.

"A sapphire ring?" I scoffed at her when she showed it to me. "Alex has better taste than to be as gaudy as that. Anyway, looks like a counterfeit to me." The size of that sapphire was unreal, and its hue was off. If she were faking this with a real sapphire that size? It would set even her family back. Then again, it seemed like something her mother would do, spend more than they have on rumors, believing Alex would eventually propose.

Justine pouted. "How could you insult your brother's gift?"

I grabbed her hand before she could pry it away. "If it is real, it will survive my flames. If it is resin or confectioner based, it will melt." I enveloped the stone in my fire magic.

Justine screamed out, so I let her hand go. My magic would not burn unless I intended it to; as much as I disliked Justine, I would never use my magic to hurt someone.

It was obvious to everyone what had burned, the fake stone. "That lit up really quick. Pine resin, I take it?"

She wiped the scalding syrup off on her finger and stormed off, others giggling. I think it is over, but I might be underestimating the girl's desperate tenacity.

December

Justine is delusional—obsessed. I thought she was fixated on obtaining my brother, becoming a princess. I'm not so sure what she is about anymore. More fake gifts came; she gushed over Alex and these stupid things she proclaimed he had written in letters he'd sent her. I know how much he is disgusted by her, but other girls lapped it up. The more I reacted, the more it made girls suspicious I was the liar. I should've listened to Lucy. She had warned me to fight back in the way the girl was fighting in the first place. I wish I had Toury's counsel, but she'd probably tell me to do something rash and unforgivable. I like that about her.

Today, I was glad Toury was not present. The rumor mill was ludicrous. All girls lost their minds in speculation. Justine was having a celebration—unofficial, since they weren't allowed in the school—with her fake friends. What was she celebrating, Joan? I will not leave you in suspense: the "fact" she had "won" Alex from Toury since "his whore" was "with child."

At the word "whore," fire leaped up inside of me. I wanted her to burn. And when the accusation hit home, I wanted to throw Justine Citrine on a pyre and see the end of her. It reminded me of Cobalt, his weaknesses, and how a lady had tried to take advantage of him with a rumored pregnancy.

Lucy had to drag me away, as Justine blew me a kiss and mouthed "sister" to me. Over my dead body. I'd sick a draca on her before I'd let her get her talons into Alex.

After I cooled down, I went to Headmistress to plead my case to get Justine expelled from school. I presented my case well. I explained the rumors, the false presents, the bullying she directed at me. Headmistress listened, but I could tell from the cold look in her eyes she had no love for me, less for Toury, and believed my brother capable of this type of behavior. And no wonder. My father and his father were never spoken of well—nor my uncles, who had both died before my birth. I understand her generation's disillusionment, but not how they view my brother. He will be the best thing to ever happen to Fyr, as the flames told me, but the headmistress seemed to think I'm a liar.

I went on defense. I was rash but clever, like Toury.

"Tell me, Headmistress, what is more important to you? Stopping treason or me acting like a lady?"

Realizing finally what I had been pointing out about Justine and possible lies against a royal and a royal-to-be if those rumors left the school—well, and Lucy for stating the laws after the woman's eyes went wide—she listened to me for once.

"You are so set on making me a lady, and although that is deeply appreciated, all I see in this school is teaching girls how to be fake and cruel."

"If Your Highness tried to make friends, aside from an uncouth girl of no education—"

"That is the Princess-to-be," I corrected.

She flushed, pinching her nose. "Yes, she is. I don't know how to please the parents who wish their daughters to be such. It's the courtly norm."

"My brother and I will not have my father's court. This false manner breeds lies and crime. Someone tried to kill Lady Tourmaline. You have not kicked Justine out, despite how these rumors prove the fact she would do such a thing."

Lucy whispered in my ear at the perfect moment. I met my servant's gaze. She really came through. I have not given her enough credit, so I thanked her.

"Lucy has told me this is Justine's third stint in this place, and how her parents are the leading contributors to your funds."

Headmistress blanched. "That's neither here nor there."

"No?" I stood. "It's everywhere, isn't it?"

She rose because she must due to my station.

"I'm leaving in the morning. I can no longer learn from someone who abides by these practices."

Headmistress scrambled toward the door. "Please, Your Highness, wait!"

I hesitated in the doorway. "I cannot stay here any longer if she is permitted to stay with all the treasonous comments. I don't want to have to write home."

"Please." She was growing pale.

I crossed my arms to show her I meant business.

"The Citrines are not people I can afford to cross. As you candidly pointed out, I cannot kick her out. I have had letters screened—all girls, except you, Your Highness."

Because I rarely wrote them and often transported to the post office just to escape the prison I was in. I saw the knowing look in the woman's eyes and the fact she "let" me have that liberty as long as I didn't take advantage to do anything stupid. Why hadn't I warned Toury about rumors in my last letters? I had written trite garbage.

"I have kept the rumors here, trust me. I have well-trained scribes to copy letters without rumors. If any got out, it is word of mouth from visitors, and that is not evidence enough. It'll be jealous girls' chit-chat."

"You're more worried about the Citrine reaction than the Sapphirian?" I challenged. Joan, I honestly enjoyed having the upperhand on her. Maybe power is not such a scary thing to wield.

"No," Headmistress looked as if she would cry. "I'm in a terrible place here. Your father is favorable to a Citrine-Sapphirian alliance. You saw I did nothing to urge our prince into that; how could I when he was clearly enamored by the now princess-to-be? I've been pressured in many directions to make things happen that I could never force. The heart has a mind of its own. I know this. Your brother saved me from having to deal with that problem with his actions, but you, Your Highness, are still an issue. Your mother will not let you leave here. I cannot kick out a main contributor of my school unless you have tangible proof."

"I understand," I told her.

"Do you?" she questioned.

"Yes."

I had a plan.

Well, I've done it. Alex came to pick me up. I did not intend to go home this way. I had wanted a loud public exposure of Justine and to set off her temper for all to see. Lucy tried to talk me out of it, but I could not deal another day with Justine. It was time to leave these ridiculous notions of propriety behind and *do* something. Joan, I'm not proud of myself—no, no, I truly am, to be honest. Justine came up behind me at breakfast and whispered, "I'll have your brother as soon as that bitch births their baseborn."

I turned and punched her square in the eye. My hand, knuckle, or finger—don't know what bones broke, but they hurt terribly. I instantly used my fire magic to mend the bones. The pain ebbed away to a dull ache.

The look on Justice's face was priceless. She had underestimated my audacity, my strength, and any hope of Alex through me—if she were that ignorant—had evaporated. Bad move for her. Why wouldn't you want my favor to get to my brother?

Headmistress came down after Justine bawled her eyes out, complete theatrics until the healer said she was fine and could go lie down and ice her eye. She acted as if she were dying as she forced the servants to carry her to her rooms, with her little entourage following after her with their fake pity.

The headmistress shook her head at me, but once we were in her office, she signed my dismissal paper with a flourish, a smirk, and a wink. If I had felt merely justified in hitting Justine, I now felt exhilarated by Headmistress's approval.

"I would appreciate if Justine could finish her *full* term here, away from my brother and I."

"I believe I can make that happen for you, Your Highness. There is just one matter that needs to be handed over—to your waiting maid, according to your mother's dictations." Then in a whisper, "Direct Queen orders, you see. Your mother insisted your suitor list will be delivered directly to her."

"Of course." My elation left me, feeling so angry about what Mother's future plan was for me.

Still, I gloated on my escape as I passed the girls watching me leave, my head held high and theirs bowed in reverence. I hate female politics, yet I am learning so much about my sphere that I never knew.

When I got into the carriage, Alex was lost in thought. I expected mother would fetch me from school so she could scold me, but a missive had arrived midday from Alex. I had been relieved, except for his weird demeanor. When pressed, he said things were complicated with Toury. Of course, that was a given. He would be a simpleton if he thought it would be otherwise.

Something else weighed upon him. I asked him where he had been, and he said at Tobias Firebrander's shop. I didn't ask after that, although I longed to. Tobias had foreseen Ruby's death too late, not warned us of Emily's at all, so what now had he told Alex to make him glum? I don't trust the firebrander—who is as good as me at it but with decades more experience. Or maybe I'm angry that with his breadth of knowledge, he had kept quiet, knowing Henry pressured me for answers. Leaving me, a former pupil of his, to grapple with topics beyond my understanding.

Regardless of my grudge, Alex was in a retrospective mood. He didn't even laugh when I told him all the silly rumors Justine invented.

He groaned. "Don't tell Toury, please. She's stressed out enough."

"No thanks to you."

"Doesn't she let me know it." Alex sighed.

"Things not going well?"

"What do you think?"

"Well, she needed time. Had you given her this whole year at Madame Mage's, she would be properly educated and refined to run a court, but you couldn't wait. Typical of the male species."

Alex's eyes narrowed. "It wasn't like that. I didn't have the luxury of time."

"Why not?" I challenged.

Alex's eyes went wide before he looked out the window. He had said too much and would tell me nothing.

"Alex, the kingdom's burdens do not have to be yours alone."

He sighed, his agitation obvious. It was not just Toury bothering him. I sensed it had everything to do with what happened to Ruby.

"So, Ruby went to Earth to bring Toury here and died there. Who killed her?"

Alex's head whipped around in shock.

"No, Toury didn't tell me anything, even though I know you two have your little secrets about Ruby. I have a brain and can put two and two together. What I don't know is who killed my cousin."

"I don't know either, but they're definitely necromancers, and likely the ones responsible for my curse. Before she disappeared, Ruby was helping me figure out the curse."

Things started clicking. My last conversation with my cousin had been in the library, and I sent her to Tobias Firebrand. Had I sent her on the beginning of the path that eventually ended in her death?

"She was looking for a cursebreaker, a savior."

"Toury?"

"Perhaps." The way he said it was clipped and the heart of the problem. How could she break his curse? Alex must know and was not sharing, which meant it was something impossible for her to do, and he deeply regretted it—or worse, cursebreaking sometimes took a sacrifice. I will watch them closely now that I am home.

Well Joan, all my worry was for nothing. Toury and Alex are thick as thieves and sickening in love. Apparently, they made up the night I returned. I don't see anything suspicious about Alex's behavior that warns me he'll do anything rash to break his curse. He is more at ease than he was when he picked me up. Toury applauded me in private for sticking up for myself and giving Justine a nice punch. I told her I had done it for her and Alex, not me, but Toury gave me that knowing look. Although we have never talked about it, I think she sees through my façade to my insecurities—likely because she is insecure herself. Whatever Alex's actions were—selfish, conniving, and downright controlling—Toury is better from life at the palace. She has grown confidence in the way only education and training can bring. Who needs Madame Mage and her etiquette? I met Toury's tutor. Alex had found another Hematite, despite Father hating him and hardly tolerating Toury.

Regardless, Father seems to have accepted her, although Alex's recounting of the day Toury met him sounds terrifying. Father's health has taken a dip; Mother fretted telling me he was dying, but I already knew. The worst part, that tore me up the most and made me pour another firewhiskey, was the accusation in Mother's eyes that I had known. How can I tell her Father's future disappears soon? These visions are—at times—too much to bear.

Dear Joan,

I must rename you. I am home, and being reunited with my best friend, my only real friend, has been amazing. I love Toury, but I know our friendship will become deeper. We'll be sisters one day, and I feel like we act that way already. I don't have a sister, but I've seen them fight, and I've seen them be each other's best supporters. That is what I have always wanted.

Anyway, Toury seems like a miracle to our lives. Why is she a miracle? I will never say. Visions have told me things, but I'm scared to let anyone know of them. I will never tell, even you, my wonderful journal. If someone reads you...the future could spin off, I think. I'm just too scared. But I know she is the very thing that our entire world needs.

Anyway, I'm naming you "Wundor," which means "miracle" in the old language. Not just because of Toury coming to us from Earth due to cousin Ruby's plans, but because Alex giving you to me as a simple gift has been a miracle. I had been lost. The miracle is I'm finding my footing. And yes, I'm drinking too much as Lucy berates me for daily, but I am truly happy for the first time. Cobalt is still my problem, and so is being the princess. If we could just shut everyone out of the castle and live in our own world—maybe I'll let Cobalt in—I would be content.

I'm renaming you because I believe in miracles. I want them to happen and see them happen. I just wish the visions were sharper so I knew they were definite.

§

I should give Lucy more credit. She had left instructions for the rag papers to be collected while we were gone and presented them last night. So many of them! Of course, there was news about Toury and my brother often. Since my brother hadn't given them much scandal, they couldn't write much until his huge act, but I'm pasting in the headlines to the duller articles:

PRINCE GIVES LADY TOURMALINE DISTINCTION OVER THE PRINCESS

THE PRINCE VISITS MADAME MAGE TO SEE WHOM?

RUMORS OF A MALE VOICE HEARD IN A CERTAIN LADY'S ROOM AT MADAME MAGE'S

LADY JUSTINE SECRETLY ENGAGED TO THE PRINCE OR VYING FOR ATTENTION?

Once I read the two articles I'm keeping a dozen times, I'll paste them in too. You'll love them. I finally see the humor in these wretchedly entertaining papers.

❦

COURTLY CUCKOLDS & CADS

PRINCE ABSCONDS A LADY

Ladies and lords, we're bringing you tremendous news first! Last night, what seemed to be a routine suitors' ball at Madame Mage's School, ended in scandal. Our very own prince, known for his scruples and aloof attitude toward the fairer sex, not only ensnared himself into an engagement, but did so publicly and quite scandalously. Several witnesses at the event said that Lady Tourmaline, known to those close to her as Lady Toury, dared to dance with the prince a second time and used his name not only without honorific but also shortened it. Only those close to him with permission can call him by his nickname. Even our daring paper will not print it.

It is known that this lady in question is not aware of Fyrian customs, ignorant to the point we must question our prince's choice or the lady's undisclosed background. Even if she had accidentally engaged herself, the prince was the mastermind, bringing her out onto the floor the second time to force distinction upon her and witnesses say he kissed her in front of all, quite passionately. Then they made a hasty escape with his magic. One might wonder, after many rumors fabricated by overreaching ladies, if he was indeed selecting his mistress, but reports said the carriages carrying her things and themselves went to the castle—not a place you bring your mistress but your future lifemate. One wonders how the king will react to this news. Now we know why the prince did not simply transport home with his future bride. He was prolonging the trip to not deal with one angry father. Let us be grateful the prince cannot burn under his father's fiery wrath.

I enjoyed this article. It did capture a lot of truth in it. Thankfully, Father seems to acknowledge he cannot win against Alex in this. Toury is growing on him too, I think. It is sad to see Father like this, deteriorating, slowly losing his fire. At the same time, it is relieving not to deal with his anger and cruelty. He's a bit softer, gentler, due to his lack of energy.

Here's the second article. I'm quite excited to make the gossip rags—and not for my drinking habits—if I am honest. All will know what happened now.

COURTLY CUCKOLDS & CADS

PRINCESS PACKS A PUNCH

Right when the kingdom believes the prince has outdone his partying sister in antics, she steals the title back for the rebellious royal. The princess has popped Lady Justine Citrine and has given her quite the bruised eye. Has the princess gone rogue? Close sources say that Lady Citrine has been creating a web of fantastical rumors that could be construed as treason against the prince and the princess-to-be. Perhaps the princess has spared the lady a worse fate, letting her off easy with humiliation and a swollen eye. We cannot pretend to not be a tad satisfied for that lady being brought down a rung.

Where is our heroine princess now? The prince picked her up, and they returned to the palace. The fact he came for her shows us many things. He supports his sister's actions, and their parents likely do not. After all, the king's best friend is Lord Citrine.

*Let it be known that Lady Justine has repeatedly sent *Courtly Cuckolds & Cads* her "news" and after fact-checking, we chose not to print her lies.

Ah, satisfaction. I think I'll end my paper reading days on a high note with this article. It's my triumph, no matter how my parents choose to view it. Lady Justine needed some sense knocked into her. Let's hope it'll last.

Wundor,

I haven't had time to write in ages. No, scratch that, it hasn't been long, just so much has happened over days that I don't know where to start. Justine, I guess, is the start to the avalanche of events. Well, Toury sought to make Justine show her true colors, and she did. Justine tried to attack her in front of an entire room of people. Toury was rattled but insisted on having the ball in her honor anyway. Alex was worse. If he was half as overprotective of me as he is of Toury, I would lose my mind.

But he had been right. I wish we had taken his concern seriously. I wish Father had listened. Justine was set free by some traitor in the castle, and they took Toury, absconded with her to the north, where fire magic works terribly. Alex went after her. He would've gone instantly if we hadn't stalled him with a plan. I swore he'd get himself killed. Love makes fools. I'm pretty bad to think Cobalt can change, but Alex and Toury are worse—reckless.

I couldn't leave the palace if Alex did. Sure, we could go down the street with a retinue with the palace army a couple hundred yards away but not across the realm. Despite what the flames had shown me, I lived in fear that I would never see my brother and my only friend again, that I would have to reign over a land I still didn't fully understand because I spent my life in protected dissipation, not bothering to learn things as "the spare." Or worse, Alex would be slain, and I would be next.

I was worried because Alex was in no fit state to do anything. From the moment of Toury's disappearance, one thing was clear to me—and everyone else: Alex's greatest weakness was Toury. They took her, and he fell to pieces. If they hurt her or worse? I'd lose Alex in some way. Just like Henry. How do people let themselves get so consumed by another being?

I trusted the visions. They were my only hope.

I made Father realize his friends were the very people who were trying to overtake the throne. Surprise, surprise, the Citrines. I was proud of myself, but only fleetingly. He would not write a command for the Citrines to be locked up for questioning, aside from Justine if she were captured, nor would he make me the Lady of the Castle in Alex's absence. Father was so weak physically that this mental upset broke him even more. He had become the shell of the powerful, intimidating man who was incapable of tenderness or feebleness. But now he was being plain stupid. I was still the useless spare, and I would remain so if something happened to Alex.

If he came back someone else, Cobalt could pull a coup, and we could say the curse made him unfit. Father had set up that rhetoric enough among the sorcerers. If Alex died, I would be trapped until Father passed. Cobalt and I decided I'd be safest playing demure and ignorant in case the worst occurred. If I wasn't an outward threat, I wouldn't be a real target. We were to stay away from the courtiers and pretend we did not suspect the Citrines. It was hard to sit on that and let others in the castle be duped or worse, but Cobalt pointed out that those who supported them were also the "sickness to be cut out from the court" as he so bluntly put it. Cobalt is creepily clever about politics.

I digress. My thoughts are so scattered. Back to what happened before Alex left and Father was in denial. Alex came to me to explain what he wanted me to do if he went dark. Then he thought he was giving me some great reveal that Toury was the savior who would break his curse.

"I know." I tried to spare Alex from explaining.

Alex's shock whipped through his frame; his confused gaze locked on mine.

Cobalt huffed. "Well, I don't have a clue what is going on."

"How does it turn out?" Alex begged me.

I had to look away. The fear in his voice clogged my throat with emotion. I swallowed several times to let out the tension from my overbearing feelings. I would not cry and alarm Alex. My weakness could alter the future.

"How does what turn out?" Cobalt grew impatient.

I took a deep breath, but put on that austere and arrogant persona we wore in public to protect myself and to protect my dear brother. "I can't influence your decisions, Alex. What if what I say destroys what I saw?"

"Then what you saw was good?" My brother's eyes were tortured.

I had never seen him so vulnerable. Father says love is weakness, and here my brother was, exposing that to many people during this courtship. Every suitor ball attendee, palace servant, visitor saw it. It would be known around the kingdom that Toury was the ticket to make my brother reckless enough to get usurped. These were my thoughts, but now I still worry about how far he will go for Toury.

"I see many things. Please, don't ask me to explain."

Alex's desperation left his eyes, and they hardened. The emotions were boiling up his curse. He growled at me.

"Please, someone explain what in the god and goddess is going on!" Cobalt snapped. He had shifted slightly to stand between Alex and I. Cobalt could sense the curse and was protecting me, while trying to distract Alex.

I was surprised in his fragile, quickly-shifting mental state that Alex answered in a coherent way. "Toury is the savior, the one to break my curse. It's a long story, but she is. If I can break the curse, the necromancers have no chance of using it against me."

"Then go get her, have her break it." Of course, the ever-practical Cobalt thought it was that easy.

"It's not that simple. I might not come back at all. I might come back your enemy. Promise me, Cobalt, if I come back not myself, lock me up—forever. Protect my sister."

Cobalt was speechless.

I knew immediately what Alex was about to do. "Alex, you can't go dark. You'll kill her. You'll try to kill me."

"Which is why I need you, Cobalt, to put me in jail if I'm not myself, and to never let me out, for my sister's safety."

"Alex—"

"No, Cobalt, promise. This must be done. The curse will let them control me. They will rule through me. It won't even be me."

Cobalt offered his hand. "I promise."

They shook on it.

After he left, time had turned minutes into hours, and hours felt like days. I prayed to the god and goddess to spare my brother from a dark life controlled by the Citrines. I prayed for Toury to come through. I prayed that if things went wrong, the Cobalts had the power to subdue the Citrines and protect me. There were many, many prayers. But those were my repetitive ones, etched into my brain forever.

It was the scariest night of my life.

We were not sure where or when Alex would appear again, or if he had the strength to transport again. If he could at all that far up north. Between prayers, I firebranded in the princess salon. Cobalt stayed with me, pacing incessantly, sword in and out of hand with nerves. He kept asking for updates until I told him off because I had none.

Then I saw Alex and Toury in the flames. I gasped.

"What?" Cobalt was down on his knees, grasping my hands, his eyes eager for news.

I could not answer. I wasn't sure when it would happen, but it was such a strong vision I knew it was soon. Worried I had little time, I grabbed Cobalt's arm, while Lucy lunged for me, and I transported us to the main hall.

A bunch of people were there, soldiers included. They jumped, thinking I was Alex. One said, "Soldiers, stand attention. Something will happen soon if the princess arrived."

"Princess Mary." Lord Citrine's chilly voice made my spine go rigid. I had to pretend I didn't know.

Cobalt gripped my arm. I thought he was trying to tell me the obvious as if I would be that daft, but instead he spoke. "Where is my father, who was left in command?"

Lord Citrine sneered. "Seize him. He is likewise a traitor, just like his father and brother."

In a split second, Cobalt dropped my arm, withdrew his sword, and swung it around over our heads to batter back a bunch of swords pointed at us—all before I registered what was going on.

"Cease and stand down!" I shouted, surprised at the boom in my voice and how it echoed off the walls.

Everyone froze. Cobalt was panting, looking around. We were grossly outnumbered, but I had fire. His eyes met mine, and he smirked and winked at me.

Although it made my heart go aflutter, I was not that much of a courtly lady to swoon. I knew what he was signaling. He screamed and started his attack while I covered his back with fire. Guards screamed and ran, trying to put out burns that did not come from fire penetrating their armor, but from the flames' heat that cooked their flesh in their metal ovens.

They all backed away from me. I turned to see a shaking sword to my throat from a very nervous lord whose name escaped me in my fright. It was the first time I used my fire to hurt any living creature. Although I hadn't thought about that until now. In that moment, all I thought of was my future with Cobalt disappearing. Cad as he was, why had he not had my back? That's when I saw him behind the arm of my scared attacker. Cobalt's boots were on the ground being dragged away with his body. I was terrified he was dead.

I pushed the sword away from my neck, glaring at the lord with enough fire intensity to make him sweat—literally. "What the bloody hell is going on?" I demanded, turning that heated stare onto the ringleader: Citrine.

My, did he cut an intimidating figure. Long white-blond hair, those eerie yellow-gold eyes, and a staggering stature—I had to find my inner strength.

He clucked at the lord, scolded him, and told him to go sit down and rethink his actions. Then he gave me a paternal, kind look—false to its core. It spoke to me in an undercurrent commanding me to shut up or I'd lose my head. But I would not be deterred. I would be strong. I would make Toury and Alex proud, despite what they came back to.

"Princess Mary." Citrine bowed. The other lords followed, but the soldiers still stood attention, not making a choice, and yet not going down on bended knee meant they were not mine to command. What would Alex do in this situation? Something smart, covert, with false arrogance. What would Cobalt do? He would fight. And die. God and goddess, he *had* to be alive.

"The magicians are attacking. The Cobalts betrayed the throne by trying to admit them," Lord Cobalt said.

"No. The magician's guild was asked to protect the castle. They would not fight sorcerers unless attacked and defending."

Citrine gave me a gloating look, as if he thought he had me trapped. "They were commanded to guard by whom?" Alex had commanded them, and our father was in charge—technically. I was furious Father held on to control he could not back.

I used my mind. I could not fight and win like Cobalt unless I torched everyone in my path. I had to think like Alex. I foresaw his return with Toury and thought it would be soon. It felt pressing and sure. I had to stall.

"My brother. It matters not. If you deny his orders now since they are not from the king, you must deny them when he returns, no?"

Citrine's smile went sour. I had him. If Alex came back on Citrine's side after denying his command, he could not easily accept it in front of others.

A voice sliced through the air. "What is going on here?" I recognized it but not its strong tone: Mother. "Attacking the Cobalts? And my daughter?" Her voice went shrill for a moment, which jarred everyone. Mother has never raised her voice or showed anger before. I felt her protective magic surround me, cocooning me. She had done that when I was young to make me feel her presence, for me to know her love in front of Father without him knowing. And she was protecting me now. "Back down Citrine. I have orders from the king himself backing up Prince Alex's discoveries. He backs his son, so obey as you should, or you will all face the pyre."

Mother clutched the letter tight. Citrine noticed and was about to grab the missive. Mother was lying, and Father had not cracked, the stubborn idiot. We might die because of his uselessness to give Alex his power.

"The king is unwell, as we all know. He has ordered Prince Alex to be the king proxy." Mother pulled the hand out from behind her back. It shook as she held out the king's medallion.

God and goddess! She was clever and likely stole or wrestled it off Father. At the same time, it was a huge gamble. If Alex came back not himself, without Toury…he'd rule as a necromancer.

No—I had seen him with Toury! I believed.

I steadied the medallion in Mother's hand, sending gentle warmth into her so she'd know I supported her crazy move. I leaned in, as some lords clapped halfheartedly, to be honest, and whispered, "He comes back whole."

Mother's shaking hand went rigid and strong. She now believed.

That's when I felt the energy in the air, and Alex popped into vision. He looked horrible, his face full of pain. He was holding Toury in one arm and fell to his knees, his other hand on a burned body: Tobias. He shouted out commands demanding me to help, and on instinct, I listened. I took Toury to her rooms. Madge was frightened. I told her to get healers, and she rushed away. I could not leave Toury either. She was a mess both physically and mentally.

When I thought she was a miracle, a *wundor*, I celebrated, but I never wished for her to go through all this to save us. She could not speak, her eyes were full of terrified horror, and I had the healers knock her out with a dram so she could mentally and physically rest. I wanted to give her time away from Alex because the bruises on her neck were evidence of what evils the curse had made Alex capable of. The entire kingdom owed Toury thanks, but we could never tell anyone the extent. No one could know how close Alex had been to losing all control, to destroying our entire sphere or the devastation he would've wreaked upon his own people. The thought of what the dark draca within him could do made me shudder. No one could know or think about that, or they'd wish to overthrow us immediately, despite me not being cursed.

When my brother came to her room moments later, walking through the door instead of transporting, likely not to further scare her, his face sank when he saw Toury asleep in the bed. I told him she would be asleep for hours, but he pulled up a chair and grasped her hand in his, holding it, watching her with tormented eyes. I hope he does not remember what he did when he was possessed by dark magic. It would be best if he never knows. I do not have the heart to ask him. I pen this through exhaustion, Wundor, so at last, I recounted the events for future me to reflect upon, and now I shall sleep.

COURTLY CUCKOLDS & CADS

A PALACE ROMANCE IN TATTERS

Reports say the whirlwind romance between the king proxy and his queen proxy-to-be has come to a halt. One must wonder if these rumors are true. Has the engagement been broken off? One can easily understand why it might be.

In true fashion, always shocking the kingdom in many ways, Lady Tourmaline, queen proxy-to-be, did it again. All along, she was the one destined by the god of fire and goddess of light to break our poor prince's curse. Now, he is free from the darkness dispelling numerous and persistent complaints to his ability to rule. As the king has all but vanished from the public eye, the proxy will likely rule soon. It was such a valiant deed for the queen proxy-to-be to save our prince, the man she loves. Or was it?

We do not wish to undermine the bravery of our future queen, but to question the actions of the former prince. Rumors surfaced about bruising around Lady Tourmaline's neck, and she was spotted in the gardens with a scarf, despite the always-pleasant Celestia weather. Seems evident enough that someone hurt her badly, and now she and the king proxy are at odds. Did the curse get to our former prince? Did he harm her? One can imagine that the curse, created by a necromancer and their old dark magic, would do anything in its power to survive.

We have a king proxy free from dark magic, the good magic in him enough to keep the fire burning and the draca at bay, but was it worth the price? Will our besotted monarch lose the love of his life? How might they heal this rupture? For all the jealous young ladies who rip our queen proxy-to-be down, we at *Courtly Cuckolds & Cads*, have quite fallen in love with the brash, uncourtly, opinionated young woman. She is a symbol of change, and many voice the sphere's deep need for that.

One might hope that the queen or Princess Mary can come up with some scheme to get our favorite royal couple back together. Then again, the former likely is pampering the ill-favored king, and the princess is likely more interested in partying and ignoring her suitors. Let us hope something happens to bring our kingdom back together. The people need hope now more than ever.

I don't know why I read this rubbish. I almost torched this article because it made me so angry. At first, I lied to myself that I was upset that they were speculating about my brother and Toury. I knew though, that I was angry because it was all true, especially about me. I should be trying to get them together. What the stupid rag didn't realize was that trauma like Toury's needs time to heal. I can do nothing until she is initially over it and not scared of Alex.

I have always contemplated sharing the papers with Toury, but now I'm glad I didn't. Her remaining ignorant of gossip is key in upping her self-esteem and finding her place in court. I'm no help in that regard, and I should take my own advice, but I'm not as strong as Toury.

I hope Alex never reads this article.

I'm pasting it in my journal so I will never forget and try to change. I want to be taken seriously and not be a negative footnote in the biography of Alex's life. I need to stop being so wild and carefree, to show I care about my people and kingdom. But where and how to start?

I'm starting to doubt the flames. Toury and Alex are in a sad state, and she was talking about leaving. Toury packed up and everything, but Alex got her to stay. Despite that, they are not doing well. He is absorbed in his work, she in her melancholy, and I am tired of them both. Yes, they have been through a lot, but you forgive, forget, and you cling to a love like theirs. I thought love was a weakness, but I see how much worse it is when it is gone. The flames are shaky, and I fear the things I have seen will not come true.

If Alex and Toury cannot work, what chance do Cobalt and I have? There's been another woman rumored to be having relations with him, but I won't bore you, nor will I condescend to read the rags about it either. I'm still not resigned, and I have this blasted suitor list to deal with. At least Mother is leaving me alone about it, after all these events, and Father is too ill to care about my marriage he'll never see. He does ask a lot about when Alex will marry. I think his plan is to live to see his heir settled down with his own on the way, but the way things are going, I'm not sure Father will make it. Not sure how I feel about his death, a man who never loved me but was fond of chastising or ignoring me. Maybe relief. Seeing him this weak and ill is upsetting.

March

Wundor,

I have neglected you. Frankly, nothing has happened until now. Alex and Toury slowly started to heal from their ordeals and were adorably in love again. Then Alex went away chasing dragons and slayers, while Toury and Cobalt prosecuted and imprisoned necromancers. Mother has made it her mission to hide firewhiskey from me, so I've been stealing it. I have been idle, useless, and too drunk to notice things right before my eyes that were transparent to others.

One morning, I came up from my bathing and dressing quarters to find the chambermaids in my room. Normally, they wait until my quarters are free to clean, but I had slept the morning away again thanks to too many spirits. I was not looking forward to Mother's reprimanding I was sure to get when I'd be forced to face her at lunch.

All worries on that avenue shifted to another when I overheard the maids gossiping. Lucy was pinning up my hair and working my circlet in carefully when the word Cobalt drew my attention.

"Flirting with her, they be saying," one maid said. I wasn't sure who since I couldn't turn my head, but Betsy and Fran are usually the ones who clean my room.

The other maid replied, "Nooo," in disbelief. "In a courtroom? Lord Cobalt must have more tact than that. It is meant to be a somber event. Poor queen proxy-to-be. After all that she has been through."

"I believe the lord definitely capable of such behavior. But the queen proxy-to-be don't push him away, mind you."

"La! Watch your mouth, Betsy. You don't want to spread false rumors and get done for treason," Fran warned in a hushed voice.

"'Tis true so not a rumor, but I'll be the first to admit she does not encourage him either. Feels more like a wolf stalking a wounded lamb."

"Someone should warn her."

"Why do you think I would dare to gossip in these quarters? I won't be sayin' em anywhere else."

Then they turned the conversation to innocuous topics. The maids should be reprimanded for the gossip, and yet there was no way of ever stopping them. At least she intentionally was warning me so I could warn Toury.

Only, after I did, she dismissed it without taking me seriously. I tried to explain his reputation, his status as an unrelenting flirt. She insisted—sort of offended—that she loved Alex and would never entertain the idea or even flirt back with Cobalt.

I cannot wait for the trial to be over so she and Cobalt never have to be together so often.

I grew weak and read the rags. They weren't as bad as I thought. A minor tiny blurb on the back painted Cobalt as an insufferable flirt, and Toury as disinterested and annoyed by his flirting. The rags were more concerned with dishing out the crimes of the guilty sorcerers with an underscore of sick triumph. I'm not bothering to keep this paper. I'm so happy the trials are over. Tomorrow is the sentencing.

Wishing the trial was over is now a regret. Toury had the necromancers snuffed and banished the ones who actually lived through the process. Toury had performed well both at dinner and the ceremony, and I was proud she had found her confidence again. She was back to the girl she was before Alex had broken her.

Then Cobalt had to knock her back down again. And me in the process.

I walked in on them kissing, openly, in the princess room, her servant not present. I stopped in the doorway. Before I could even react—my first instinct was to torch the place—Toury shoved him away.

She gasped. "Get away from me."

Cobalt tried to coax her back into his arms. "Toury—"

"Don't touch me!"

I stood frozen in shock and pain as she planted a nasty punch right into his eye, so hard, her face screwed up in pain from the contact, and he staggered a step back.

"How dare you take advantage of me!" she shouted.

Finally, her maid entered the room—she must've come up behind me in the doorway when I was distracted—and came to Toury's aid.

My eyes teared up as rage built in me. Holding the fire inside me to not hurt those who had just wounded me was one of the most difficult things I have ever had to do.

Toury was surprised to see me standing there, and then her face went from anger at Cobalt to guilt and sympathy when she met my gaze.

"Mary, I'm—"

"Don't." I cowardly transported back to my room, unable to face them.

I cried for some time. In between bouts of that, I cursed them. I was convinced it had been going on all along. My mind turned against rationality. Wasn't Cobalt on her suitor's list once? She had liked him. She was going for the throne and wanting Cobalt as a lover too. And Cobalt was a cad. To stab his friend in the back just because he wanted to bed Toury? No, rationality poked holes in this theory. I resolved on the fact that they were in love, and too late into her engagement to Alex, Toury realized. They would run away together to avoid Alex's wrath.

I was going wild aloud, because Lucy started telling me it made no sense, so I told her to be quiet. Still, she went on, telling me it was Cobalt who was to blame. I didn't want to hear he was the cad I always knew him to be. Why did the flames have to show me things that would entice me and make me fall for such a person? I dismissed Lucy and drowned my sorrow in cups, only to feel worse in the morning due to them and a lack of sleep.

What an entry. Sorry, Wundor. At least you do not judge me in my weakest moments.

So much has changed in one day.

Toury came to my room, and I let her have it, but she insisted on explaining. I could not stay mad. It all clicked now that my feelings were dulled through exhaustion and a raging headache. Cobalt had magnetized her—he has used his powers to attract and seduce women who find him pleasing but have scruples. I had to hand him over to her on a platter with the truth that he does this all the time. Toury was disgusted and enraged. Then I became rightfully so, not because he was "mine" or I was jealous, but her reaction showed me how wrong this was. Her Earthly views of men and equality always help me situate right from wrong in this world I grew up in, with men like my father at the helm, thinking us women have few purposes but to be beautiful and marry to have children. Toury is a miracle for my sphere in so many ways, Wundor, and I can't wait to see how she changes it for the better.

But I digress. We confronted Cobalt together. I almost forgot my anger to laugh at how terrified he was, but then, I dropped that sentiment. Alex could banish him from court, from the sphere completely; snuff his magic, making him ineligible to marry me, or he could even have him executed. It was treason to accost royalty, after all.

Toury tried to get straight to the point, but I could not wait. I had to hear the truth from his mouth. It would be the only way I'd know how to proceed with these stupid visions of our supposedly happy future. I straightforwardly asked if he had magnetized her.

He fumbled for an answer, so I pressed, "Cobalt, own up to it. I know what you do. I hear the gossip." It was harsh, but he deserved it.

As his face turned as red as a beet, I gloried in how much power I had to make him feel bad. I finally understood the aloof and austere persona my brother wore. It wielded power that could cut like a knife and shield you from anyone seeing your pain.

"What you must think of me," the cad muttered. Then he looked at me—not Toury—me! He worried about what *I* thought about him, not the woman who held his life in her hand.

This shocked me enough to let my Alex-façade slip. Why was he caring about what I thought now, after all these years, after never flirting with me or looking at me the way he looked at other women, after treating me as a mere acquaintance?

I deflected his comment, and then he switched topics to what would happen to him, what we'd tell Alex. Then he tried to persuade Toury not to have him punished too severely. She was crumbling. Her great heart and inability to hide it would be her weakness. I loved how she was not like the other courtiers, but sometimes, you have to wear a mask and throw on a fake smile or scowl.

I had to intervene. "Banish you? He'll probably want to kill you, Cobalt. You tried to steal away the person he loves most in this world."

Cobalt went pale and touched his head, hands shaking. I went too far. He must be imagining Alex torching him, literally. I was thinking about how it was a possibility. My brother didn't know my feelings. He could react horrifically and end my future in a couple seconds.

"Oh, don't look so pale like a debutante having a fainting fit. I'll help you."

"Mary?" Cobalt was astounded. The gibberish that came out of his mouth was dracaberry candy to my ears. I felt weak for loving to hear it. "You want to help me? I thought...I thought the way you reacted yesterday... It has bothered me more than anything."

Toury cut in and pressed for him to admit why. I gave her a death glare. She shouldn't have forced him to say anything further. Cobalt needed to deal with Alex, then me.

"I've asked that myself a dozen times," he whispered, his gaze intensely burning when it met mine, the same way when he beheld other women.

I was flattered, sadly. My pulse beat erratically. How had we gotten from me saving him from sudden death to this dance around feelings?

"I don't want to hurt you, Mary, never." He leaned toward me, his face warring between eagerness and nervousness. "And the way you reacted makes me think I've already done that. What I did was stupid and unforgivable, but it didn't warrant that reaction unless..."

I could not look into those cobalt eyes. I gave Toury a darting look, for she was about to leave. I nonverbally pleaded with her to stay. I could not trust myself with Cobalt. I was weak, and he deserved to be punished, not rewarded.

"Unless what, Cobalt?" I pressed.

Our eyes met, and I swear there was a connection, an intense flicker of understanding.

"Nothing. I'm being an absurd, egotistical fool." Cobalt stood. He was upset about something and turned his back on me.

I needed him to say it. I needed to know he could love me as I have loved him all my life because the stupid flames made me promises I long to live out despite everything.

"I could never hope to attain...I'm undeserving." He turned and looked at me, appalled.

I didn't like his expression. Why was he looking at me so...repulsed?

"I'm a scoundrel. I'm tainted, impure. I've broken so many hearts, and there's one in this kingdom I never ever want to break."

My heart sped up at his confession. It was all true, and I wanted to sardonically agree with him, and yet he was scared to hurt me. Why? He has already broken my heart repeatedly with his actions. He is so thick sometimes, but god and goddess, for some reason unknown to myself, I love the cad.

His eyes bore into mine. He was taking deep breaths, showing how nervous he was, which made me even more anxious, and I could no longer keep my eyes trained upon his intense gaze that spoke of love and lust and hope. I felt woozy and wanted to laugh at how I was about to swoon like every silly damsel in a book. I gave Toury a look, but she seemed confused about my expression. What was I supposed to say?

"I think that would be for her to decide, Lord Cobalt, don't you?" Toury said.

I took a deep breath. I needed Toury to divert his attention to gather my thoughts. I looked up to find he was staring at me.

"Mary?" his voice pleaded with me to say something. He'd take a scornful dismissal rather than this silence, so why couldn't I speak?

He rushed over to me and squatted to my sitting level. He took up my hands, which were shaking in his cooler clammy ones. "Is that true?"

I could not let him be forgiven so easily with a yes that would make him happy. He has hurt me again and again. I didn't want revenge, just not to reward him so soon with what he wanted, what we both wanted.

I pulled my hands away and got up. It was easier to talk when I wasn't looking at those deep blue eyes. "It won't be that easy, Cobalt. You are a scoundrel. You don't deserve me."

I had an idea though, a way for him to earn me. I opened the desk and motioned Lucy, who knew what I was up to. She grabbed a quill and inkpot.

"Mary, I know. God and goddess, I know. Had I ever known you might even think of me in any other way than just a friend or a brother—"

"You would've behaved? Not likely." I laughed, but it was hollow. I handed Cobalt my scroll of suitors and the quill in the inkpot. "But you will behave from now on if you want it to come true."

Cobalt looked at the scroll, his face blank and bewildered, and asked, "For what to come true?"

I met his gaze trying to act alluring as I see flirty court ladies do, and my, Wundor, it worked. His eyes lit up and stared at me as if he saw a woman in front of him, not innocent Mary. I wanted him to look at me like that forever, but I finally tore my eyes from his and sat again, this time next to Toury before I figuratively slapped him with the truth. "What I've seen in the flames. Why else would you think I'd have been sweet on you?"

"Sweet on me?" Cobalt was lost, and I was enjoying toying with him too much. He did deserve to squirm.

"You never had a clue?" He had to know on some level. I couldn't believe he would be that unobservant.

"Well, when you were little, yeah, but when I became interested in girls..." He had to look away, for we both remembered exactly the moment I found out how interested he had become in women when I caught him with my maid. The thought of her and of others made me insanely jealous, so I lashed out.

"When you were caught having your fun with a chambermaid?" I fired a barb at him, trying to wound him as the memory of it still twinged me.

Toury stifled a laugh. I guess she didn't know that tidbit until now or maybe she was enjoying watching Cobalt squirm.

After Cobalt swallowed his pride, he pushed for answers. "That, yes. But even then, you started to ignore me."

"And you paid attention to my cousin." I kept throwing what I could at him to wound him because it had wounded me.

"That wasn't...I don't think anyone knew what my relationship with Ruby was like."

Toury's mood went sour, and she accused him of courting her right after Ruby went missing. I knew this morsel of info because he had admitted it, but I had believed he did it to push Alex to sign as well since Alex was obviously enamored by Toury. The games this boy played.

"I'm a scoundrel, and I know you both think ill of me, and I deserve that, but Ruby would not be upset by my forsaking her. Ruby had a secret that I caught onto. We decided to pretend to court to lead to a marriage of convenience. Aside from occasional heirs, we would not be in each other's way when it came to the women we wanted to dally with."

My mouth dropped. I had never known that about my cousin. I now regret our last conversation. I had believed she would take Cobalt away from me for some selfish reason when, truly, she had only desired to love whom she wanted, in private. She was willing to accept a marriage of convenience and the continuation of the Fyrian line in exchange to love women. It seems a strange notion to me. I hate most women, but I have heard tales of romantic entanglements between two women or two men. Being an innocent still, I'm not sure why it is outlawed or how it became that way. Shouldn't any Fyrian love whomever they chose? I know firsthand you cannot control whom you love. I love a cad I want to throttle.

Back to what happened: the silence was broken by said cad as he examined my suitor list in his hand. "How many men are on here?" He was jealous, and Wundor, that felt good for it to be him for once.

"I am the princess, Cobalt, so every man who is single?"

Cobalt's lips pinched together, displeased. "I don't see you as a princess, not like they do. To them, you're just a step up in society, in power, a step closer to the king's ear."

"I know."

He finally signed his name on the list, where it should have been from the start. He blew the ink dry and handed it back to me, the flirt purposely brushing my finger. It was such an innocent touch, and yet nothing was innocent between us anymore. I felt my face go red, and I had to suppress a grin. It would've been a huge triumphant smile.

"So, lovebirds," Toury teased us. "What do we do about Alex?"

Great. With my brother's name, Toury doused any good feelings I had about Cobalt and me. What will my brother do?

Of course, the gossip rags reported Cobalt and Toury's kiss. One of the servants who had witnessed the kiss must've leaked it out to the public, but it didn't make the next day's paper, but the following day's. Lucy, always thinking ahead, had the rag for me that morning. My excitement of having Cobalt as my suitor diminished. I knew to expect this, but I had thought I might get at least a couple more days before facing reality. Here is the awful article that I will reread often to remember Cobalt's faults. I cannot get engaged to or let alone marry him until I trust him.

COURTLY CUCKOLDS & CADS

PROXY AWAY, COBALT PLAYS

Reader, today we have a salacious rumor directly from the castle. There were several witnesses to confirm what we had thought was a vicious rumor.

While the king proxy has been after dragon slayers down south, in the capital, his queen proxy-to-be has been busy with the necromancer trials, but apparently also other pursuits. She has been assisted by Lord Stephen Cobalt during these trials, but now accusations are rising that he helped her with much more. Let your memory wander with that one, dear reader, we are sticking to facts.

Several witnesses saw the lord mentioned above kissing our queen proxy-to-be, only the kiss was punctuated with a fist to his face. Yes, lords and ladies, our future queen—if we can call her that still—can pack a punch. It appears on the surface that the kiss was neither wanted nor asked for. And we all know the Cobalts' magical gift of persuasion. However, it cannot be ruled out that the kiss was mutual, and she was trying to cover it up to save face once company discovered them.

We should presume she is innocent in this situation. All that awaits now is King Proxy Alexander's return and reaction. Will this break off their engagement permanently? More importantly, what will our ruler do to his best friend, the court's favorite cad?

Cad indeed. This will take a long time for people to forget.

Unfortunately, Alex returned before another scandal could steal the headlines. He also had heard rumors in the city before any of us could explain what had happened and the turn in events. I was truly terrified that Alex would kill Cobalt on the spot. I had never seen my brother like this, so I stood ready to block any fire if I had to. I would protect Cobalt. He deserved punishment, but not death. That would break my heart, and Alex's too, even though he was far from seeing it that way at that moment.

There was no need for my protective magic. Alex was more hurt than angry, just as I had been. I could see it in his eyes, the rage shimmered with excruciating pain. The idea of losing Toury ripped him up inside. I understood more than the others in the room.

I can't wait until Cobalt loves me that much, so much that he will feel like dying rather than live without me. Sigh. Call it revenge, but I want Cobalt to suffer as much as he made me. Then, I would heal his pain with my love. It is only fair, right?

My thoughts were in the clouds, because the next thing I knew, my brother ordered Cobalt's banishment from the castle. Eventually, Alex will forgive him; it's not in my brother's kind nature to hold grudges forever, but it was hard to let go when I had him in my grasp. Cobalt will be my lifemate. I want him here with me, yet I know I am still young. Plus, he is too wild for us to settle down quite yet. He is on my list. I will be satisfied with that. Distance will make him prove himself.

That's not all, Wundor. I did something reckless. I was determined to see him before he left. I knew Cobalt would be marched out the front gates. Alex probably wouldn't demand the shame of it, and I thought perhaps Cobalt would sneak out the way of the stables, but Cobalt is the type to face the consequences, take the embarrassment if it means he can win back his lifelong friend. And me. Right now, Alex is the one he has to win over. Cobalt has time to win me. God and goddess, he will need to do a lot to have me forgive him. The distance will help as a test for his commitment to me, a cooling period for Alex, and a slow down for my excitement that he finally knows my feelings and visions.

I hid by the entrance of the Great Hall, which is rarely used these days. Lucy followed me in. I forgot about her. Great, an audience. There was no getting rid of her either. After the Toury incident, Lucy would never leave me alone with Cobalt—even if on my suitor list.

I heard footsteps and peeked out. Cobalt had his things in a rucksack, and a servant carried his trunk. He was leaving, and I would not see him for ages; it felt like a bitter sting, having just come to an understanding about our feelings. My feelings. I know Cobalt used to see me as the childhood friend grown up, and I'm sure he found me pretty, but I wanted him to look at me with that passionate fire in his eyes. The way Toury and Alex look at each other. I needed him to leave thinking about me every second of the day, much like he forced his way into my mind all too often. I had a sliver of it when he realized my feelings, but I needed more.

When he passed the room, I yanked Cobalt's arm, scaring him and making him teeter off balance. His stumbling allowed me to pull him into the room. His vibrant blue eyes, lighter than my own, bore into mine, his expression scrunched up, hurt, and confused.

After such an act, I feigned a regal air. "Load his belongings into the coach. Lucy, stand watch outside the door."

Lucy opened her mouth to speak, but I glowered at her. I was getting a goodbye memento. Cobalt and I were alone.

"Mary, what's going on?"

I closed the door and spun around to face him.

"Alex will kill me, literally, if he sees me in here with you...alone." He swallowed hard, his hands clenched at his sides, terrified.

"Then I'll make it quick. You may write to me." I had wanted to tell him things, unleash my feelings, tell him the future, but nerves overwhelmed me. There was also a niggling voice in my head begging for him to suffer and not to soothe him yet.

"You want me to write to you?" he questioned. His lost face was adorable.

"And I will write to you. It may be some time until you're allowed to return."

"I'm going to return?" Now he was eager, hoping I had seen it.

At least I could give him that smidgen to live off. "Of course, do you think Alex will stay mad forever? That I would let him banish you for good?"

Cobalt took up my hand impulsively and kissed the back of it. His warm lips left a spot of tingling, and my heart started to beat furiously in my chest. "I'm more worried about you staying mad at me."

"Oh, it'll take me a while. I will make you pay for it." When the teasing came out, his grip on my hand tightened, and his eyes dilated. His eyes roamed.

That was the moment I realized the gravity of our loss of innocence when simply talking. Teasing words had now become sensual flirting.

"Please do," he whispered, his gaze lingering on my lips.

I knew what he wanted because I did too. I moved closer to him. He took a ragged breath. Good, he was feeling the same sweet tension I was.

His other hand smoothed an errant strand of hair that had escaped my hair pins and moved it behind my ear, his fingers brushing my skin, sending shivers down my spine. It was a classic Cobalt flirting move, but my goodness, it worked. I leaned into him, pushing up on my toes to close the distance between our lips, and closed my eyes.

Cobalt let me kiss him. My lips touched his softly. His lips were warm, gentle, and it felt like my heart was doing flips in my chest.

But he didn't react or respond. Something was wrong. This was not the kiss I foresaw. Was it later? No, it was this moment—the room, our clothing; it all matched my vibrant visions. Or had I tried to make it happen with my foresight and it was supposed to be later? Doubt crept in. About everything.

I pulled away, frowning. "Did I...did I do something wrong?"

Cobalt's blank face transformed into worry. "No!" He lowered his voice, "Not at all, Mary. I'm trying to be a gentleman here. You are...beyond tempting." His eyes suggestively roamed down me, making me blush.

"Well, you're not a gentleman, but a cad. I want you to be a cad right now. And I foresaw it, so give me my *real* first kiss now." I actually stomped my foot. I thought he was going to laugh at my bratty tantrum and mock me for it.

Instead, his intense eyes stared me down for a second, before he lunged out and pulled me against him by the nape of my neck, making me squeal. His lips crashed roughly into mine. I pressed my lips against his. My stomach dipped, and I felt dizzy as he moved his lips over mine again and again, falling into a coordinating pattern. I wound my arms around his neck; as his hand cradled my head, his other was touching my side.

All too soon, he pulled away, meeting my gaze. His eyes were filled with that amorous intensity I saw between others. Finally, he saw me as a woman and not a girl. He backed away and straightened himself up. "Better?" He raised his brows. Oh, he was so cocky. Sadly, I found it cute.

"Better, but I think you'll improve your technique over time. One day, I'll get the real cad Cobalt."

He laughed nervously and looked away. "I think you're a bit young for that."

"Am not!"

Then he looked at me again with a wry expression. "You're ready to get married right now, then?"

It was a cold dose of reality. And it felt like one. He was telling me we have to take it slow. He inadvertently insinuated to me that he does indeed habitually seduce women all the way. We should wait because I don't trust him not to stray.

Still, I did not want to ruin this moment with accusations. "You're no fun." I pouted.

Cobalt laughed. Too soon, it faded. "Do write to me often, Mary. I will miss you."

I nodded, trying not to let him see how sad I was. It will be ages—or feel like it at least—until I see him again. After that kiss, I want to see him every day. "Go be a good boy, and earn a reputation worthy of a future prince-to-be."

"Yes, Your Highness. I will adhere to your every command from here on out." He bowed and showed himself out.

And now I sit here writing to you, already missing my silly cad. I await his first letter to come because I will not admit I miss him more than he misses me by caving in and writing first.

I did not expect a letter for a fortnight. It would be the typical male thing to do to avoid seeming overeager or easily manipulative. Knowing Cobalt's history with women, I didn't doubt he had an arsenal of tricks to gain the upper hand in the relationship.

I was greatly surprised when I received a letter within the week.

Now this is the dedication a princess deserves. Let the time apart tell if he stays constant or if he strays. I'm praying to the god and goddess he will not let me down again. Not knowing about our future was one excuse, but there is nothing now to defend his actions if he seduces women.

Cobalt Estate
Nigh Ludford

Dear Princess Mary,

I know firsthand how stubborn you can be, and the last thing I want to do is anger you by waiting to write. Now, you can write to me and proclaim you have me under your spell, following your every demand. I am no great writer, so I'm sorry if my letters are brief and not the literary composition of a poet to impress you and make you swoon. I promise to make this one as long as possible. You know that already because you teased me relentlessly about my poor penmanship and terrible style during lessons long ago. I think you said, "verse more boring than the histories," and that was always your least favorite subject. I am told the first letter of a courtship is a keepsake cherished always. At least my little dreamer of a sister Margaret insists it is. She nonstop talks of boys right now, which I find alarming and difficult to not get overprotective about. She's so eager to marry and only fifteen! I'm sure you'd argue otherwise with me and say it is a suitable age, and I'm being a tedious older brother because you've always loved scolding me...

Lucy had the audacity to tell me to get out of bed for my bath full-knowing the letter was important to me. I withheld my temper even after she said the letter would keep but not the temperature of the bath water. I swear she lives to pain me. She knows I can heat the water myself with my fire. Apparently, Mother needed me ready immediately. It ended up being gown fittings. Irritating interruption.

Then there was the whole Toury debacle that kept me from the letter. I had let her move in with me, settled her in. She was withdrawn completely and didn't bother with her friends. Unopened correspondence piled up in just a couple days. Her moping was irritating enough, but then Mother had expected me to cheer up her and Alex too. My brother and Toury are hopeless and miserable without each other. Something has to give soon.

Finally, I got back to Cobalt's letter.

That reminds me. I meant to tell you before I left—but someone distracted me with a kiss, one I cannot forget about and long to reenact. I'm utterly distracted again by the mere thought. What I was trying to say to you was I can't wait to be prince for one big reason: I can tease you back just as mercilessly as you tease me and not get punished for it.

You are totally going to hit me for that comment, aren't you?

I'm staying busy doing landlord duties for my father. I never realized how much I'd miss him or my brother. Being here with only the women of the household is a bit dull. I love my mother and my sisters, but all they do is read, gossip, paint, and play music. You know how interested in any of that I am. I've also been at the palace so long that I don't know any country gentleman close to my age or a decade older. The closest place with anything going on is Ludford, so I might check it out and try to make some friends. I never knew how much I relied on your brother for friendship. He was literally my only real friend. I don't dare write him. How is he? I don't want you in the middle of this but long to know how he fares. I miss him.

More importantly, write to me how you are faring. I always missed you when away from the castle, but I cannot forget what you said about us and the future, and I wish I could embark on that path now. I'm glad you told me. The burden of it must have been terrible for you. The wounds I unknowing caused you torment me. I want to start making it up to you, but I'm stuck here, away from you.

I long to know what you are up to. Try not to party too much without me, my darling wild princess.

Your cad truly,
Stephen Cobalt

112

Considering Cobalt is no writer, the letter was longer than I had anticipated. Other than that, I wasn't sure what I had expected—poetry, words of love, that nonsense that makes girls giddy? Part of me was disappointed, but then I chastised myself. Would I have wanted flowery words from him, the same language he used to seduce others? Words he likely never meant. Or do I prefer this, the real him, the boy I know and grew up with, the friend? It doesn't feel like a keepsake, but I pasted it in here in case I look back one day and love this letter.

Of course, I reread it a dozen times and picked up on the importance behind his mention of the kiss and our future. He realizes how much his dallying has hurt me, saving me from the painful admittance I thought I would have to make. His deep contemplation on my feelings—ones he unknowingly has hurt—is showing me promise he can change his selfish ways.

I concluded it was a good letter for its hope and honesty.

I instantly started writing back. But what to tell him when it came to Alex and Toury? I'm watching her read in my room as I write in you. Perhaps she needs a journal, a Wundor to spill her heart to. I should get her talking about things, but it's awkward. Alex is my brother, and I'm not sure I want to hear about a side of him intended for privacy. I sure know Cobalt would never talk to him about problems with me—if they were on friendly terms.

After a few false starts writing Cobalt back and four crumpled papers, I put it off a couple days to think. As long as I write back within a week, he will not worry.

It took me more than a week, and I do not think it is a good letter. I did not dare ask Toury for help or to look at it. Perhaps I am no romantic either. How doomed are Cobalt and I in this letter writing business then?

I broke down and asked Lucy. She said it wasn't overly romantic but thought that was good in the circumstances. She thought he deserved to be berated for his behavior but how it also lacked hope. The important thing, she said, was that my letter was honest and from me. She then told me tales of letters men pay to have written while courting that leads to disappointment for the ladies after marriage. What a horrible concept. I am now glad Cobalt's letter wasn't full of poetry and promises. I know he wrote it. Here it is while I try to think of how to end it.

The Sapphirian Palace
Celestia

My dear cad,

It is funny that you don yourself with the very pet name I gave you in private? I am loath to admit it, but I cant forget about that kiss either. By the way, arent we past the title business? Call me Mary. I thought a kiss would show I was allowing informality.

You are right that I love to tease you, and if we ever get engaged, you have the law on your side, but the law protects me from punishment too. Retaliation is not fun, dear cad.

Be nice to your sisters and mother. A woman's life is idle because we are taught to be useless pretty little breeders. I cannot condone that. Help them understand your interests. Forge a bridge between your mind and theirs so that they make better companions for you and you for them. Our world will change, Cobalt. I feel it. Toury is the key to so many things. But I think she will have a huge impact on women.

I can imagine you rolling your eyes at that. But you only would refuse change because women are easy to conquer as is. You need not think that way anymore since you are courting me. I will not tolerate you trying to control me like so many men control their wives. Not only because I am second in line but because a marriage should be a partnership. Toury and Alex's little tiffs over control have made me see it is better to be a team than to exert force over each other. It is best I tell you this now: you will not rule me, and in return, I will not rule you. That is if we marry.

As to answer your question about my brother, Alex and Toury are not doing well. I'm sure you expected that. I'm not going to downplay things to pamper your ego. You should feel the brunt of the blame for it. She is now living with me in my quarters, and she and Alex ignore each other. They are both sad and broken.

I didnt get to add to it. My letter was already pretty long, and I wanted to crumble it up and start afresh. My inaction came from my worry over whether I should even be with him. The elation from our kiss had faded, and I wondered if it was only that great because it was my first kiss ever. Then I started blaming myself. Why hadnt I told him about us when we were kids? Would it have ruined *things or prevented the whole catalyst to his behavior when I found him with my chambermaid? Was she the first one even? When you're idle and knocking back firewhiskeys, your mind becomes your worst enemy.*

I went to bed and woke up with a headache. Determined to rewrite it. I looked it over after lunch. I didn't crumple up my letter to Cobalt. I decided to end on a more positive note as Lucy mentioned.

Then I thanked her. I don't think she knew what to do with my kindness. I have to start treating her better and not take my worries out on her. Here's the end of the letter:

As I scold you and fill you with guilt, my heart aches that you will be hurt by this news. Don't despair, Stephen. The flames tell me they will reconcile. I'm just not sure how long it will take. I also long to see you. And yet, I must admit, this is good for us. We know each other well. But not in a romantic way. Perhaps forging our feelings apart will help us not get tangled in all the feelings kisses could bring.

Yours truly,
Mary

Mother came to me. I should've known that she had schemes to get Toury and Alex back together.

In the princess salon, she brought me into the fold. "A surprise birthday party for Toury. It's just the thing to push the two of them together enough that will induce a wedding, I hope."

Mother is ambitious. I just want them back together, my rooms to myself, and Cobalt back. There was a big problem with her plan too. "But how will we hide it, and isn't her birthday a long way away?"

"Five months away, so I can plan this slowly under her nose. Closer to the time, I'll find some excuse or way. We'll have to get Alex involved. He's too shrewd not to notice."

"I want to see his face when you tell him."

"I was hoping you'd go in and break him a bit."

"Ah, taunt and distract him, so he doesn't realize you're coming to attack. I like this."

"No. Don't anger him or upset him, just ruffle his feathers."

"Easy to do these days. I'll simply tell him what I've seen in the flames."

"Tell me—No, don't," Mother struggled.

I gripped her hands in mine lovingly. "You love the good surprises. I cannot rob you of those. I cannot break your heart with the bad ones either. It is best not to know, trust me."

Right then and there, I wanted to tell her about Cobalt, but couldn't. She is dealing with a lot. I cannot add to her concerns.

I did as I was told and ruffled Alex's feathers. I told Alex I saw him marry Toury, just as I would marry Cobalt. He did not like that at all, but at least I preserved Cobalt's life on this sphere. Alex cannot banish or execute him without destroying my life. He loves me too much, and he'll realize soon enough he cannot live without his friend.

Alex is still in absolute denial about Toury, but he caved to the party when Mother entered. He really can't handle the two of us ganging up on him at once. I imagine if Toury banded with us about an issue, he would do anything we say. It feels powerful to manipulate a king, not that I would often exploit my brother. These are our futures and that of Fyr on the line.

I left him a note that would override his denial by mentioning his and Toury's future kids. Hopefully, it at least planted a seed of reconciliation—I hope.

Today, Lord Cobalt and Lord Thomas Cobalt came to visit me in the Princess Salon. Toury conveniently asked Mother to take a stroll in the orchard with her after she seemed puzzled by their appearance. They are usually busy with orders from Alex, compensating for the many lords who were punished in the necromancer's failed coup.

As she left, Toury winked. I'm glad to see her happy again.

I invited the men to sit. Then it dawned on me who they truly might be one day: my father and brother by law.

Lord Cobalt spoke first. Although Cobalt looks more like his mother in coloring, the way his father speaks and moves, his mannerisms, reminds me very much of my Cobalt. "Princess Mary, I apologize for intruding on your afternoon, but I have a letter from my son he has asked me to deliver. It was enclosed in one for me. He has informed me of some circumstances that I see my Queen Dowager is not yet aware of. We came to pay my respects, and frankly, I wanted to know if you told the king proxy of this possible future marriage to my son to save him from death."

I glanced at the fire. "They say the future shifts with the flames, but that has been the one constant in my firebranding. For better or worse, I have only seen Stephen, often, since I was six."

Thomas whistled out, shaking his head. His father gave him a look.

"What?" Thomas shrugged. "That's a hard thing for someone to carry with them and keep secret. I'm impressed we are only finding out now."

Lord Cobalt sighed, unhappy about something. "Forgive me for saying this Princess Mary—about my own child, especially—but you deserve better. I know who he is, and I love all my children, but you are *the* princess."

"I am well aware of his reputation. I saw to it that he will not be severely punished."

"May I ask what will happen to my son?"

I frowned. "I actually do not know, but I think pushing for that answer is unwise. My brother is cooling down, and he and the queen-to-be are mending what issues divided them. I think it best to wait and see. He was my brother's best friend and is my future. Some reconciliation will happen at some point."

Lord Cobalt smiled and nodded. "Thank you, Princess." Then he stood.

Thomas did as well.

"We will no longer trespass on your time."

I nodded to allow them to leave. In the doorway, Thomas stopped. "Tell my brother I said to get over himself, and 'I told you so.' He'll know what it's about."

As soon as they were gone, I tore open the letter.

Cobalt Estate
Nigh Ludford

Dear Princess Mary,

I am more than overjoyed you wrote back to me. I was worried at first, not receiving a letter soon after mine. That kiss and you asking me to write...but you needed time. I understand.

I'm sorry, Princess, but I will not drop your title, since I'm not engaged to you yet. Did you forget how your brother urged the queen proxy-to-be to drop his title and trapped her into an engagement? Not that I would complain about being trapped by you. That would not be fair to you if it occurred.

I am truly sorry things are so bad at the castle. If only there were a type of magic to turn back time and undo my mistake so I could be there for you. It is a punishment to know that most of the negativity around you was caused by me. That pains me more than anything. I hurt you the most in all this. I will make it up to you.

In my desire to earn your love, I am behaving. I will show you and all of Fyr that I can be steadfast and change my ways. Only a few of us know the prize I'm reaching for. I hope it was acceptable that I told my father and brother. My sisters noticed me writing—odd for me as you know, so I slipped this letter into my father's so they'd stop asking questions. I do not want "us" to be idle gossip.

I'm bored here. Last week, I took my sisters to a country ball. I forgot how informal those things could be since I've been spoiled by Celestia's finest for so long. You'd be proud of me. Lots of country lasses there, and I didn't dance with one. I only danced with my sisters. Mother is relentlessly trying to marry Holly off. At twenty-one, it is getting Mother worried, but lots of women marry later. She's a bit plain, but I don't think anyone would dare say Holly wasn't pretty. I just think she hates being in public so much that men overlook her. Poor Holly.

As for the rest of my family, I did get some nasty letters from my father and brother. My father's was the worst. He's disappointed in me and threatened to disown me if I embarrassed my family again. He's threatened this many times before, but I think it is true this time. My brother said the same. He will inherit the Cobalt estate and fortune one day, and father has wanted the monies portioned out. Thomas threatened to take my portion, split it, and give it to our sisters.

It doesn't matter. I will have no more indiscretions that could embarrass them. I'm waiting for you no matter how long it takes to win you over. I'll wait until I'm an old man if needs be.

Your undeserving cad,
Stephen Cobalt

I devoured his letter. It made me smile, but I long for a time when I will no longer need to chastise him nor him beg to be forgiven. Time will close that, but I can't easily forgive nor forget. His promise to wait touched my heart, but I worry how long he can last before he slips up—if he does misstep. I should not assume since no flames have shown me anything of that sort.

At least he is behaving right now. I checked more than the flames. I had Lucy—who admitted she likes reading them—devour the gossip rags to present to me anything that involved him. The only news she brought was that there was a tiny article about him in the country keeping his hands to himself and speculation on how long that would last. Then silence.

I pressed her, but she got into a tale of a Lady not of my acquaintance having an affair and her children's paternity coming under question due to eye color. It sounded like too much drama to bother reading, but at least it turns an eye away from the palace and us inhabitants.

No news also means Cobalt did not spread the word of why he stopped chasing lightskirts. Only a few in our families know. Like he wished to take time back and change things, I wish to press it forward through all this waiting. I want to punish him but not myself in all this time apart. Too bad that isn't possible.

I wrote back to him at once.

The Sapphirian Palace
Celestia

My dear partially-deserving cad,

I appreciate you refraining from dancing. As much as I want to forgive you for your past actions, since you had no idea about my firebranding findings, I must admit even if I could forgive, I am still not ready to marry. You are right that your one sister is too young and the other is not too old.

I feel I am too young—perhaps both of us. Not from maturity or a lack of desire to secure a lifemate, but because it brings children. How shaky this world is and my brother's tenuous proxy rule, the fear of people such as necromancers and rebels—it's a bit terrifying to imagine bringing a child into this world, when I still feel as if I haven't left childhood far behind.

I must stop these maudlin thoughts. The point is, one step at a time. You heal this rupture with Alex when he is ready. You apologize to Toury after that. Then maybe we can get engaged. I don't want to admit it, but when that happens, I think we should wait the full two years of the engagement. I need to see years of celibacy and control to trust you if I give my life over to your love and care. I'm sorry I'm talking about such things, but you and I need time and honesty. A rushed marriage will not do us well, lies will ruin us. I hope you don't think I'm backsliding. I just want assurance.

Anyway, your father and brother came to see me. Your brother told me to tell you to "get over yourself" and "told you so," whatever that means. Your father told me I deserve better than you. They were worried you would be executed or banished, but I assured them, and you now, that Alex will not pursue either, so that is positive at this stage. How could he when his stubborn sister browbeat him into dismissing both punishments? He needs time, and I think that will heal all things.

Your father believes my influence is the only thing that keeps you alive. let the sphere think that and not see Alex has a soft heart.

I wanted this letter to be full of humor, but look at me now: full of reproach and sadness. I will go and think of better things to write in my next letter.

Yours truly,
Mary

120

April

After that depressing letter, I doubt I will hear from Cobalt for some time. Everyone truly is weighing me down, and the drinking is worse. It makes me feel so much better and chases the sadness away, but it always comes back tenfold the next morning.

Today, I was in the library, trying to find something to read to stifle my boredom, when Mother came in, her bodyguard standing with mine by the door.

"I think my little plan is working."

The look I gave her must have been disappointing because she huffed at me and crossed her arms, very unlike her. "It's not? You live with Toury. Don't you think they are on the verge of at least getting on speaking terms?"

"Aside from 'please pass the potatoes' at supper?" I raised my brow at her. Wundor, she has so much hope, and I cannot see why she does.

"Mary, perhaps you do not see the nuances, not ever being in love yet. The way they ask for things in each other's presence, the fleeting looks when they had been stoic in ignoring each other. They need another push, although I know whatever clever thing you wrote on that paper, my darling, has done something to Alex. He's been meandering. First it was the nursery, which greatly shocked me. Then it was the orchard. He's gone there often. He's thinking about the future and of her. He watches that little servant Toury brought in—Duric—pick the dracaberry Toury is so fond of. He chats with the boy. It is quite adorable and definitely a lovesick thing he's doing."

It did sound a bit pathetic and made complete sense. Except for one thing. "Have you been spying?"

"Not at all. I merely asked a servant to get information from David."

My mind went numb, and my stomach dropped. Does Lucy tell her things about me?

"Don't give me that look, Mary. I don't spy on my children regularly. This is an extreme circumstance. David is concerned about Alex as well. He's not himself without Toury." Mother frowned. "Plus, how is it different from you kids spying into the future? When will you tell me anything about what might happen?"

"Mother, I explained before. Won't that take the fun away?" More like I don't want to scare her—or worse, hurt her. Some terribly difficult things are heading our way, but they are too vague and changing to admit them aloud. But the strongest thread I see in the fire is happy, healthy lives for us after the storm passes. How long this storm will last, I'm unsure. Father is not in these visions at all. Although I know Mother can tell he will pass away soon, I could not bring it up.

She gave me a chiding look. I had the power of the future in my hands and felt more like the adult in the situation. It was strange.

"Mother, it is best not to know really, isn't it?"

I could see questions burning in her expression. "Is it?" She bit her lip.

I had to give her something, anything other than my father's death and the horrors that are coming. "I will marry Cobalt, but he has been an absolute cad."

Mother gasped at my impulsive admittance.

"It is horrible knowing what will be and not seeing why and how the events unfold. My future is mapped out without me. I can't fight it."

Mother stared at me and touched my chin gently. "Mary, never marry unless for love. I do not look like a fighter, but I simply choose my battles and fight them in private. Your father has not pressed Alex or you into marriage as soon as you were of age as he had wanted, because of me. I have kept him at bay for a couple years, and then the illness stole his fight."

I was stunned. I knew my mother was not a weak woman, but she hardly protested against my father. I never thought about what they spoke of in their quarters.

"Mary, women have little control in this world—"

"Alex and Toury will change that."

She smiled and closed her eyes, tipping her head up to the ceiling. A smile lit her face. When she peered down at me, she blinked back tears. "I could not ask for more." She wiped her eyes. "It's in your voice, Mary. I hear when you are unsure. I hear it and see it in your gaze when it is the future you are certain of. Ever since you could speak, I could tell."

I was stunned by Mother's admittance, how much she was sharing with me. She views me as an adult now, able to handle these deep topics. Our roles are shifting. How odd to know more than your parent about things. It is an emboldening feeling that drops off into worry about who can help me if I need it.

"All I want is your happiness. Both you and Alex. When you talked back to your father for the first time at eleven, remember, when Alex came of age? I knew you had seen that waiting was paramount. Maybe you hadn't seen Toury yet, or maybe you had, but you saw that Alex's path was not to be planned out by your father. Nor your own." She took a deep breath. "I fought him on your marriages and waited for love matches." Mother took my hands in hers. "You see, Mary. I saw a seer, a renowned one, while your father was courting me. I was told the cold, hard truth of my future marriage. I still chose it. I want so much better for both of you."

Mother's admittance hit me hard. I had always known it was not a marriage of love but convenience. I saw few loving words from my father toward her; even in his weak state, he lashed out in anger rather than thanking her for all the care she personally was giving him.

It makes me worry about Cobalt and me. Will we reach a loveless state of indifference like my parents? I can imagine if he strays, has a baseborn child—we could end up that way. It isn't the flames, but my insecurity is leading me down this mental path. My parents and their terrible relationship brings it all on.

"Why did you go through with it?" I managed to squeeze out, my heart thumping, worried my mother regretted her entire life.

"Because I was told I would have you two." Tears built up in her eyes again, and now in mine. "I was told if I did not marry him and beget you, Fyr would never flourish. But now..." she sighed. "I wonder—"

"If the sacrifice was worth it?"

Mother laughed and wiped away her tears. "Ah, Mary, any sacrifice is worth seeing your child in your arms. One day you will learn that. But I will not let you think ill of your father. He treated me well enough. It was a different time. He has never struck me or hurt me. He was faithful in marriage. This was a time we did not marry for love. I married for a prophecy I was sure of. I'm sure of it now more than ever. I do not mind being a small stepping stone to a wondrous future. I was born to be a queen, to serve my country in the only way a woman could the last generation."

"A mother to Alex."

"Yes, and you. Stop underrating the ability you have to control this sphere. I pushed you to become a courtly woman in hopes you could learn to own them, change them, mold them into something better than the falsities they exhibit."

"If you told me that..."

"You'd listen?" She gave me that maternal look that accused me of the opposite. She is right. I have been downright oppositional. I wouldn't have listened or understood.

I threw my arms around my mother, stealing a hug. She happily sighed.

"Anything you want, Mother. I'll go in there and force him into his destiny." Like she gave up her life for Fyr by marrying father to ensure Alex would change the world, I will ensure he ends up with Toury. I know they are meant for each other and will be the exact pair that will change Fyr forever.

❧

Cobalt Estate
Nigh Ludford

Dearest wild, lovely Princess,

It looks as though we are in agreement: we should wait. I'm not going to propose for a good while. I need the people, Alex, the queen proxy-to-be, and you to forgive me before I can think of asking. More importantly, I want to prove myself, my worth, to everyone, but especially you. I will not ask for your hand until the sphere is convinced I am a devoted future prince and not a wicked philanderer. I would never have your name dragged into that.

As for not being happy in your letter, please don't ever take that for me. I need to know how you are. I need the truth, even when it hurts me. Princess Mary, I want to take on your problems as mine, so never apologize for them. Chastise me when I rightfully deserve it. Let us promise each other full disclosure and honesty. I think that's the only way for you and me to make this work. When I see you, my wild princess, I'm going to make you vow that to me—after I kiss you madly. I can't stop thinking about you and the future. It gets me by all these lonely nights.

So you know, my father came home to properly chastise me for you. He speaks so highly of your kindness and honesty and made sure I knew I was lesser than the mud on your boot. I already know this, my darling Princess Mary. His reminder makes me feel even more unworthy.

Of course, I groveled, but I also assured him I was a changed person and that I would do anything he wished if it kept me on a path to courting you. I kind of promised I'd name one of my future kids after Father—and my brother since they share the name—to appease him, but that's something to talk about way later. Sorry, I always get ahead of myself when I'm excited about something. We are going to wait. As I promised and we both know, it is the right course.

I miss you.

Your cad,
Stephen

I put the letter away quickly when Toury entered. I do not like him being so sad, but I know he has to feel terrible before things can be mended between us.

If Toury saw me hide the letter, she did not call me out.

I glanced at the ever-so-long suitor list sitting on the shelf. I really need to weed out some. I cannot select Cobalt only. What if he slips up?

"How is he?" Toury's voice was void of emotion.

"Huh?"

"Cobalt." She had a harder time saying his name without a touch of venom, but I could tell she was trying to remain kind for my sake. "Every time you get a letter from a courtly lady, you roll your eyes several times, scoff, and critique them aloud. When you get one from him, you're off in another world and pensive or hide it if I startle you."

I had not realized she was so observant while she attempted to embroider, with little improvement, or walked in the room.

"Fine as he can be, I suppose." I didn't know what to tell her.

"So he suffers as we do here? I guess that is good."

Her comment bothered me at the time, but I didn't want to fight.

Cobalt deserves punishment, I know, but perhaps she thinks he is getting off too lightly.

"Yes," I allowed. "We are all being punished, which is not fair, but please know he is feeling the full brunt of punishment. Alex is his everything. Together from infancy, best friends, primed to be his advisor. He messed up, and I'm sorry it was you who got entangled in it. But now he knows about me. I'm becoming his everything as well. To be severed from that is acute enough. Don't you feel that way about Alex? That part of you is missing by this separation?"

Toury's lips were firm, and she yanked the thread until it broke. She threw her project onto the floor and glared at me. "I cannot pretend I'm not glad to hear Cobalt suffers. The problem I have, Mary, is he made the mistake. I did not, and now I suffer."

"Go to Alex," I pleaded.

"And what? Apologize for something I didn't do?"

"No. Just go to him and tell him you miss him, that you love him, that you can't stand to be away from him."

Toury stood, her fists balling up. Great. She would not see reason or truth. "You'd never understand. You have rose-colored glasses on with your new feelings of love. It turns bitter. It hurts. It gets tainted and ruined. Then it is gone." She stormed out of the room and slammed the bedroom door, the room that one day will belong to Cobalt.

I don't know what "rose-colored glasses" are, but one of her Earthling expressions, no doubt. I caught the meaning of it though. In Fyr, we say people have a rosy view of things, so Toury was cruelly saying I am naïve and seeing love as an idyllic process rather than what it truly is. Little does she know how much pain Cobalt has put me through.

The Sapphirian Palace
Celestia

My Cad,

Full disclosure? Are you sure? I have nothing to hide. But you have a list of sins longer than my arm. I would ask the worst questions possible.

I will help your sister Holly if she wants to marry. Perhaps she doesn't want to. If she wants to remain unwed, let her live with us and dote upon our children, including a Thomas. Clever promise you made, and I happen to like the name. I don't mind talking and dreaming of the future. I'm not scared of it, just scared of rushing into it. I have a bad feeling things will be rocky with us for a while—for all of Fyr. I want to start our lives after the storm passes. Please don't ask too many questions about what I see. Every day, the flames shift, seemingly with my brother's mood. He has no idea the power he wields to control all Fyrians' futures. Everything hinges on his decisions.

Here I am getting too grave again. I will write when in a better mood.

In all honesty, if your sister would be in agreement, send her to the palace to be a companion to me. I have no friends. Like you had only Alex, I only had Toury. She is not much company these days.

The letter is short, but not much is happening at the palace. I am bored out of my mind and wish everything was back to the way it was. Even more so, I long for Cobalt's return. I cannot tell him that though. It is hard not to instantly forgive him when his letters cheer me so much. I can't let him know how much I rely on him for happiness. I cannot make promises I might not be able to keep. I don't want to push, but I am terribly afraid of his history. I can imagine some nasty lady telling me about her tryst with him or even reveal to me a baseborn child of his. My imagination is cruel to me. I have envisioned all terrible scenarios. It is best to get the truth from him now—even though I would hate it. I'm starting a list of questions I should ask him.

Cobalt Estate
Nigh Ludford

My wild princess,

Never apologize for your moods. I want to know them. I would know just seeing your face, if I could be there. I miss you and hate that I cannot be there.

In response to your letter opening, ask away. Do your worst. I deserve it, and you deserve the truth. I would hate for women to come cause embarrassment after we are engaged. You need to be ready to battle them. At least, I'm assuming your questions would be about women. If they aren't, now I just set myself up for the slaughter. I have no other sins I am aware of except my past weakness to give into my lust.

My ambition was to serve your brother as an advisor. I messed that up. With you, my dearest, I want the rest of my life to be devoted to you. If Alex will never trust me, I'll be your personal servant, tasked to always make you happy. All I can think of are those lost hours when I was in your presence and could have spent time with you or simply admire you longer.

I won't lie. Here is my first admittance for honesty's sake. When I attended that suitors' ball at your school, I asked you to dance to occupy my time—at first. While we danced, I admired how beautiful you looked. I think you realized I had acted oddly, and it was because I saw you as a woman for the first time. I berated myself for even thinking of you that way. I put those feelings elsewhere. Had I not, had I confronted you, or taken my time to show interest in you...perhaps things would be different. Or not. I thought myself undeserving then, as I still do.

I will earn my way back to you. I promise.

Last, Holly is thinking about your proposition and is flattered, but there is a baron dower in Fieldstone in need of a wife to care for his two daughters and still wants a son. He likes the Cobalt social connections. She's interested, but he's waiting for this uproar I caused to die down. I have hurt too many women in my life.

I deserve it all. I only write this maudlin news so you know I am being justly punished for all I've done.

Your repentant cad,
Stephen

May

Cobalt and I continued to write, but our letters both got shorter and a bit repetitive. I don't have the guts to ask him questions, or more likely I don't have the strength to bear the answers. I stopped writing him so often, explaining I had nothing to add but to repeat myself. Just like I stopped writing in you, Wundor. I had nothing to say. Everything was the same.

He continued to write me short messages twice a week, but I wrote to him once a week.

When May approached, finally, something happened in my dull life, and I was able to write him a real letter.

Wundor, I have to explain. Alex came to ask Toury on a "date." Don't even ask what that is. It was a special Earthling word for having dinner or alone time with someone you like—according to Toury. It was hilarious. He was all nervous, and she was confused.

I tried so hard not to laugh, but after he left, I could not withhold it. I told her to give him a chance, and she fired back, saying I should quit drinking.

Wundor, I was offended at first, but I struck a deal. Surely, not drinking to get my brother and Toury back together would be worth it.

Day one without firewhiskey: I am miserable. It's kind of like when you know you can't have something, so you want it ten times more than you ever had before. I was fine all morning. Lucy had gotten rid of the bottles in my room. Mother had already cleared them out of the princess salon prior, so I was fine until lunch.

Neither Lucy nor I thought to tell all the staff not to serve me my usual drink. Once I saw it placed in front of me, the urge took hold. I took a deep breath and asked the servant to take it away and give me a water.

Mother's eyes went wide in surprise, but I know she'll be happy with me.

Toury patted my hand as if she could sense my struggle.

I am proud of myself.

In the afternoon, I started lashing out at poor Lucy for overpampering me. Then I was cranky at Toury because she was disappointed Alex was too busy to spend time with her but hesitant about joining him to hear the grievances.

After calling me useless, I came with her. I was positive she wanted a buffer from Alex.

There was no need for a buffer. Their eyes met, smiles spread, and the heavens aligned. I am being facetious. I am jealous. I wish Cobalt were here, smiling at me and staring at me with the adoration these two give each other.

Their progress will lead to my own. I have to simply be patient.

It felt like ages until Alex noticed me and asked if I were lost. I came because I was bored, but I showed him by taking things seriously.

The first couple grievances were boring. A dispute for an unpaid bill Alex ordered a man to pay; the second complaint was about fake stones being sold and money not returned. Alex gave the man one week to repay all five counts of counterfeit or to choose time in a labor camp to earn the monies owed back. He chose the latter. Another was a cunning folk, Mister Baker, whose grievance was against a poor man who stole bread to feed his family. Alex was able to swindle a deal: the baker gave the man a job in turn for a free hour of work to pay off the bread.

Once the man left, I said, "Ingenious Alex. Not only will he have a way to provide, he can take the stale bread home to feed his family."

Alex smirked. "I do know what I'm doing, Mary. But thanks for the compliment."

When the first nobleman of the day showed up, Lord Ruby, I perked up. His brother had been a necromancer who had died when stripped of his darkness. Not that I remembered all necromancers, but since his surname matched my late cousin's first name, it had stuck.

"Your Majesty," the man bowed, fidgeting with his round-brimmed cap, his fingers adorned with a jeweled ring on each finger. He was gaudily dressed beyond trying to impress. "As you well know, my late cousin has tainted our family name beyond repair for his heinous crimes against our sphere. I would like compensation for the loss of favor."

I was not sure what was more offensive: the fact he did not address the female royalty in the room or that he was making demands of his king proxy for something a criminal brother had done. Maybe it was his appearance and the slight against Toury and me, or the mood I was in after quitting drinking—likely all three—but I reacted. "Forgive my ignorance, but you expect us to 'compensate' your estate because your cousin's crimes affect you? How does that have anything to do with our actions? I suggest you stop spoiling yourself with more jewelry than I would wear at a ball and sell them to fill your coffers."

Alex's mouth quirked, and Toury bit her lip. They were holding hands under the table. Sigh. When is my turn to have that comfort?

"That's enough, Mary," Alex halfheartedly murmured. "But my sister is right, Lord Ruby. By association, you will struggle to find your influence again. I suggest making some moves to secure favor with other nobles and us."

The spoiled brat of a lord had the nerve to ask in a nasty tone, "How do I go about doing that?"

"Your land is near Hollyhaven, no?" Alex somehow kept his stoic, calm act in place.

Lord Ruby's eyes darted around madly, confused as I was about where Alex was headed. "Yes, but Your Majesty—"

"And you've not come to aid, to take any survivors in? Even after I asked any nobles who could to do so." Ah, there it was. He was finding an excuse to berate or deny him.

"I don't have a place to, the means—"

I snorted. I could not contain my distaste. The man spent more on his appearance than any lord I had seen before, and that said something because the Citrines had been pretty bad.

Alex's shoulders went tense, and his eyes locked onto the man, an intimidating place to be. Why did I find this fun? "Your cousin's estate lies empty. His assets are now yours. You are childless and feel you need two estates? Why is that?"

The man looked to Toury for help, likely because she hadn't said a word yet. I was about to speak a possible judgment, but the way Alex looked to Toury, I knew to keep my mouth shut. He wanted her to dole out the verdict. He was giving his lifemate power, and I would not stand in the way of that. Plus she needed it. She needed to feel his equal as much as I need Cobalt to eventually feel mine.

She stood with confidence. What an excellent power move. Standing, she was more intimidating than sitting and holding my brother's hand. "What His Majesty is saying, Lord Ruby, is that you ought to have bent over backward to help those in need, considering your precarious social position." She walked around the table, closing the distance between her and the Lord.

I was loving this, and Lord Ruby was grappling to understand what was going to happen. I waited with bated breath to hear her verdict.

"You find it in your heart to use your cousin's empty estate to temporarily house some of the victims of the dragon attack, I might find it in my heart to visit your sister," Toury said.

The man's face went through shock, confusion, and stopped at jubilation.

Toury is a genius for playing into his greed for social climbing. A huge concern for any gentleman is to marry off a sister well. A sister who is visited that far south by royalty will have all suitors in the area coming to call. One visit could equate solid marriage prospects, of course, if followed by a couple invites to events at the castle. So easy for us to do and so powerful and life-changing for them.

"If I find myself at liberty, I'll join my sister-to-be," I threw on.

The way the man smiled at Toury made me realize how this might ripple throughout the court. Sure, these selfish lords might be performing charity to get attention and favor from us, but at least they will be helping others rather than letting them suffer and "die off" as Father always states.

"Thank you, Queen Proxy-to-be. Thank you, Princess Mary. You dispel all my fears and worries. I will at once set up the place to house these poor souls, until His Majesty decides where they shall remain."

Alex stared at his hands and quietly dismissed the man—not without having to hear his false flattery and groveling.

Before I could tell the soldier to send in the next victim—err—nobleman, Alex put up his hand to halt them and asked to see Toury in private.

Way to spoil my fun. I growled childishly, but it was the first time I felt stimulated in ages, useful, partaking in something that could make a difference. "I came here for Toury's sake. I'm gone. Do all the talking you want. I'm leaving."

"No, Mary, don't go." Alex stopped me from rising. "It is so much easier with people behind me. See the next person, if you will. We'll only be a moment."

He stood and took up Toury's hand, walking her to him and then sneaking into the hidey-hole for who knew what.

I was excited at the prospect of serving these spoiled brats my justice. "I quite like this!"

I'm not going to lie, Wundor, it felt amazing, powerful. Perhaps I don't hate politics after all.

The Sapphirian Palace
Celestia

Dearest cad,

I finally have some good news after these past few months. Alex came to take Toury on a "date." It's this Earth custom where a man asks a woman to dinner or an activity to get to know each other better. I think it's like a starting over thing for them. This is good for us. But I still think it'll take time. Alex still clenches his jaw when he hears "Cobalt" in reference to your brother or father. But Toury and Alex's healing relationship is a good sign.

At first, Toury was wary of getting back together. When I urged her to give him a chance, she got mad at me. She had the audacity to say that I should give no drinking a chance. I couldn't believe the nerve. But just to show her, I had Lucy get rid of the hidden firewhiskey in my room. It has been a few days since I drank. I had been worried it was becoming a real issue. But Toury helped me realize that it was from a feeling of uselessness and not loving myself. I was the spare, and no one had expectations of me. Deep down, I think that bothered me.

Can you believe I went and heard grievances? Even wilder, can you imagine how I loved putting spoiled lords in their place? I have to go but will write to you soon. Dreaming of the day I can kiss you again.

Your wild Princess reformed,
Mary

Things in the palace are becoming routine. Toury and Alex are getting along. I want Cobalt here with me but also am afraid it could ruin everything. They are working so well together too. I joined them for grievances, where they'd let me take over as they escaped together to be happy. Still, she is getting involved in reports and fully dedicates herself to learning to be his partner. It is everything I wish for them. Still, she will not move into his rooms. I know why. They don't want to face the Cobalt issue or the dragon-slayer sister sitting in the dungeon. My brother is busy, but he has to do something about Toury's sister soon, or the people will find him inept to rule.

✦

Cobalt Estate
Nigh Ludford

Dear Wild Princess,

So glad to hear the queen proxy-to-be is officially a
to-be again. I am glad you've kicked the habit, but you are
no reformed girl to me. There are many ways of being
wild, like referencing kisses in a letter and getting me all
worked up. I miss you to distraction, and that damn kiss
plays through my mind daily. I do and will remain faithful
to that memory and you, longing as well to feel your lips
on mine.

Enough of that. You make my mind a mess. I now
understand what Alex meant when he told me love did
things like this. I'm not professing love, because I want to
do that in person, but this writing was a great idea for us
to get to know each other on this level. Girls, by your
nature, are distracting, but now I see when the heart is
also involved, it is beyond that. I can hardly function
because my mind drifts to you so often. This has been
building for a while, but I thought I should finally tell you.
However, Mary, please do not rush this. I've been celibate
for you these months, and we need to start our
relationship slowly. Your brother's situation makes me
think we should do this Earth thing of dating. Being in
public will make me behave.

Your cad in heart and body,
dreaming of a wedding night
tonight,
Stephen

To be honest, Wundor, I was appalled by the end of his letter, with its
suggestive —well, candid tone. But I hate to admit my heart was racing, and
I've reread it a dozen times. Each time, I wanted to read it more, searching

for some kind of satisfaction for the fire that burned in me. I do not know the details of a wedding night, but I have been educated about the workings of where children come from. The idea of it all is enough for me to understand a shred of why Cobalt fell victim to lust.

The next morning, those feelings had me thinking. I'd loved him since I was little. I am an innocent. He is far from that.

It is time to demand the past before I want him and love him too much.

◆

The Sapphirian Palace
Celestia

My loving cad,

Your last letter I will cherish always. I long to hear the words from you as you promised. My situation is quite different. I knew from the age of six that you and I would be lifemates. This perhaps will explain away a lot of my weird childhood behavior towards you, and the distance I created when I found you with my chambermaid.

On that topic, I'm including my questions. I'm sorry that after a response of deep feelings I'm disrupting that. I know I wont like what I hear, but as you said, I need to know. Perhaps the answers will slow us down once we meet in person. I know I cannot hold the past against you, particularly because I never told you we would be together, but it will still hurt to read. All wounds heal in time, as I have seen with Toury and Alex. Please be honest and patient with me.

1. How many women have you kissed?
2. How many women have you bedded?
3. How many baseborns did you father?
4. Do you have a mistress?
5. Do you intend to keep a mistress if we marry?
6. Do you realize I will never let you bed anyone else for the rest of your life?
7. Do you realize if you do, you will lose what is between your legs?
8. Will you still marry me after those terms?

Please answer these honestly for both our sakes. After your letter, I hope we'll drop the subject until we meet in person. I so do like love letters better.

Not yours "in body," yet, you cad—
a scoundrel I couldn't help but love
my entire life.
Mary

I did it. I told him I loved him and dared to ask the questions I didn't want to hear answered. It will be a bitter sting, and I likely will need a lot of time to process what he might tell me. I had to give him that love before I might need to send a letter of hurt and anger. He needs to know how I feel deep down before this hurdle in our relationship.

His letter has arrived. He had to have responded and sent a messenger express for it to arrive within two days. He wants to get this over with as much as I do.

I cannot open it, Wundor, so I write in you to delay the inevitable.

"From Cobalt?" Toury asked, putting her book down. She was in a much better mood and said his name without any disdain. She and Alex are together again, but there is still tension, which shows me they are ignoring the issue instead of talking about Cobalt head on and getting it over with.

I nodded. What will Cobalt tell me?

"But you're not eagerly tearing it open per usual." Her confusion shifted to worry. "Oh no, did you have a fight? Look, I am not his biggest fan, but I am your friend, and I will listen and help you with anything. I hope you know that."

"I do," I squeaked out. I swallowed hard. "We swore brutal honesty, so I asked him about his past, you know, with women. He agreed to tell me everything so the women cannot catch me off-guard in public or at gatherings. Well, this letter has all the answers."

"And you don't want to know."

I shook my head. I longed for her to tell me what to do.

Toury mused for a moment, then said, "I think he is being smart. You do need to know. You are sensitive, Mary. It will hurt to read it. Likely, you'll be jealous, despite it being the past. But imagine if they came up and publicly embarrassed you. It would be mortifying and a constant reminder of what he was like."

I appreciate her honesty and how she is willing to believe he has changed.

"I will go down, make excuses for you at lunch, since your mother invited some ladies. I will send lunch to you. I will be back this afternoon if you want to talk about it. If not, no problem. I am here for whatever you need."

I thanked her, almost weeping for her understanding and kindness. I truly have a best friend in Toury, a sister. I am thankful she came into my life. I had been afraid that I'd lose my brother when he found his lifemate; then, I was worried Alex would steal my friend, but I am learning firsthand the heart has room for many and that there are many ways to love people. The more people you love does not diminish the feeling from another. It grows and blooms like flowers on a dracaberry tree.

This was a moment I would need a drink, but I had promised. It would dull my pain. I need to feel this disappointment and hurt. I need to grasp it all.

I tore open the letter and dove in.

Cobalt Estate
Nigh Ludford

Dearest Princess Mary,

I am moved by your admittance of loving me. I know I do not deserve this. I feel acutely the pain I might bring you and fear of how it will end all of my hope. I will not lie to you, as promised. Know that in light of everything I have done that I would never have done so had I known you cared for me. No—absolute truth. I would have done those things. I'm a passionate man, but I would've stopped it all after that coming out ball. The day you were presented to society, and I saw you dressed in women's garments for the first time—Wow. You were beauty itself. Something beyond me. My feelings felt wrong, not because the shift in your role in society but because Alex took offense at my ogling, and rightfully as we have seen from my behavior toward other women. Then, the suitors' ball at your school. You had my heart then, but I had to grow up. I still do. I know I can if I know I keep your heart after this. Here are my grievous crimes against the fairer sex.

I can't recall the number of women I have kissed. This is the hardest question to admit, but it had been my favorite pastime and an easy prize from a giddy lady at a ball. Know that I did this way more than worse acts, and they meant nothing. Know that my heart was only involved with two kisses in my life, and one woman I bedded. The chambermaid you caught me with was my first kiss, paramour, and love. I was young and inexperienced, and she was older than me; honestly—not trying to defend myself—but looking back, it was predatory. She manipulated me and tricked me into believing I was in love for hopes of monetary gain as a mistress. I did not realize until later that her experience, how I was the learner and she the teacher of seductive arts, was an obvious oversight about her character and previous romantic entanglements.

It was young, silly love of no substance, and my father chastised me, broke it off, which was easy because she was dismissed. Unfortunately, I feel as if what happened with her set me up to become a predator and not be hurt again. I felt love's sting acutely at the time, although looking back now, it only causes me shame. Even more so because I understand the expression you had when you caught me. I despoiled an innocent girl's eyes and had thought that was where your anger came from. I now realize you hated me for destroying the visions of our future happiness. Had I known about it and still did this, I would steer you far away from someone like me. I did not know. I also take into account that my ignorance does not lessen the pain I caused you that day.

The second kiss that meant something was you. And Mary, it was beyond any of my many experiences before. I want no lips but yours now. I will vow that to you, if you will still have me after this letter. I never knew what love was until now, and I know it will grow even more if given the chance. Love and lust are very different things. I want you to realize that because you have not experienced the full brunt of lust. It is instinctual, simple gratification. Love involves emotions, friendship, and caring more for someone than you care for yourself. I cannot fathom and one day I will take the trip with you to see how both together form an unbelievable bond.

Sorry, I'm looking forward to our future too much. I know I might be destroying it with this letter, and it terrifies me. Regardless, back to my charges. After the chambermaid, I was intimate with other women, and I'm not proud of it. You and I have our vices we'll both overcome. This was mine. Counting them is making me full of shame: eleven women all together. I have nothing to say about this except the past cannot be changed. I cannot undo my mistakes, but I can promise my present and future will only add one more woman for the rest of my life. I vow this to you.

In light of all you have said, my past feels like cheating on you, having mistresses behind your back, even though we had no agreement yet. At the same time, I shamed these women, and thanks to your questions, I'm realizing my actions have hurt them, despite their loose scruples and desire to socially climb through lustful means. I was a selfish cad for enticing them and making them believe I would be interested beyond a night together.

As for baseborns, there are ways to be careful, and I always have been. You should've also asked about disease. I am healthy due to precautions. This limited things. You know about the girl who had lied, I'm sure. Her lover claimed her, and the child has his eyes. She was after money and tarnishing my family in revenge after I decided she wasn't for me. There was another suppressed scare with a lady I had been with, just last year. The child did not have my eyes, which I know is not foolproof, but they matched a Citrine's, which was not near her own eye color.

Stupid to mention right now, but this makes me think of our children one day. I'd love to stare into my children's eyes and see your Sapphirian ones staring back. Sorry, that's unfair to tell you my terrible deeds followed by wonderful thoughts. I'm not trying to manipulate you. I just feel so much, and it all conflicts. I'm telling the truth but trying to make you not hate me. I fear I'll be unsuccessful and lose you forever.

Continuing your inquiry, I have never kept a mistress. It seemed like a hassle, and I was more about conquests, sadly, than maintaining something. I am changing for you. Never would I want a mistress if I can marry you. Never in my right mind would I dare to start keeping a mistress if married to you. I would hope that I could seduce my lifemate frequently enough that straying would never cross my mind. If I ever feel the inkling to stray, well, I'm not doing my job properly as a lifemate to you. I love a challenge, and one would be making my lifemate always in the mood for a paramour. Here I go again. Sorry, the topic makes me think of you.

To end my long letter—go figure, my crimes end up being the longest letter I've written you—I understand you'll cut off my parts if I hurt you, have the authority to it as well, and I will vow to it—in privacy, I hope—that I will stand by that. I will never stray from you, my princess. I give myself over to you to command. I have not stopped thinking about you, and us, and this dream will keep me on course. I will marry you no matter what restrictions you put upon my life. You have always been my family. Now you've added layers of love and passion. How could anyone deny all three wrapped up together with a beautiful and powerful woman? I truly think your lot are descended from gods.

Your humble criminal who
does not deserve the goddess
I'm writing to,
Stephen

I have not answered him. In a way, I expected worse, but part of me hoped for better. I cannot write back. My heart is broken. He was my first kiss and will be my first everything. He has been through so many women intimately, shared his body. It is not promising that he could do that. I cannot fathom how someone does that without their heart involved in it, but I do believe he told the truth about his crimes. I'm not sure I truly believe he loves me. His desperate attempts to reel me back in with words of love and promises interspersed between his crimes just doesn't elicit my trust either.

I'm second-guessing myself and my visions. I'm falling out of love with him. I've realized that I never gave any other man a chance because I was convinced since childhood that Cobalt was for me. Eleven women in three years? There are worse men, I am sure, but there are far more better.

I could not talk to Toury about it. She did not press me. I did not sleep that night. But Wundor, I did not drink. I think that speaks volumes for my strength through this.

I sought out my mother. After the heart-to-heart talk, I thought she might be able to help me more than Toury. I knew Toury would not have an unbiased opinion about Cobalt's past indiscretions. She might even get mad Alex didn't warn her more. I could not upset their healing relationship.

I told mother what I had asked and that I was upset by the answer to his number of women. Mother refused to give me her opinion, and barely reacted to that number of women. What she did suggest was I pull the Toury-Alex thing and entertain my suitor list by having these Earth-like "dates" at the palace. Her suggestion was so I could give these patient men a chance while angry at Cobalt and to trim my list down. It was such a rational answer that my emotional mind clung to the plan like a lifeline. She wanted me to be sure of Cobalt, to never regret my choice or miss out on a possibly better love match.

I'm not sure how Cobalt will take my seeing men. I'm not sure I should care. And then I feel guilty. How can I punish him for his past? How can I come to terms with his character though?

Mother's advice wasn't enough. I felt overwhelmingly guilty even though I rationally knew I shouldn't. I broke down and vaguely told Toury. She advised to write Cobalt and tell him the truth. What would I say? I'm angry, need space, and am dating others? He would not take it well. He might do something rash, like come to the castle if I told him I needed a break from writing to him. I am his lifeline to the castle, to Alex. It was cowardly, but I thought maybe things would take their course if I just stopped writing.

She thought that was a terrible idea. She thought Cobalt would see the dating as "dumping" him, another Earth term that is what it sounds like. Getting rid of someone as if they are garbage. What a horrible thought that is for human beings. Then Toury went on about time healing wounds and got all sentimental and sappy because she had worked things out with Alex. I am glad for them, but it was sickeningly sweet and not what I wanted to hear. I need someone on my level. Few people live in the castle. None of them could understand.

Sleeping on it did not help.

I went to Alex. Who else would understand? Oh, he'd be biased, and yet he is the most leveled-headed person in my life: a true ruler who would undo the last few ancestors' damage, including our father's, and outshine them.

"Yes?" he asked, putting the quill down as I sat.

"You busy?"

He smirked. "When aren't I? But never too busy for a gloomy sister. This won't do. You're supposed to be the free-spirited, happy one. I'm the brooder. Since my time is never my own these days, let's get to the problem straight away so I can fix it. What's wrong?"

"Something you don't want to discuss, but Mother is no help, and Toury, whom I normally confide in, is starry-eyed and too romantic to hold logical conversations."

"Is she?" He was way too eager to hear that. A large smile spread across his face. Ugh.

"This is about *me* for once."

Alex's smile fell. He straightened his posture, and then finished his letter quickly, sealed it with wax, and sent the messenger away. "There we go. You have my undivided attention now as long as you need it. I'm sorry if you feel slighted, but you seem to be enjoying responsibility recently. Would you like more?"

I huffed. "That is not why I came here."

"Mary, I love you. I'd do anything for you, but you have to get to the point. I'm just a bit lost."

I wanted to smack him, but I know his time is precious, and he always is quick to the point with most things. He has two jobs: overseeing the kingdom and undoing every terrible thing father and our grandfather did. I know from visions my brother will change the world for better, so how could I take up his time?

I blurted out the short of things. Cobalt admitting his wrongs and Mother urging me to "date."

Alex stared off, actually thinking it over as if it were an important as a stately matter. That is what is beautiful about my brother. He could have blown up. Cobalt is a touchy subject still, and he flinched at his name. When a friend wounded you deeply, it must very much be like a relationship breaking up, a "dumping" as Toury called it. Alex and Cobalt are hurting, part of them missing. I have worried about Cobalt, thought about Toury, but not enough time has been spent thinking of my brother.

Alex deserves a more caring sister. I wonder how I could repay him for this moment. He'd help me, so I must help him. No matter what, he would tell me the right thing, even though he hated and loved Cobalt as I did. He would still, no matter what, be honest with his advice. Alex would not let his bias interfere with this. I trust my brother more than any other being on Fyr.

He blew out a breath. "I'm astounded by his honesty. These things he has done I wanted to warn you about. There's no way you could enter a happy marriage without knowing. These courtly "ladies," would tear you to shreds and ruin the many happy years you deserve. However, to be honest, I don't know many men who would marry as pure beings, so—"

"Don't tell me you aren't?" I blurted out.

Alex's cheeks flared red. He could not meet my gaze. This was a weird conversation, but if he didn't explain the ways of the world to me with actual honesty, who would?

"I'm a rare exception, Mary. Most of it was fear: a woman trapping me with a child, the curse passing on to my child, and the flames not showing me a future with them."

"But you never would have to marry them. Look how many fire cunning-folk are out there. Our grandfather's generation never married their mistresses, never were trapped."

"Let me rephrase. I'd feel trapped, bound by principle to marry the woman who carried my child."

"And Cobalt?"

Alex sighed and paused, giving it thought. "I don't know of any children of his, but he would have enough principles to take care of the child. Remember, he almost bound himself to that woman who had lied about her baby. Look, Mary, he's not a bad man. He has his weaknesses, but I think if he could truly love you, he would be a good lifemate. I cannot promise he wouldn't stray or fall victim to his vices again. My experience is our nature can change but not so drastically that you should let your guard down. Only time would convince me people can wholly change, and I have not been on this sphere long enough to see it yet. What you need to think about is how much of that you can take, your limit and set it. Look at Mother. She was a puppet, not herself in front of father or in public. Oh, she loved him, but he used her for her beauty, progeny, and power. Ask yourself what you can handle, and give him ultimatums according to what you're comfortable with."

"I did. I told him no mistress, no one else, or I'd cut it off."

Alex laughed loudly. He couldn't stop laughing until he wiped a tear away and said, "Oh Mary, thank goodness you are not queen. Most men would never be the same if you made that a law. Did he agree to your terms?" It was good to see him amused once more, despite it being at my expense.

I nodded.

"There you go, then."

"What?"

"Any man willing to marry a woman who will cut off his bits is promising loyalty."

"You hate him though."

"Yes, and I was speaking to you as a king. It is a good match in social station, monetarily, and you seem to care for him. Now as a brother, I will admit you are way too good for him. Go on these dates. Be sure no one else suits you. You'll figure it out by doing that."

"Figure what out exactly?"

"You won't be able to help comparing each suitor to Cobalt. They will fail in comparison, or they will prove he is not for you." Alex said it with confidence. Was this what he had done in the months he and Toury had been apart: pine for her when no other woman in Fyr matched her? Toury was a force all of her own. I foresee her power growing. There is no replacing her, not for Alex and not for the kingdom.

Could Cobalt be the same for me?

Alex looked down at a missive. "Don't do that either." He wasn't even looking at me. I was lost. "Don't ever compare your relationship with anyone else's. You and Cobalt are different people with different roles in society."

God and goddess, my brother was good. I never realized his intelligence and empathy until now, how much he had matured.

"Thank you, Alex. You were honest and fair despite your personal feelings. You are the best person I know." I got up and hugged him.

"Don't let your heart rely on visions. Seek out how you feel first before you test the flames. Trust me, they change with every thought we have."

"How do you bear it?" I dared to whisper.

"I would lose my mind if I kept looking. When you feel sure, confident, then look. Only then. I've learned the flames do not tell us the future; they only confirm the results of our decisions and choices."

I kissed the top of his head. Then I hurried out of the room. I didn't want him to see the tears forming in my eyes. I am going to hurt Cobalt. It will hurt me as well. I have to do it in order to know what my future holds.

June

I entertained a few men. I decided to start easy with suitors I definitely wanted to cross off my list without meeting them if I could. Lucy pointed out they held a shred of hope all these months, and I should give them a chance. I sent out five invitations for the next two weeks. One came back from a baron, a Lord Crystal, who was flattered but already had entered an engagement with a Lady Diamond. I did send back a letter of congratulations and invited them to a luncheon. It felt like the right thing to do, and I could give the girl distinction. After all, I had met her father before, and he was a horribly stodgy old-fashioned man on his third wife, who tried to marry off his many daughters, this one the youngest. I didn't owe him any favors because he was horrid at dinner toward Toury and about Alex, but I could extend my charity to save his daughter.

The dates were what I expected: awkward, the men trying to show off, thinking that would woo me. I was doing exactly what Alex predicted, comparing them to Cobalt. It wasn't because he suggested it but my nature. I was weighing destiny against my opinions.

Not long after the round of gentlemen's visits where I crossed them off my list, I received a letter from Cobalt. I was afraid to read it, but braced myself for his anger. I worried that I should've warned him as Toury had said I should.

Cobalt Estate
Nigh Ludford

Dear Princess Mary,

Seeing you have not written me back in a fortnight and are entertaining men at the castle—many men—and they are the ones on your suitor list, I take it my honesty about my past was too much for you to bear. I cannot change what I have done. I think, though, as a gentlemen who has an understanding with you, I deserve a response or explanation, particularly if you wish to remove me from your suitor list.

I expected silence from you. When I sent off that letter, I expected not to hear from you for a while or at least be reprimanded and told how upset and angry you were via some form of communication. I guess you entertaining others is a sign for me to quit the field.

There's nothing I can say except I will remain faithful to you until you marry another in hopes you might change your mind. I will remain faithful to my future king and hope he will return me to the fold one day. I know Alex well enough that he needs me. I thought you did too, but perhaps I thought it in earnest. I hope if I do return one day, and you are married to another, that we can try to be amicable. I think it will be a struggle for me not to murder the man who steals your heart, who takes you away from me, but I would refrain for your sake, for Alex's sake. I made a stupid mistake to lose your brother's favor. I did worse throughout my life and thoroughly deserve to lose you.

I love you, Mary. I wanted to say that in person, but you need to know in case you're heading down a path that will irrevocably change our futures. I don't want you to regret your decisions, especially if you are unsure of my affections: they lie with you alone. I cannot fathom the idea of you married to someone else. You got my attention, Mary, and that kiss sealed the deal for me. You are all I think about. Please just write to me. Don't leave me in suspense. Even if it is to dismiss me forever, let me know.

Your humbled subject,
Lord Stephen Cobalt

The letter cut deep, but what hurt most of all was how he signed it with his formal name and addressing me with mine. No more Wild Princess and Cad. That was ruined now.

Of course, Lucy informed me the rags had written about my suitors. I was sure that was how Cobalt heard about them. They could not report that most of these men I had to entertain were droll. Cobalt could not know my feelings.

I cut down my list, but there were fifteen gentlemen left, including Cobalt. I saw five more after his letter, trying for ones more eligible this time to figure out how to answer Cobalt—I still didn't know if I could tell him. I admit I liked hearing about his anger and pain. Toury told me it was a natural feeling but not to partake in it too long. She was the one who suggested to see the most eligible, the ones I could imagine marrying if Cobalt didn't exist. I think she thought it would push me in one direction or another, and it did. I booted four of them off my list. One stayed because he was pleasant, attractive, and what I imagined a solid backup plan to be. He was malleable. I could make him into the prince and lifemate I would want him to be. That was politically using Lord Serpentine, not love. How could I love a man like him, one without a spine, even if he was attractive? Those green eyes didn't quicken my pulse like those vibrant blues did. I missed Cobalt and hated him for it. Alex was right; I was comparing every man to Cobalt. Even though he was a cad, he was my cad, and no one could compare to him.

Still. I kept Serpentine on the list because he would never try to control me or usurp my power. In my head, I call him the Ruby plan. A marriage of convenience. It would be better than Cobalt tearing my heart apart with his potential cheating, creating scandals for Alex to squelch, or worse: forcing Alex to banish him. Alex needs him, and Cobalt needs Alex's friendship. If I refuse to marry him, he should at least be able to do the job he was brought up to do. For my brother's sake alone. I started understanding how Mother could sacrifice her life for the future and those she would love after she gave birth to us. But her message of warning and desire I marry for love was looming.

I sent more missives out to suitors. I was trying to open my heart, cast Cobalt out, imagine I never saw the future in the flames. The batch lined up this week seemed pointless, but word got around I was giving everyone an interview, and news spread that I was doing this to make my choice and marry soon. The pressure was overwhelming. But their excited gossip of me seeing men told me one thing: they will not accept Cobalt right now as my prince-to-be. They want someone better. Time is needed.

July

Cobalt, however, was not handling the time the sphere needed to forget his crime against Toury, particularly because he was only banished from the court. He was not kicked out of the sphere, executed or imprisoned. Lucy said his crime stayed out of the rags, as he did as well, his behavior boringly chaste for their liking. I was happy with that, obviously, but I could not resign myself to write him yet.

He caved in yet again, wanting an answer. By this point, Wundor, he probably deserves one—or at least an explanation.

Cobalt Estate
Nigh Ludford

Princess Mary,

I am writing to beg you to put me out of my misery. I need to know if you will ever find it in your heart to forgive my past actions or if I should prepare for the worst. Please write me as soon as you get this. I'm in agony knowing I hurt you and caused you pain. I know if you were merely mad, you'd let me have it by now in a letter. Please. Even if it is a letter of hatred, I long for it. I need to hear from you.

Your humble servant,
Lord Stephen Cobalt

Before I could even write Cobalt back, Mother burst into my quarters, excitement on her face. She was grinning ear to ear. I gave her a wary look.

"Toury?" She questioned.

"With Alex, why?"

"The preparations are in full swing. It will be hard to hide the party from her, but I was thinking...what if we pretend it is an engagement party for you and Cobalt?"

She scrutinized me, and her face fell in realization Cobalt and I were no longer on good terms. "I thought crossing out suitors down to ten meant you forgave him. The thing is, there is nothing he or you can do about the past. You must focus on the present and future."

"But what if Father had told you that?"

Mother looked away. My words stung. "I didn't have pleasure of my lifemate telling me his exploits. Instead, a woman showed up at our door with a child. He was born before our marriage, but it still hurt. Your father denied the relation, but I made sure the child was taken care of. I was ridiculed and laughed at in court. It is acceptable in court, unfortunately, for gentlemen to have lovers, mistresses. Your father's curse put a stop to his infidelity. After you, there were no more children and no more straying from our marriage."

This was more than I wanted to hear, but I longed to hear more. My poor mother's suffering all these years. Cobalt would not command me as Father did Mother, not use me. He has the king's ear—or had prior—so he wasn't using me for power as a few of the last batch of dates were obviously after Alex's influence. He'd never fall for these sycophants' flattery. I wonder if Alex could tolerate Serpentine. The court is changing.

Mother hadn't even tried to persuade or evoke change, or maybe she did in her subtle way. Father was too powerful, too controlling, but Alex is malleable. Without Father's dominance—and, to be honest, disappointment I was a girl—I could be whomever I wanted to be. Except Alex hadn't forgiven Cobalt yet.

"We have to get Alex to summon Cobalt."

"I was hoping you'd be up to the task to tell your brother that."

"Great. Why do you make me do all the hard talks?"

"Because you listen to each other. You have a bond I cannot forge."

I huffed and got up. It was a command, and the look on her face said, "Do it now," even though her voice was gentle.

I found him in his office, rubbing his temples. He was already weary of being king.

"You look like you need a break."

He looked up and gave me a small smile. "Father left me a mess: rebels, some necromancers, and a lot of irate nobility. I feel like I'm holding the kingdom together with thousands of frayed strings. One breaks, and it all falls apart."

Not the moment to mention Cobalt, but it had to be done. "Delegate better. Let me take over some matters for you. I love putting those pissants in their place, so I'll do all grievances if you let me."

"Tempting, but I cannot let them hate us. No offense. You chastise a bit too well. That will be beneficial one day, but things are shaky. People want us dead."

"Cobalt warned me of that. By the way, you have to forgive Cobalt in private before you publicly do so. Summon him so the ruse isn't spoiled for Toury's birthday."

Alex groaned. "You're marrying him?"

"To be honest, I don't know. You need this more than I do. Alex, I need to see him to know...to know how I feel. I miss him."

"Me too," Alex whispered quietly.

"Bring him back, sort it out in person. If you cannot get over it, then we figure out another ruse. Mother is right in that Toury needs this surprise, to see that people care about her."

Alex nodded and took out parchment paper and his quill pen. He started writing.

I got up to leave.

"Stay. I am making it a generic summon. I don't think I have it in me to send it off or to say more. Could you put it in your letter for discretion? Maybe a few lines of what to expect."

I nodded. "What should he expect?"

"I don't know." Alex blew on the ink, making sure it dried, then dusted it with powder before he folded it and sealed it with wax pressed by his emblem. "I won't kill him or banish him from the sphere as promised. But I think he'll be more concerned by what to expect from you."

I took the letter and left. Several hour later, I enclosed it in the hardest letter I have ever written.

The Sapphirian Palace
Celestia

Lord Stephen Cobalt,

It seems you are needed. Enclosed is my brother's summons for your return. You are to be a diversion for something my mother cooked up for Toury's birthday.

I am sorry if my silence distressed you. I thought you'd assume I needed time to digest, to understand, and to move on from what you have told me. Sadly, it has not been enough time yet. You remain on my suitor list as I weed out the gentlemen I could never stand. Most are not living up to my expectations because they are not you. We promised honesty. There it is.

Don't get false hope from that truth. I know you cannot change the past. But that past makes me worry about the future. How can I be sure you'll never stray, never mess up? Women are your weakness. How can I be sure you won't hurt me as you casually hurt most of those girls simply for your own gratification?

Please don't answer this with false promises. Don't answer me at all. I forbid it. Come work things out with Alex, and then I demand your attendance in the princess salon. I think one look will be all it will take for us to know where things stand. Unfortunately, I don't know, even with my flames, how it will work out.

Sincerely,
Princess Mary Sapphirian

I cried after I sent that letter. I couldn't focus all day on a book, embroidery, what Toury was saying, the grievances—nothing. I finally just gave up and tried to lie down. Sleep did not come. The urge for firewhiskey to soothe my anxiety grew.

I would not drink.

I went to the orchard and picked dracaberries. I think Toury could eat the whole orchard in a season. We would see soon enough. It was something to keep me busy.

After I filled a basket and a half, enjoying the engrossing tedium, a maid came running out to Lucy, whispered something to her, and hurried back inside.

"What was that about?" I called down.

"Come down!" Lucy called back.

Great. Something was wrong. I climbed down.

"Betsy was to inform me when Lord Cobalt returned, so we could ready you and await him in the princess salon as you instructed me," Lucy said in a guarded tone.

"He's here already?" I shrieked.

Lucy nodded.

"How?" I didn't wait for an answer, dropping my basket and running inside, through the castle, to my quarters, Lucy racing after me. I didn't expect him until the next day. He came in such haste that he must've read the letter and summons and readied his horse and rode at full speed. His eagerness to be back here, his rightful place and home—maybe—was telling. He missed us as much as we missed him.

I changed out of boots into slippers, while Lucy powdered my face.

"Let's hurry," I pressed as she was starting to pin loose hair.

Lucy pressed her lips together, trying not to laugh as she met my gaze in the mirror.

"What?" I demanded.

"In your haste, you forgot you can transport. You could save us another run if you'd like, Your Highness."

Ugh, I was so distracted by the news that I had forgotten my very magic and nature. I was as addlebrained as Toury and Alex. Just great. I gave Lucy my best death stare, grabbed her hand, and transported us to the princess salon. Then I paced.

"Don't leave me alone with him. Even if I command it."

"Even if you push me into the hallway again?"

How dare she? "Until I'm engaged properly, you are not to leave my side. Get that smug knowing look off your face, Lucy. This is not funny to me and should not be for you." It probably was cruel, but in my anxious state, I could not take any mocking. I needed to see him.

Lucy's face went blank, and she stared at the ground.

It felt like ages, but I heard someone coming. My heart thudded in my chest. I became dizzy, and all the chidings and the welcomes I debated over in my head left me. I had no words to say to Cobalt.

He crossed the threshold, and vibrant blue eyes met mine. I couldn't catch my breath. I felt so many things, but what overrode everything was love. I love him. I wanted him to never leave my side, to hold me, to soothe me, to hear his lips say he loves me.

Walking was too much, so I transported a few feet just to touch him.

"Mary." His voice cracked, and his eyes teared up. He thought he had lost me. He almost had.

I couldn't even speak to tell him words of assurance. All I had left was action. I yanked his neck roughly and crashed my lips into his.

He cried out and pushed me away an arm's length, his warm hand resting on my shoulder. His other hand dabbed his lip that I now realized was split and bleeding. Then he chuckled, moving his hand up my shoulder to my neck; then his thumb touched my cheek. My traitorous skin prickled into goose pimples under his touch.

"My contrary Mary. I expected another beating."

Another? His lip was split, his clothes a bit disheveled and hastily put back together, and his eye was red and starting to swell.

"I've missed you so much more than any words could express." Cobalt smiled, his lip preventing half his mouth from rising, giving him a lopsided grin.

"Another beating? Did my brute of a brother do this?" I was ready to go punch Alex for this. How would my level-headed brother turn into a temperamental jerk and beat up his best friend?

"Don't." Cobalt squared my shoulders. "I instigated it. Got him to do it."

"Why? Look at you. You're hurt."

"Alex needed it, Mary. We needed to get his rage out, or it would fester. He feels he got his retribution, and now I am allowed to remain. Didn't broach the topic of you and I—well, because I didn't know how things were between us. I didn't want to push my luck either."

"Let me heal you." I put my fingers to his lips, but he yanked them off, squeezing my hand gently.

"No. No offense, I hate fire healing because it hurts a bit at first, but really I don't want a healing. I'm going to wear this as a badge of atonement. I'm going out to the pubs all this week to regal the tale of my beating."

"Why?"

"It'll make Alex look good."

"But make you the villain."

"That's the point."

"But they'll never support you marrying me one day. They already hate you!"

He sighed. "Can we sit down and talk? There are things I need you to understand, and you're a bit worked up already."

This sounded ominous. Was he no longer going to court me? I motioned him to join me, and then I sat across from him. He dabbed his lip again.

"You well know that I am the villain in all this. I must make amends. You don't understand men that well, Mary—that's not an insult by the way, so stop giving me that look."

I stopped glaring but kept my arms crossed to show him my displeasure.

He sighed but continued on. "Nor are you used to cunning folk. There are more magicians in our world than sorcerers. Sorcerers turn a blind eye to indiscretions, although they would try to use it against Alex any way they can. Cunning folk judge a king off his strength in all things. This might seem like a brutish thing to you, but these marks show his primal power. It tells people he can protect his queen and will do so; he will fight for what he wants and what is right. To forgive me without a fight, they would see him as weak and spineless."

It was logical, and I could see the perks for Alex, but he still hadn't answered my question. "What about the sorcerers, then? Your reputation?"

"The latter will heal over time when I prove myself faithful to you. The former, the sorcerers, Alex will need to take in hand, but you and the queen proxy-to-be could help with the ladies. Men listen to their women behind closed doors. It'll take time, but us, we are salvageable. That is...if you want it to be."

I nodded, not knowing what else to say. He had thought this all through. No one else would do. I only wanted him.

"So that leaves one more thing to discuss. What do we do about us, privately?"

"I hardly know. I didn't intend on forgiving you or kissing you, but when I saw you I just..." I shrugged.

He got up and walked around the table. He kneeled before me, taking my hands in his. He kissed them and stared up at me with those adorably pleading eyes. "Mary, please. Give me a chance." He should not use my name so, and I would remind him later, but now, without public witnesses, we were not bound. But we had to be careful, if anyone heard or saw us kiss, we would be engaged.

"I will." I said, knowing now exactly what to say next. "I have nine more suitors before you to see to determine if they stay on my list."

He frowned and then it crept into a smile. "I like a challenge."

I knew he would.

August

As you have guessed, none of the suitors were for me. I compared them all to Cobalt. I kept two on my list in the end, aside from Cobalt. It was Toury's idea that I have a backup plan, and the bonus was, it drove Cobalt insane with jealousy. He said he loved challenges, but I don't think he thought it through that he was actually still competing with others.

What didn't sit right to me was how unfair it would be to lead these men on. I spoke the truth to Lord Antony Serpentine and Lord Phillip Quartz. The former was happy because he didn't feel ready, but his parents pushed him to sign and found me the best girl in the land but didn't feel he deserved me. The latter was a bit miffed and told me Cobalt was trouble and Lord Phillip would, being young, wait for me to marry before he pursued a lady he felt would be second best. Both were eager to stay on the list and be allowed to see me and take me on outings. Admittedly, it was a good idea. They would gain societal and political benefits of being one of the princess's suitors, not be pressured to court other ladies, and both seemed to enjoy seeing Cobalt squirm.

Cobalt was livid when he heard about the list. I still did not trust him. He was so busy helping Alex and then spending every free moment with me that there was no time for him to stray, but I was still worried. At the surprise ball for Toury, he only danced with me, and we were limited to one dance by royal custom, then his sisters, whom I invited, and then the cad made his mother and then *my* mother dance. It had been ages since Mother danced because Father was only so fond of it and now could not even stand to be able to do so. She was so happy.

What I don't trust—despite all this time getting to know each other—somehow without kissing—is his constant heart. I have this horrible feeling that he doesn't love me or that he wants this palace lifestyle more than his feelings for me. He was such a playactor with women that I wonder if he is doing that with me. I feel like our relationship has fallen back into a friendship. It isn't going anywhere. I know it is because of my age, because we agreed not to rush things, because if caught, we'd be engaged and forced to marry within two years. Sadly, I am more insecure than I had thought. I think it all started at Toury's party. One lady approached me and said I should keep Cobalt on a leash. Another dared to suggest I remember that whatever I would enjoy in my marriage bed was taught to him by others. I know they are horrid girls, and if Toury had been by my side, I would have had the fortitude to come up with some quip rather than pretend I didn't hear the barb. All I could do was roll my eyes at them and pretend their comments didn't bother me.

It was Toury's day, not mine. And she was ever so happy.

Toury and Alex set the date. They will marry soon. Mother is in her element, pleasantly distracted from Father's poor health. Father smiled about the news, the first time he has made any expression in weeks. I think he feels at peace mentally now, knowing Alex is marrying and will beget an heir soon. Still, I have this looming feeling of fear and dread that something bad will happen to start the landslide of terrible visions I have had. I feel like we are atop a mountaintop, ready to fall a long way down.

So much has happened that I don't know where to start. I am numb and not sure how to form the words to record what I must. Father is dead. Rebels attacked, stopping the wedding. Toury was taken by her father and the rest of the rebels. Alex almost died. He is not awake yet. I write this for I cannot sleep. I think I will get up and talk to Cobalt. I need to start listening to my intuition more. It tells me many bad things are coming our way.

Add engaged to that list of many things.

I was Lady of the Castle but went to bed when Mother forced me away with the news of Father. I tried to sleep then, but I was unable. Not wanting to wake Lucy, I transported.

I knocked on Alex's study, the place I had left Cobalt after we sorted out security of the castle and a plan to track and find Toury. Then I slipped in, closing the door behind me.

"Mary?" Cobalt asked groggily. The fire was low, and the lighting in the room only consisted of a few lamps since no one really used the room late at night. The full glass-windowed wall gave enough sunlight for the study's purposes. I stared at the dark windows, finding it odd I had never been in here at night.

Cobalt was pouring over correspondence and maps still.

"You'll go blind in this light," I chastised while I lit the fire in the grate.

He was completely alone. *We* were alone. "What are you doing here, alone...wearing that?"

I was in my nightgown and a robe, hardly risqué, but the way Cobalt ogled me suggested otherwise. Finally, he was seeing me as a woman again.

"Is Alex...all right?" He could not utter "dead," but the fear was in his eyes.

"He's alive, fighting the remnants of poison, but not awake. I had trouble sleeping, so I came to help."

"By yourself?"

What a silly question to ask when it was obvious.

"Mary. Your Father just passed away, your brother clings to life, and you are traipsing through the castle without your bodyguard? It's dangerous."

"Well, I transported."

"It's not safe. Anyone could be an enemy, even staff."

I could not argue. I should've taken the guards stationed outside my door and walked there. "When you put it that way..." I didn't want to admit he was right.

"Mary," he sighed. He was tired, frustrated. He came over to me and pulled me into a hug, tucking my head under his chin where I just fit under. "Nothing can happen to you. You are the 'spare' as you often condescendingly say, but that makes you the most important person in all of Fyr at the moment. You're a—"

"Target. I get it. I'm sorry. The Sapphirian rule just crumbled in a mere night." I was annoyed but tried to hide it. I had thought he was about to profess he could not live without me, but no. He was all business.

"It is still there. You are the ruler for the moment. Alex will rally. Toury will be found. But, yes. No risks, my Mary. Some only remember the young party princess." He pulled away, still holding my arms in his strong hands. "We need Alex awake. We need your cousin to return. We need a united front of strong families supporting us."

"Us?"

"Oh." Cobalt let go. "I wasn't trying to presume."

"No, I liked hearing you naturally talk about you and me as an 'us.'"

He gave me a sad smile and leaned his forehead down upon mine. "I love you Mary, and you'll trust me one day, and 'us' will truly be one unit."

"How about two years from today?" It just came out of my mouth. I couldn't take the suggestion back, nor did I want to as I processed it. I was trying to force him to admit more, to say more, to feel more important than his job. If we were engaged, I'd get that.

Cobalt pulled away, his eyes locking on mine trying to puzzle out my thinking. "A wedding in two years?" Then it clicked. He started to ramble. "So, are we...are you asking me to propose to you, or are you proposing to

158

me right now? Because you know I have to ask you first if I'm allowed to, but you can propose, instead, although not always custom for the girl to—"

I stopped his nervous chatter with my hand. "I suggest we enter an engagement, right now, yes. I think it would strengthen *our* rule. If the rebels think I'm on the path to marriage, and in time, heirs, then it's a backup if the worst should happen to Toury or Alex. It'll strengthen my reign in this annoyingly male-run world to have a man with me at the helm. Annoying that I need you for that, but it is the way this world is at the moment. When Alex and Toury both are ruling again, four is stronger than three."

"This feels like a business agreement. Mary, I know things with us are different and the circumstances not ideal, but you deserve to get engaged when you are ready. It should be something, I don't know...romantic."

"It's engagement, not marriage. It gives us two years to figure 'us' out, and plus I get your added security by my side...in my quarters."

Cobalt swallowed hard at that and broke away from me.

"I'm almost sixteen. This would put our marriage at me being almost eighteen. I think you and I need to take things to the next level. We have drifted into a friendship, a business deal as you said, which is fine, but we need to get to know each other more intimately."

He was wide-eyed.

"Wipe that shocked look off your face. I don't mean sexually, you cad. I mean romance, feelings, everything but the final part that edicts claim is only suitable in marriage." I took a shaky breath, everything that happened catching up with me. "I want to go to my quarters right now and sleep on my settee with you holding me in your arms. I need you right now. Not as an advisor, not as a friend, but a lover consoling me."

Cobalt came over to me and took my hands in his, his face serious and earnest. "I would like that more than anything in this sphere. But we will do it right, starting now. Princess Mary, would you condescend to enter an engagement with a lowly scoundrel like me?"

I nodded, not trusting words, and I cried for so many reasons but one of them, mixed in with grief and fear, was happiness. I was not alone anymore.

Cobalt kissed me gently on the lips and then whispered, "Take us to your room, my engagee."

I transported us at once. Exhausted, we lay on the settee as I described. With my head on his chest and his arms around me, I fell asleep instantly in the warm and loving embrace.

The next morning, I awoke to Cobalt snooping around, mainly around my bookshelf. He blushed at being caught and had to admit he had never been in my room before and was curious to explore it. It would be his home too, so I could not censure him. Until I had to throw a settee pillow at him when he mentioned I had too many romance novels, and he wanted space for his military books. I told him to build his own man-room upstairs. I didn't like the idea of him hiding himself away in a room, though, and took it back. I did not think this engagement stuff would entail compromising from day one, but it gave me an idea.

"Well, I need romance in my life, so every gesture I deem romantic, I will lose the need for one book, and you can use its place."

"Deal." He grinned. He loved challenges, games. I could have fun with this.

"To a point," I said sternly.

"Yes, my Mary." He gave me a smirk.

He can publicly call me by my name now. I like the idea of that. No more hiding kisses and worrying about titles. So much freedom.

Moments later, Lucy came in, shocked and holding a dagger after a male's voice had been heard. In hindsight, the first thing we did that morning should've been informing her, not bartering over book space.

Alex is awake! Oh, Wundor, another miracle. I have to go but will write when I can. My brother is alive!

No time to write. My brother is the hero of the day. They are calling him Draca. Chanting it. He gave the speech of a lifetime without prepping while he was barely able to stand. I always believed in him, but today he made the world believe. I have faith in him, Toury, and a golden age for us to come. Hail the Draca!

I go to bed now, on the settee again, in the arms of the man I love, to dream of better days.

LISA BORNE GRAVES

COURTLY CUCKOLDS & CADS

THE DRACA RISES FROM THE FLAMES

It has been a dramatic time in our history, but King Alexander has added his flair to a somber event. We lost our king, but we have gained a new one who has proven himself already at the age of eighteen. If today's pyre service is any indicator of what our recently wounded and poisoned king is capable of, we shall have our queen back and the rebels obliterated.

For those who could not attend, King Alexander lit his father's pyre as is custom, only he did it whilst inside the flames. The former king's magic gone, he burned quickly, while his son stood over him, giving the crowd a menacing stare—or dare we say challenge. It was a formidable sight and yet...inspiring. Then he went and comforted his sister and mother, hugs, kisses, and what looked like words of comfort. This show of affection is not one our former king would have condoned.

This goes to show that King Alexander Sapphirian's kingdom will be nothing like his last couple predecessors, something the rebels might not want to overlook. It seems their cause is slipping, and the only thing protecting them is they have our queen, for that is who she would be by now had their wedding not been put to a halt.

May the god and goddess guide our king and return his lifemate alive and well.

The euphoric high my brother rallying the sphere gave me was blighted out today—hopefully temporary. Today was my father's pyre. What made it worse was Cobalt, being the best tracker, went after Toury. I know he'll be successful, but I need him. Today was heavy. It is an awful feeling, mourning someone who never deserved your love, but duty forces you to care. I would not shed another tear for Father but would take all that undeserved love I had been bound to give him and give it all to my mother.

161

I cried at the funeral for her, for Alex and the burden he will have to bear for the rest of his life, and for Toury, who was still missing.

Perhaps if Alex loved her less, those who sought to destroy him would not tear at his weakest link, but it is not in his nature to half love and hide the best parts of himself. It is not in his nature to underestimate Toury either. This is a battle they must fight separately, conquer their own enemies, which might be the same but enemies for very different reasons. I have faith that Toury's parents are more loving than my father was. They will not hurt her. If they were like Father, she would be doomed. Father would've traded my life up to keep his medallion. Never would have hesitated.

I don't have Cobalt to soothe me, and Alex is still weak and fretting about Toury. Mother is numb. I feel alone. I know it will all work out one day, or at least I hoped the flames don't let me down.

I also have to wear this blasted "Prince" medallion in public. I know I have to because it strengthens the Sapphirian rule, but it presses the weight upon my shoulders that Alex always had to bear. It is eye-opening to say the least. He better get Toury back, marry her, and throw this medallion on a baby cot soon. It is not for me.

COURTLY CUCKOLDS & CADS

NEWS ON HOLD

We have decided to halt all gossip from our newspapers until the queen is returned. Instead, each day, we will publish leads people give us to finding her, news about rebels, and full stories on those who assist in the capture of rebels. Spread the word: the Draca is coming for them.

I'm exhausted and only recording info for the sake of it being needed one day as evidence. Today, Alex received a ransom letter for Toury that she specially coded. He had hard decisions to make. I tried to see truth in the flames, but Alex's mind kept wildly shifting, changing the future. He was not stable, which frightened me. I watched my poor brother at his desk. He was beyond exhausted but could not sleep. He needs Toury to function. Is this what love is? God and goddess, I hope not.

Through all of this, Wundor, I would like to pride myself on only having a social drink here and there in toasts. Alex said moderation is key, and he hardly drinks a thing. My brother accepting my problem and being pleased that I am making strides and allowing me in the worst times to give myself an allowance—everything I needed. I found the stuff not as gratifying anymore. Even the slight numb feeling one drink gave me was useless when it ebbed away. I had no clue because I had drunk so much before. I felt abstaining was a way I had proven myself...to myself. I can't wait to tell Cobalt that I could have one on a special occasion without falling victim to my former vice.

Under the counsel of Mother and the Cobalts, after Tobias Firebrander's advice, I made a decision. I answered the ransom letter in Alex's stead. It would not look great for Alex, and yet they might see it as him being elsewhere doing other things against them. I had to take this task on for him because he would give up everything for Toury. I could see it in his eyes, in the instability of the flames to show me what would occur. Alex might possibly give up everything—including his life—for Toury. What would it take for Cobalt to love me to that level?

We rejoined Alex in his study, where I told him it was done.

He barely reacted from how exhausted he was. He simply was worried I had made myself a target, but I have always been one. When usurping a throne, you don't keep the spare around. Henry would be in danger too—wherever he is.

Then I got to the point of why I returned. Cobalt's coded letter in his and Alex's secret language from childhood to avoid the tutor's interpretation. Once translated by Alex, it didn't sound good. I was to go bring Toury back. But what of my Cobalt? I wouldn't be able to leave him behind with his men to die, and the honorable cad, at least when he chose to be, would stay with his men. If I didn't think of something, I would lose Cobalt. I told Alex to stay put, although part of me wanted him to be rash and save Cobalt. I knew he shouldn't, but he would have a hard time letting him die too.

Lucy suited me in armor, but I was impatient to get there. I envisioned the place and used my magic to transport to the top of the rocky plateau of

Dragon's Rock, where I knew I'd be safer, then peered down. Cobalt and his men were cornered below.

Lucy tried to speak, but I cut her off by transporting us right behind Cobalt's army. He was in the front, the foolishly brave cad. He was holding his own, despite it looking like two-to-one with no way out, no path to retreat. I threw out an arc of fire and saw a flame to my left. I lost track of Cobalt, but he had extracted himself and raced back to me. He threw up his visor to gaze upon me, grabbed my neck to pull me close, and kissed me hard on the mouth. It was awkward, with all the armor between us, but he was saying goodbye.

Not if I could help it.

"There." Cobalt pointed to the person throwing fire. Next to the fire lasher, for it went around in a whiplike fashion, was Toury. She was alive and fighting off the enemy. "Take her and, Mary, do not come back."

"You know I don't take orders from a cad like you." I gave him a smile and transported to Toury, only hesitating a second to get ahold of her arm, before using my dragon's trapdoor magic to go back to Alex's quarters. In that moment, I glimpsed the stranger who could wield fire. He looked like my father, like Alex. I knew right then, I had to go back, for Cobalt and, apparently, a relative I never knew existed.

I let go of Toury once I saw Alex was there, and I transported back to Dragon Rock. Lucy yelped as she grabbed on, not realizing I'd go back. I appeared right where I left Cobalt and threw flames through the enemy, splitting them in half, lessening who was attacking Cobalt. In hindsight, it was a terrible move because it drew half of them toward me. They would do anything to kill me. I'd be a bonus. My baseborn brother—I assumed—was whipping around fire to the back of the army. Anyone who came near me, I lit aflame. The first few soldiers, I felt a bit bad about. I had never killed anyone. It is not in my nature. When I hesitated, though, a rebel got so close to me that Lucy had to parry his sword away. Wundor, I'm not proud of what I did, but it was to save my life, Cobalt's, my soldiers, my people, my brother, and Toury.

I lit the entire scene up, being careful to avoid my men.

Then I noticed more fire, extremely powerful flames, with white balls of light firing near the flames. My brother and Toury had come too. This felt like a final stand, and Wundor, I thought we would die. I thought it was the end and the flames had lied to me. I felt the happy peaceful life with Cobalt and our brood of children slipping away. It made me desperately fight harder.

Alex managed to extract us all in turns, getting us and his men away from the rebel army. Surviving, I wanted to cling onto my man, but Cobalt had to ruin the moment by thanking Alex and not me. When it came to Cobalt, would I always be second-best to my brother? I could never deal with that. Cobalt is going to get a talking to. I need to be his primary concern if he wants to continue working as Alex's Ealder Advisor. He will be a lifemate and father before his role in Alex's kingdom.

I know I sometimes ramble about believing in miracles, but how my brother transported us out of there was very much that. He transported an entire army. He single-handedly saved us all, with a little light power charge from Toury, that is. I am in awe of my brother—this seemingly undefeatable Draca. There is only one explanation: the curse had always held him back.

We were alive, safe at the palace thanks to him. Still, I called my brother a show-off to lighten the mood and check his pride. There will be time to thank him later. He was hardly able to stand after his exertions. He left Cobalt and me in charge of the army, and he and Toury walked inside. The fact he did not attempt a simple transport, so close to his quarters, just showed how drained Alex truly was.

My brother Alex is okay, and Toury was able to revive her aunt. I met our brother Craig, and he seems nice, like a softer, kinder version of my father, or just like Alex, but not raised with all this pressure on him. His eyes do not match ours, and his hair is lighter than mine, an ash-blond. He appeared scared of me, or maybe just intimidated. I wanted to assure him all would be well, that we could accept him, but without the eyes, Mother's definite distaste of him, and Alex being too tired to talk to him yet, he is in a precarious position. I understand Mother's resentment. Even though Craig is older than Alex and born before her marriage to my father, it is exactly the way I felt when I feared Cobalt had baseborns. I hope this is the child mother knew about and there aren't others.

In other news, the last amazing thing was Henry returned safely with much news.

All seemed well, but it was not. This wasn't a happily-ever-after tale for us. I had to order a task force to capture the retreating rebels, and they successfully captured Toury's parents. I have to boast that I bravely retrieved them using my dragon's trapdoor to transport to them and back into our dungeons. Cobalt had not wanted me to, but we could not risk escape, and Alex was wiped out of energy at the time.

This would be difficult for Alex and Toury to deal with. Execute them, as they deserve, and Toury would hate him. Let them live, and he'd weaken his rule to the point the rebels, necromancers, and even the sorcerers would usurp him one way or another. I do not envy my brother's choices.

Thankfully, Mother realized a way to get him out. If he were related to her parents through marriage, he could pass the ruling onto the guilds to decide, claim a bias.

The rest of that day, Cobalt and I worked together on orchestrating the capture of the rebels. It was strange that we were able to focus, to work, without getting distracted and without bickering. I felt like thinking we would never see each other again, for even a moment, had solidified us more. There was friendship, and there was love, but now a comfortability between us brought on by duty. I could imagine us carrying out duties to the kingdom together, rather than Alex stealing his time from me.

I must've been staring, because Cobalt stopped writing and looked at me. "What is it?"

"Huh?"

Cobalt smirked and winked at me as if he knew how distracted I had become. I know, Wundor, right after I was thinking how well we got on.

Cobalt finished writing the order and handed it to a messenger. Then he dismissed the few people remaining until it was just me, Lucy, and himself. He turned in his chair to face me and took my hand in his. "I told you not to come back for me."

"And I don't have to listen to your orders."

His face scrunched up at that.

"I'm not one of your men but *the* princess. I wasn't about to live without you."

Cobalt's lips crashed into mine as if he lost all self-control, his hands wove into my hair, messing up Lucy's hard work. I squeaked when he pulled me onto his lap.

He stopped kissing me and just stared into my eyes. "I know that. But I can beg of you not to endanger yourself for me ever again?"

"On one condition."

He groaned, leaning his forehead against mine. "What?" he hedged, his voice dripping with dread.

"You must have a bodyguard as a prince-to-be."

"I'm a soldier, and—"

"Not even the best soldier can watch his own back. My brother has one. If you don't find someone to watch your back, then it will be me. I'm no warrior, but I have fire."

"Yes, you do." The way he said it was somehow laced with suggestion.

I gave him a look that said it was an ultimatum, and he sighed. "Fine. As long as you stay out of trouble."

"Trouble? Never. Battles, fine by me," I told him.

Alex won't let me near a warzone ever again. I am still the spare until his first child is born. Later, Cobalt and I will have children. I flushed at the thought. I was on his lap. Suddenly, it all clicked on how we must not take things too far.

I stood. My adorable cad frowned.

"Sorry, I...it's nothing. My thoughts strayed to the future with kids and all that."

He laughed lightly. "We have two years, my princess, before that is even a thought. This is why we should take this slow like we are."

"Because I'm so young." I threw in an eyeroll, so he would see my annoyance at being treated that way.

"Not just that. Let us be aunt and uncle first and have children when we want them. I told you there are ways to...be cautious." Then his mouth dropped. "I, uh...meant after the wedding. Being careful then, not now."

I raised my brows at him.

"You make me a babbling fool, and I feel like a sad little pup scrambling at your feet." He stood and placed his hands on my hips, staring into my eyes with those beautiful ones of his, so vibrant in color.

"Why is that?"

"Because I'm in love, Mary. I've never felt this way before. It is all new and fresh to me. When you came back for me, I was mad and worried for your safety, but I knew then you loved me as much as I loved you. I would've done the same."

He kissed me soundly and only stopped when a knock at the door interrupted our bliss.

◊

I wish I could've stayed in that moment with my cad forever. I should rename him like I did you, or maybe call him Stephen, but he smiles at the teasing moniker, and I adore that smile.

Ugh. I definitely am a sad sort of girl in love when I get lost in nicknames instead of telling the awfulness of what I just learned. Toury's parents were murdered by my uncle, of all people. He fled. I felt so bad for Toury, but I didn't get to see her until the next morning because Lucy insisted that I read the newspaper. I only read the headline:

THE KING ELOPES AND MAKES LADY TOURMALINE QUEEN

Then Alex left. Apparently, my draca of a brother is a cad as well. If Cobalt left me after our wedding day, there would be no marriage. He'd be dead. Ugh, he wouldn't. I love him too much, but he'll pay for a long, long time.

True, my cad left me too, but was ordered as one of the best trackers. He had to help Alex find my uncle. At least he did not slink away in the middle of the night. He woke me, gave me a long, promising kiss, and said duty called. He also said there was a note on the table. I was too tired to care then and drifted back off. When I awoke, the letter informed me of the hasty wedding and how Alex and Cobalt left to track her uncle. The best part of the note, I reread again and again:

> Since I must leave you, my wild princess, I wanted to give you a gift. I only had a few moments to contemplate as Alex is ready to leave instantly. I thought of ordering Percival—I hate having a bodyguard by the way—to delegate and get you something nice, but it felt wrong. I know you hate thinking of my past, but giving expensive gifts was my forte. I cannot buy a princess anything she cannot buy herself. Plus, I've known my wild girl her entire life, so I know that gifts would never make you happy without thought and deep meaning. What I give you now is something that belongs to me, means everything to

me, and I gift it to you. I'm going to wonder and worry you do not like it while I'm gone. I hope I sized up my wonderful princess right. I do not want to give you false poetry and fine words but always be direct. It is what we have always been, candid. I'll never forget when you made me first see you as a woman—one out of my reach, I had thought. In the box is a token of my love. I long to secure our happiness, even though we said we'd wait. I'm of two minds, but ready to be led by you in anything.

Your faithful worshiper who
is trying to get back to you,
Stephen, your cad

In the box was Cobalt's signet ring. My heart thumped wildly. A lord never gives a ring to lady, even an engagee. It is like giving away proof of identity, his name. He would give up his name in marriage and become a Sapphirian, but here he is pledging his life to me now.

I could not think of a better gift or deeper form of affection.

I cannot wait for Cobalt's return.

Mary Elizabeth Sapphirian,
Her Royal Highness, Princess of Fyr
(the one and only),
aged 16 years

September

Wundor,

The flames show so many conflicting and chaotic things, it makes my head spin. I'm frightened. I have seen war. I've seen strife and pain, but I also see bliss and happiness. The worst is that firebranding doom is only half of my problems. Cobalt, as always, is my greatest problem. Wundor, before you chastise, it is not his fault completely, and it is not me fixating on his past anymore either.

Cobalt had moved in after our engagement, and then, it was new and awkward. I thought some time would make it normal, but living with a man was far different than living with a woman like when Toury had lived with me. Cobalt and I had been somewhat settled, and then Alex stole him for a few days, and then Toury put her foot down and they stayed to sort things out. No one told me that, but from Toury's upset mood shifting to one of silent gloating, I knew she did something to force them to stay. She is a queen indeed. I need to ask her how she got Alex to heel.

As always, there I go off topic. So, the short separation with Cobalt and I was like starting over. He was weird around me. For example, I would enter the sitting room to have my tea after a morning bath, just as I always have. I like to enjoy my tea, in my robe before I dress, but now Cobalt was there, eyes wide, stuttering excuses about the shower being open. He'd flee and then come back after we both were dressed for the day. We would talk, joke, but things seemed frictionally formal. We'd have breakfast with the family, then he'd be off to assist Alex, and I would go to do grievances or tea with the ladies of the house. It went on awkwardly for a fortnight, and I started to fret about the future with us. How will we marry and have children if we barely interact daily? If he can't be in the room with me half-clad? Is he not attracted to me? Regretting the engagement?

When supper with the family was over, we would always part ways. Alex had seemed to want to continue family nightcaps after Father died, and I thought he stopped for my sake. It was becoming clearer that he wanted Toury time instead. I wanted Cobalt time, so I understood. It was strange. Cobalt was such a part of the family, but there was little romance between us—his letters had been, but now...

It started to irritate me when I'd see Toury and Alex all sweet, staring in each other's eyes as if no one else in Fyr existed. And it angered me to see their stolen kisses because Cobalt never instigated any kisses. It was always me followed by him redirecting himself to some task that "needed" doing—a rebuff. I gave up.

Here we were again, awkwardly together before bedtime while he'd read over reports or polish his weapons before Percival—his newly appointed bodyguard-valet—would take them away in hopes he'd act more princely. The servant entertainingly got in a huff when Cobalt did anything for himself as if personally insulted.

I, on the other hand, wanted Cobalt to act completely unprincely in a very different way.

"Percival, take Cobalt's sword and have it cleaned. Lucy, you are dismissed until my bath."

Percival was confused. Lucy gave me a knowing look, smirking as she slunk away. Likely, she was preparing my bed because there was only so far I could—or was allowed—to take this. She knew, but from the look on Cobalt's face, he didn't know what I was up to.

He frowned adorably. "Why'd you get rid of him? I have things to go over."

"So do I," I countered, standing up.

I sat next to him, close. He straightened, and his eyes examined me in wonderment. "You have things to go over...with me?"

He was adorable in his stunned state.

"Yes. After such a promising letter and giving me your signet, one of the greatest things a lord owns, you returned to be cool and standoffish. You don't show me you love me, and I don't think I can handle that."

"What?" His back stiffened, and his fists clenched, deeply offended at my accusation. But then he sighed.

I was terrified it was coming. He'd tell me it was all a mistake. I knew it wasn't, but perhaps my telling him pushed him too far too early. Maybe he still had a lot of growing up to do. Lucy always told me I was young, to be patient, and the engagement would get me my man. I have never had much patience though.

"I'm sorry I'm no poet. I could give you a million sappy-sweet words, but that was what I gave those girls in my past, girls I never truly loved. Am I to do that to you? Playact? I think not. I thought you wanted open honesty."

"I do but Alex and Toury—"

"We aren't them, Mary. Don't compare us."

"Why? Won't we ever have that? He loves her to the point of distraction, and she him. When they're together, no one else exists."

"We will have all that and more." He gripped my hand in his and kissed it before he met my gaze. "Something better and more suited for us because we are different people than them."

"You said you wanted to marry me in your letter. You said many naughty things."

"I do, god and goddess, Mary, I do. But while we were apart, the more I thought of it, the more I believed we should wait. I must prove my constancy."

"You have, haven't you?"

Now, I was worried he had strayed while away. To say it aloud would accuse him and break his heart if he was innocent. If he was guilty, he would break mine.

"Of course!" He growled and rubbed his face. "But see? If you question it, even for a second, the entire kingdom does. I know what you were asking. There were no other women. None since the day you told me you wanted me to sign your suitor list."

He stood with unspent energy. "Mary, I will not have you marry me and anyone think you a fool. I need to prove myself with time and loyalty, our full engagement."

"And I am young, so automatically, I must be foolish."

"No, stop. I don't think that. The older folks might. They always do, don't they? Mary, we have time."

"I know, it's just..." I sighed, not sure how to phrase myself for him to understand me well. Women are not supposed to be brash and upfront. "You don't want me the way you wanted those other women."

I said it, Wundor. I had to. I cannot live in a marriage that is completely contrived of social roles and duties like my parents. I want that strange, almost obsessive love Toury and my brother share. I want Cobalt to look at me like every part of him would die if I didn't return his gaze. I don't want him to grovel, but I want him as weak for me as I am for him. I razed things to the ground with my fire to save him, and he doesn't deserve it—yet. I fear he would not do the same for me.

"I don't want you?" His face screwed up in a bitter expression as if tasting something unpleasant. Sensing moods, perhaps my attitude literally stunk to him.

"Cobalt, don't be dense. You know what I'm talking about." In case he didn't, I leaned toward him like one of the flirts of the court to display my bosom to him. Of course, he stopped pacing, freezing on the spot. His eyes flickered down, and then he yanked his gaze to meet mine as if enjoying the view would get him punished. This wouldn't do. Why, when I needed a cad, would he not act like one?

He swallowed hard, "Princess Mary."

Determined to get a reaction from him, I said his first name in a seductive whisper, "Stephen."

A sharp inhalation was all I received. He was weak, frozen in inaction, so I acted. I stood and pulled him by his doublet collar to me and kissed him. Only, not being that experienced with passionate kisses, I did it a bit aggressively. He chuckled breathily and pulled away.

He kissed my hands and stared at them, not meeting my gaze. "Mary, forgive me. I've never been good at self-restraint with the fairer sex."

I scoffed at that. "You more than restrain yourself with me. I'm not sensual enough for you."

"You are!" He protested, grabbing my arms. Finally, I saw intensity in those vibrant blue eyes, matching the fire in mine. "I mean, I have to *try* to be good, and it's very, very hard." His lips crashed into mine, deepening the kiss, his tongue invading my mouth. He moaned.

I pulled him against me, lacing my fingers through his hair, but before I could take control over our battling tongues, he yanked himself away. His eyes were wild. He was breathing deeply. "I'm sorry, Mary, if you were misled by my lack of outward passion lately. I don't trust myself with you. Just that kiss makes me want you more than I'm allowed to."

"How much? Show me. I need to know."

He attacked me with kisses, his hands wrapping around me, running down my back. I let him lean me back until we crashed on the settee. My heart raced. When his hand ran up my stockings, past my knee, to touch the flesh of my thigh, I realized I had taken this test too far.

At the same time, Cobalt yanked himself away. He stood, and turned from me, his arms frustratingly folded behind his head. Quietly, he said,

"See, Mary? I want you as my lifemate in every way, but we must wait." He turned and met my gaze, but first his eyes fixated on my legs.

I covered them.

"I cannot mess this up. You must be pure when marrying as your edicts state. I can barely control myself, so please, don't temp me like this again. The only intimacy issue we have, as far as I'm concerned, is I can't have what I want until we marry."

It struck me how hard I had read his lack of lust so wrong. "I'm sorry."

"It is my fault." His eyes were full of guilt, a confession coming. "I don't know how to be romantic, not if I'm being genuine."

"Honesty," I said quickly. "Just tell me how you feel about me."

"But you know already."

"Do I? How? Aside from your letters and a few kisses, you've been more of a friend living in my quarters than an engagee."

"Mary, I don't trust myself."

I stood to go to bed but stopped in my doorway. "Stephen, can't we come up with some boundaries? A way we can let this develop into something affectionate and wonderful without crossing the line?"

His eyes met mine, and he smirked. He always loved a challenge. I just hoped he would see the challenge as behaving and not eschewing the rules we would make. There was only one person who I figured knew what rules could work and how far to take things: Toury. But then I wasn't sure I could stomach the idea that her experience was with my brother. Gross. Who else would I turn to though?

As Lucy brushed my hair, I realized that maybe she would know. A waiting maid-bodyguard would be an innocent, according to her job requirements, but servants talk, and Lucy would be instructed in multiple subjects to be able to assist me.

"Lucy?"

"Hmm?"

My cheeks burned. "I need help with a very embarrassing topic."

Her hands froze, and then she continued brushing. "Did Lord Cobalt turn down an advance of yours? I could see what you were up to."

"Then, why did you let me?" I turned and looked up at her with anger and desperation.

"It is not my place to tell you how to maneuver your relationship. That is something personal between two people and is different for each couple, from what I hear." She sighed as if having a change of thought. "May I sit, Your Highness?"

"Yes. Please. Get a chair." Relief swept through me that maybe I had a confidante who could answer back—no offense Wundor—and not make things super gross by talking to my only friend. Even if Lucy didn't know the answers, she could find them out discreetly.

Lucy scooted over the chair she sits in by the door when she guards me in my room. Ever since Father's death, she is always in the room when I am awake.

She sighed and looked at me and then down at her hands, not wanting to make eye contact during this upcoming discussion. "As you know, I'm assigned to watch over you, so I'm trained to notice everything anyone does around you. Princess, you do not see the look in that man's eyes when you are not watching. I think, forgive me if I'm wrong, that you believe his lack of initiating a physical relationship is worrisome. But I do research to help my charge more than you know. He has been absolutely faithful to you. Because I have to stay close for your safety and I see more than you do, it is obvious he cares for you. He does not want to ruin this marriage so is likely trying to take things slow."

It was the reassurance I needed, but I had to ask more. "I was taught where babies come from. I was taught what the line was not to cross to keep my purity. Lucy, what I want to know from you is...there has to be some kind of in between compromise. Don't make me ask Toury. It would make me sick."

"Riiiiight," Lucy pondered. "I know only a few things I've heard, but I know there are books written for ladies in the same situation. I will discretely procure one for you."

I grabbed her shoulders and hugged her tightly. She froze at my show of affection. "I'm sorry. This just...I needed a friend, and I'm sorry I never went to you first with things. That will change."

Her eyes went wide, and I thought the warrior woman would cry. She squeezed my hands to show her appreciation. Why have I been so obstinate to someone who only wants to be my ally? I am not that far away from marriage, but I have so much to learn about everything and everyone. At least I could learn some things from a book.

Lucy got the book the next morning. That meant it was somewhere in the castle or in Celestia already—easy to find, which surprised me. And, Wundor, I don't dare write what I saw on the pages for another person to accidentally read if they find this. It is beyond risqué. It is descriptive enough that they are directions on how to seduce a man. I could never do half these things! At first, I made Lucy read it to me, but then when she blushed and stammered, we flopped on the bed and read it quietly, giggling like little girls. Then it got uncomfortably bad. Lucy excused herself.

Not long after, I stopped reading since it got worse and worse. I figured if the earlier things happened between Cobalt, and I and he were able to control his lust, then I would read on. At least I know what to expect and know the things that start the actions toward the act. Ignorance is what I wager gets women in situations with unplanned children. I am glad for the education to make proper choices.

I'm furious with my brother. It's his fault I cannot become closer with Cobalt.

Cobalt and I just had mended things by being openly honest. We had gotten flirty after our conversation, and I learned ways in which to subtly gain his attention. At first, I thought he was teasing, being mean, but I realized Cobalt had always been a flirt. Even when he teased me when we were young, there was always something playful about his tone. That playfulness was still there, laced with a cocksure smirk and seductive eyes.

But Alex disrupted this nice shift. He made Cobalt stay in a room next to Henry to watch him as if Henry were the enemy. He is a Sapphirian, not an Emerald. I swear Alex did it on purpose to keep Cobalt away from me. I miss his presence. Knowing he was there in the room next to me was enough for now. But not having him there the moment I wake, having breakfast in private—it cuts deep. I feel like I am losing him, not to his duty and job, but intimately. He is busy and consumed with his work. I understand he just wants to protect me, to protect Alex, and Toury. He has labeled us the "core four." I love him for it, but if I don't do something, he'll forget me.

So, I asked him to come to my rooms—well, it was more of an order. He walked in, agitated.

"Mary, what do you need? I can't be off watch for long."

"Where is Percival?"

"On watch, so I could be here."

"No."

He stared at me confounded.

"You have a duty to me as an engagee. One of those duties is to have your bodyguard watch you at all times so you live."

"According to you, there is nothing to fear since Henry is oh-so innocent."

I did not care for his tone. "He is not the threat. But anyone could try to hurt you at any time. Just like you see Toury as a weakness to manipulate Alex, *you* are the same for Alex *and* me."

"Mary, Henry is the greatest threat. I'm trying to protect all of us. I need you just to think about it and stop reacting like all three of us are attacking him."

"I didn't bring you here to talk about Henry. You have pushed me aside. I will not marry a man who has no time for me."

"Mary, come on. This is my job!" His angry and scoffing tone spoke volumes. He was belittling my outburst as if I were unhinged, asking way too much.

I calmed myself so he could not blame me for being hysterical. "Is that more important than being my lifemate?"

He huffed out air, his eyes examining me. "An ultimatum? I quit, or you won't marry me? Is that what this is?" His face was guarded, and in that moment, I feared he would choose duty, Alex.

"No!" I feared his answer, but it also dawned on me how unfair an ultimatum would be. Reversed, it would be tantamount to him asking me not to be a princess. "Cobalt. When will you learn to delegate? Alex put you in charge and asked you to move to watch Henry in his quarters—"

"A subject you think silly, and I think serious."

"Let me finish." I added, "please," after I heard my nasty tone. "When is he in his quarters aside from morning and night?"

Cobalt opened his mouth but shut it.

"I take it that it is rarely? Delegate to be informed the moment they hear him transport out of the room—which you'd not be able to stop—and if he returns there at an odd time. Secondly, you ignored my one point. Percival is *your* bodyguard. What do you think my uncle could do if he got a hold of you?"

"But—"

"I would do anything for you, Cobalt. I showed you that at the Dragon Rock."

"Okay, okay," he said and pulled me into his arms. "Mary, I love you. I love you. But you and I are not seeing eye-to-eye about Henry right now. We've been fighting. I thought the space might help until things play out."

"I need you. Alive."

"I know." He cradled my face in his hands, and his eyes spoke the truth. His lips told me we were one and always would be.

He eventually broke away with a sigh. "I've missed you so much. I will delegate, so I am yours—as much as I can be—except the mornings and nights your brother demands of me. But of Henry—"

"I do not wish to argue again." I closed the subject. "You believing the worst and me the best will likely find the truth as in between."

I believe Henry is good, but it was a compromise. It would be foolish not to have someone think ill of him and watch for our safety, but that person who would think the worst will not be me. Dear Henry who watched over me and helped me when I had no one else.

"I'll make time for you every day, here on out. It will be different and unannounced times. I apologize for that, but just in case, no one should know our plans."

I understood why but did not want to discuss people trying to watch our lives to kill us. To shift his perspective, I said, "It will be more romantic if it's spontaneous."

COURTLY CUCKOLDS & CADS

THE PARTY PRINCESS'S BIRTHDAY BALL

Attendees said the entire day's celebration was a lovely affair. The princess actually did not party hard as she had been oft to do in the past. She seems to have grown up on us overnight, working for her brother and taking herself, her kingdom, and her people seriously. Although she will give us less gossip to bander about, we at the newspaper are proud of her, as I'm sure the entire kingdom is.

Her party consisted of a ladies tea and luncheon, a fashion show with women's pants—we are eager to see the prototypes!—a dinner, and a ball. Throughout the night, most attendees who spoke to us said they would not be surprised if a prince or princess was on the way. Apparently, the king and queen are adorably in love.

Speculations on a wedding date for the princess and prince-to-be were a recurrent topic of gossip. No one had seen the princess or Cobalt so happy. A source quoted, "They only have eyes for each other."

Which will come first lords and ladies? A baby Sapphirian or another wedding?

If they were Sapphirians and could read the flames, they would know it will be Alex and Toury's baby. To get us to that point though, I see so many awful things. I will not get grave. I cannot share this burden with Cobalt. He already worries so much. I cannot disrupt Alex's happiness. If only I could figure out what exactly kicks off all the strife to warn them. The flames do not cooperate.

I will smile and think of the wonderful day I had yesterday and cling onto the good times to remember them for when they get bad.

October

It's with a heavy heart I write this. My uncle is dead. He was a traitor. My poor brother had to execute him, due to the edicts and my uncle's request. Alex is composing himself together well, but I can see in his eyes that he is shattered by it. I'm not sure what I can say or do to help him, so I say nothing, hoping Toury can keep the pieces of him together. I have nightmares of what I think he saw. I cannot imagine the horror of real memories haunting him in his dreams. Henry has left. I get it, but I refuse to think the boy who was so kind to me is gone or in cahoots with his father's terrible plans. Henry has a good heart, and I wish people could see it as I do.

The only saving grace I have is Cobalt is back in my rooms. I hold onto him and make him hold me together. He does not understand my fear of an unclear future, but the flames keep changing so drastically that I'm not sure what will happen to us anymore.

November

I have no words to describe what has occurred, but I'll try. I feel so much it is hard to put down here. So much has happened I don't know where to start. I guess I should lay down the facts of what occurred so I can reread them and process it all.

We were attacked by Henry and a small retinue of soldiers. He took Toury and I. Foolishly, I still had faith that he would not hurt us. Seeing how broken my aunt was kind of woke me up, and Toury insisting we could die. When I reflected upon her position, I realized Henry would want her dead, and Alex, but likely not me. But how could he be ridiculous enough to think I would want to live a life without my brother and best friend? Stripped of my princesshood? I don't show it often, but I care about my people. And what would Cobalt do? Incite a revenge war?

I'm happy to report my love is still alive, and my brother, but Henry took away Toury after Alex besieged the fort. I fear for her and try to imagine she is alive since the flames tell conflicting tales.

The only time we were let out of prison was for supper with him. The way he behaved set me on alert, as if he wasn't himself, not the Henry who took me under his wing three years ago. He has changed, so much so that Henry poisoned us. Nothing to kill us, but to kill Toury's unborn child. It was horrible. It opened my eyes to see we are not dealing with a changed and battered Henry. We are dealing with a monster. The Henry I knew died with his wife. Cobalt tells me Henry was always evil, conditioned and abused by his father to become what he is now, but I knew the boy who was there for me. When he lost Emily, he went away on a mission—we had falsely believed. I must admit, now, that he was changed when he returned. I was just too blind to see through his playacting.

I pray now to the god and goddess for Toury's safe return. My brother is in pieces, and I have been ruling in his stead as much as possible—with Cobalt's help. I'm so scared this will be the future if the worst happens. I'm so scared Alex will follow her if she's dead. I don't know how to console him. The flames are tediously ever changing. I saw them with kids, but the flames can change. I also pray that Henry finds his humanity again. Spares Toury. He seemed somewhat infatuated and proclaimed he wants her to live. I pray that is the truth. I cannot write more. I'm beyond exhausted, but sleep barely comes. At least I must snuff the flame of my candle, which is keeping Cobalt from deep sleep. The gravity of everything and our exhaustion makes him behave, and he's able to share a bed with me. I admit being held and not sleeping alone keeps the nightmares away.

I am utterly worried about my brother, who does not sleep. If he is searching the flames as I am, I know why he is up all night.

I don't even know how to describe the fear of dying. Of a war directly outside your home. Or worse—maybe—thinking everyone you love except your mother is dead, and you'll have to transport via labradorite to Earth, a place you have never known nor studied well, described to be magicless and full of weird contraptions. I didn't want to leave Fyr, but it was the emergency plan. And for what? Obviously to save my life and my mother's, but what would we do? Remain there until our deaths? Try to return someday, not knowing what we'd walk into? Come back and discover what Henry would do to the sphere? Or more likely, the necromancers who would slaughter him the minute Henry snatched the medallion off my brother's neck.

How had I been so blind? Henry cared for me. I couldn't believe he didn't. And yet, a person who would kill everyone you love could not truly care for you. It took him finally making a move to attack to wake me up to see his real self. I should've known he was a different person from when I was younger, a different person after he lost Emily. Even now, I could not look back and see the signs. I should've known their love was that strong—that without her, he lost the will to live and became a puppet for my uncle to control. What other purpose did he have if he could no longer love anyone, not even his dear young cousin? What is a life without love?

"Mary, it will be all right. Alex will win this," Mother assured me. Her shaky voice did not soothe me.

We were secure in the safeaway, and I hadn't heard anyone breach Mother's rooms above us yet. I figured I should pass the time and just maybe I could foresee our fates to give me conviction to leave if I saw our deaths, or—hopefully—assure Mother she was right. I lit a fireball in my hand, focusing on Alex. He would be the key. If he died, all was lost; if he lived, all would be well.

"What are you doing?" Mother asked despite knowing. Her voice was tense, as scared as I was of finding answers we would not like.

I grew the flames in my hands until I could form a ball. "The future should get more certain every moment. I can't be idle and wait."

Poor mother couldn't see in them and didn't dare further interrupt my firebranding because too many times Father had scolded her for it. Now we knew he could not see well from his curse, but he blamed interruptions and other nonsense on my poor mother.

So many variations, but in a couple, I saw draca entering the capital. I didn't understand how or why. Would Henry or Alex release them from the Firelands? Would the draca even obey a Sapphirian? There was a treaty with them.

At one point, I fell asleep. The noise dwindled outside, and I think that was what woke me: an eerie silence. I shook Mother awake. We did not speak much, knowing that whoever came to the safeaway would determine who had won, determine our future, or it was clear the battle outside was over. Would Mother and I have to start a new life on a foreign planet, with everyone else we loved dead? Would Cobalt come to me with his secret codeword to say all was safe?

There was noise in Mother's quarters above us. Hurried footsteps. Mother gripped my arm. I grabbed the pouch around my neck, our escape route, my heart thrumming outside my chest. I could not leave. I could not. I would need to see the fate of Cobalt, Alex, and Toury. I belong here. Nowhere else. I couldn't live without my magic. I dropped the pouch, letting it rest on my chest. "Mother," I whispered.

"I agree, my darling. For better or worse, we stay here. I am with you, no matter what." She kissed my temple.

I began to cry for her love and dedication to me, my choice, even if it meant her death. Tears flowed, but I choked back the sound so whoever was racing down toward us would not hear me.

"Mary!" It was Alex!

I stood, but Mother gripped my arm, shaking her head. It could be a ploy, at knifepoint, to get me to come out. Cobalt had drilled it in our heads to await the password.

"Time changes as much as the flame flickers."

I raced up the steps and unlocked the sealed door with my fire magic.

"Alex!" I crashed into his arms, hugging him tightly—as tight as I could because he was still in his battle armor. He squeezed me back before he let go and embraced Mother, who was now bawling.

Then it hit me. Cobalt was not here.

"Are you all right?" Alex demanded.

"Yes. Cobalt?"

"Wounded. He's fine. Superficial. I sent him to the infirmary."

"I must go to him."

"Not yet, Mary, sorry. There are a few of Henry's men still in here being rounded up. Henry is dead." From the way it rushed out of his mouth, devoid of emotion, his eyes fixated on the ground momentarily, I knew my poor brother had been forced to do it himself. His eyes snapped up to meet mine. "I must go, but I will be back when all is safe enough for you to unbar your door. Mary, Mother, Toury is alive!" A smile took flight upon his exhausted face, despite all he must've gone through.

Then he was gone in a ball of flames. Mother sighed in relief, weary but relaxed. I could not. I paced. Alex would tell me if it were serious, wouldn't he? He wouldn't lie to keep me here, would he? He'd have ten guards take me to the infirmary if it were dire. I must wait to see my love, my future. So I sat down and penned this onto paper that I will later copy into your pages, Wundor, to pass the time so that waiting would not be so much torture.

Alex came back as promised, lifetimes later, or roughly an hour as Mother said. I raced to the infirmary. Cobalt was being tended to by healers, being pushed onto a cot, blood all over his head and face. It looked horrific.

I raced over to him, shouting at the healers I knew not what. Likely my thoughts. *Why hadn't they healed him yet? Why was half the blood dried up, and they were just now cleaning the cut now?* I looked him over to find no other wounds.

"Mary, stop!" he pleaded. He took up my hand. "It is no one's fault but my own. I disobeyed my king and helped wipe out the scum inside the castle. I had to protect Queen Toury, who foolishly left her rooms to get *food* of all things. You'll be pleased to know—"

"Then I have her to blame for the scar you'll have."

His face fell as it finally dawned on him that he'd be scarred because there was only so much healing magic could do if not healed instantly. Even my fire magic would likely leave a nasty red, puckered streak down the side of his face.

"You could heal me, no?" His voice was tentative, knowing how much pain it would cause him.

My willpower to hurt him was low, even if it could save his face. "The pain...I couldn't. My brother?"

"I cannot ask him. He has too much going on, and he is with Toury. The fire lasher?"

"I can ask if he can heal. Not all fire magic works the same."

Lady Edwina was in the room, healing a soldier across from us. She came to us briskly. "It will scar by now regardless of the treatment. Fire will leave a melting mark, puckered up discolored flesh. I will use my light instead. It will be a cleaner scar. You will not want to be present, Princess."

"I'm not leaving." I stayed despite his screams and squeezing of my hand.

He tried to keep a brave face, but she was literally using light magic to mend his flesh back together as one would stitch a hemline. When she was done, so was he—half-conscious, moaning rather than talking. There was a part of the wound that was still open and weeping, about two inches long down his cheek, and the rest was an angry red color with a crease through the middle.

"I can do no more, nor would your magic. This must be healed another way. I will talk to Tobias Firebrander, the smartest man I know. He is sure to know non-magical healing. I wish Toury was okay enough to tell me Earth's customs for such a wound, but I would not dare disturb her and the king."

"No wait! I can find him faster." I ignored her perplexed face and closed my eyes, locating first Alex and Craig's whereabouts in the castle, then Aunt Anne's. After that, I searched for the smallest little pull with a desperate hope. Alex was right. Tobias *is* a distant relation. I transported to that little pull. He was in the library, of course, and jumped at my arrival.

"Sorry. Come. You are needed." I did not wait for a response but grabbed his wrist and transported him back to the infirmary with me.

Tobias instantly looked at Cobalt's face.

"What can be done?" I asked.

"Light did not fully work, so I doubt fire. Anything Earth-like, non-magical?" Edwina asked.

Tobias's eyes flittered as if he were pouring through mental books he had stored in his mind; likely, he was. "Yes!" He was excited. "Thread—braided silk if on hand—firespice whiskey, and a curved needle."

"Curved?"

"The princess can bend it with her power if I cannot."

Lady Edwina rushed from the room. It would be faster for me, but I had no idea where to go. My embroidery threads would not do, and I had no firewhiskey in my rooms. I hoped Cobalt had not used it all up during the war with his fire plans he had been so excited about.

Edwina was smart. A servant entered with the thread and needle, a second with Edwina behind carrying a jug of the spirit. She had delegated to not waste time. I quickly heated the needle and bent it as Tobias instructed, while he wiped the thread with firewhiskey. I had heard of using the alcohol in a bind to clean wounds, so I guess it was a similar tactic. Edwina dabbed the wound with a cloth soaked in the whiskey, making the barely conscious Cobalt thrash about. I wanted them to stop, but I understood it was to prevent infection.

I looked away as they worked. Once they were done, I saw his sewn-up face. Such beauty despoiled. I was so upset, but knew it mattered not. I love him, not for his face alone although it was a rather attractive one. I ached for the pain he was in and how he might react to his gruesomely sewn face.

"He waited too long," Edwina touched my shoulder in apology.

"He fought instead of getting healed." I expected no less from my future lifemate.

"I believe he fought valiantly." She left me.

A healer placed stones on him to ward off infection and to alleviate pain. Then she drew a curtain that separated the beds around us for privacy. I only then noticed it was full of soldiers, ones I should visit and thank for their roles in us winning.

I could not. I felt like crying but held it in, thinking of the soldiers around me with worse injuries than Cobalt's. It does not matter what he looks like. I have always loved him since the flames told me I would. I had not foreseen the scar, but had I, it would not lessen my adoration for him. No, I have loved him since I could remember in a very innocent way, like a brother, until it shifted to infatuation when the flames told me so. I often wonder if I could not have seen my future if I would've ended up with him. My heart tells me yes. I have always been fond of him. I love him, and we survived the turmoil I had foreseen. He is alive. I will become his lifemate. The sadness crept away, and I felt stronger, happier. I kissed his hand and then opened the curtain. I would not leave him, but I would do my duty and talk to all the soldiers while I waited for him to wake.

At some point, I woke up, not realizing I had fallen asleep. It took me a moment to realize what had woken me was someone touching my disheveled hair, tangled around my circlet. It came back to me. Cobalt, infirmary, a healer begging me to rest after seeing every soldier in the infirmary and down the hallway. I had insisted on sitting next to Cobalt and must've drifted to sleep, my head on his cot. Cobalt!

I looked up to see him awake, peering at me, his wounded flesh in the shadows. He had turned his head toward me, which must have caused him pain.

"Don't turn your head so. You're in pain."

"Mental pain more so."

He turned to look up at the ceiling. His face, from his forehead diagonally down to the end of his jaw, was blemished, starting with red sealed skin to the sewn area on his cheek, then returned to pink. In the pink areas, the skin still was interrupted by a thin line. It would all scar.

Then I registered his words. "Mental pain? What has happened?" Had someone died? Alex? Toury? Mother?

His eyes darted over to me. Then he sat up, facing me. "Look at me, Mary!" He motioned his face with his hand. One side was so beautiful and smooth, the other mangled. It mattered not. He was still gorgeous with the scars to prove his bravery.

"It looks like it must hurt, so you should rest."

"Don't take me for a fool, Mary. I know I look hideous. Please release me from the engagement. You cannot marry someone like me. Princes should look noble and attractive."

Fear clutched my heart, squeezing it. What if he was using this as an excuse to be free of me? No, no. I know him, and I was confident enough that he wants and loves me. "And if I find you noble and attractive as is? Is that the only reason you want to end our engagement?"

"Mary, please don't lie to me. Don't pity me. I cannot bear it." Cobalt stared into my eyes, his shining. Tears were forming. He was afraid to lose me but was being silly.

I stood. "Obviously, you are still in shock from the pain, because you're talking nonsense. If you don't stop wallowing and pitying yourself, I'm going to leave. I will not hear it. Many soldiers died, and many are much more wounded than you. Cobalt, I love *you*, not just your face. You *are* noble. The scar is proof to all how brave you were. And you are beautiful, you fool. I'm going to have to beat the ladies away from you. Many women love scars. It speaks courage and danger."

Cobalt smiled but then it dropped to a wince of pain. He took my hand in his. "It only matters what one woman thinks."

"Good then. Engagement on. No more disparaging yourself either."

"Yes, Your Highness." He teased, giving me a soft grin.

I leaned over and went to kiss him, on his forehead and the start of his wound. He flinched under my gentle kiss.

"Did it hurt? Sorry."

"It only hurt me here," he pointed to his chest, his heart.

"Hurt?"

"I once mocked Alex that love was like pain to him. Now I know he was right. I love you so much, I want the world for you, and I feel too inferior to give it."

"Well then," I said lightly. "You'll have to spend the rest of our lives trying to compensate."

Then I left, knowing I had lit up his mood as he always brightens others' who are down with his magic. I have always seen him as a resilient and strong man, overly confident with others, particularly women. Maybe he had relied on his looks far too long. Wundor, I have realized that it's fine for me to stumble and feel insecure at times, but overall, I feel more in charge of my life than ever. Perhaps it is the thought of losing everything that ignites the drive to fight for it, to keep it all, to shape my own future. I'll take charge of my own life.

We had the celebration, finally. The one for Alex and Toury's marriage they never had. Toury is already showing. I can't believe my nephew will be here in about five months. I'm so excited to become an auntie. I marvel over her strength to save her child from poison and danger. One day, I want to be her equal in her power and strength. Speaking of power, she can transport and make lightning. Tobias and Alex obsessively discuss it, trying to figure it out. If only they'd listen to Cobalt to begin with. She is Bladesung, the legend of the land that would save us. And she has in so many ways. I'm most thankful in her seemingly innocuous challenge to give up firewhiskey, which made me save myself.

Alex caved in and believes Cobalt; you cannot deny Toury is the ultimate savior, but he and Tobias are obsessed with *how* it came to be. I don't envy that task. No one gains powers that I know of, but Toury did through her baby it seems, or maybe Ruby, or both? Strange.

Mother keeps begging us to set a date for Cobalt and my wedding, which is awkward because when Cobalt blushes, the scar becomes redder each time, although most of it is a thin groove in his flesh now. The stitches were taken out, and that area is still pink. He is beautiful, but unfortunately, now all the women are trying to talk to the wounded and valiant soldier. I trust him, but it still bothers me in the back of my mind of what he had once been like and how the old him would take advantage of this situation.

I digress. Everything has been wonderful for all of us once the aftermath of the battle left us, the dead were mourned and given up to the god and goddess swiftly through many pyre ceremonies done by the guilds. This included Henry's body—done privately by us family without any distinction or ceremony. I had been foolish, and I watched his shrouded body burn, thinking of how careful I would be in examining someone's honesty in the future.

COURTLY CUCKOLDS & CADS

THE END AND NEW BEGINNING

Reader, you well know the war has ended, and celebrations are in full swing. It feels like the start of a new age. Necromancers and rebels gone, draca out of the Firelands but peacefully, and the Bladesung Queen with our Draca King are all recipes for a powerful reign. And that reign will continue.

Attendees at the long-awaited wedding feast reported that the queen wore the prince's medallion and sported a baby bump, indicating we are to expect the long-awaited start of the next generation of Sapphirians. To keep the line going, this king and queen will be mighty busy if you catch my drift, but seeing as her fertility is under no question, there should be no problem creating a large family of royals.

Good times ahead of us, if the royal's use of Golden Age of peace can be believed. Reader, we believe.

We hope that here on out we can return to our comical stories of ladies cuckolding their lifemates and cads who do the same.

Celebrate your hearts out.

January

Wundor, it has been two months since the war ended. Everything is a normal blissfulness. Toury found it a bit boring, likely because Alex does not let her do anything. I can't say I blame him, so I have kept to the castle as well to keep her company. I've invited Toury's ladies in waiting over, luncheons in the orchard, secret sparring lessons where she helps teach me how to properly defend myself, long walks, and even a secret shopping trip Alex never found out we transported to.

I understand Alex's concern. The kingdom knows the way to get to him is through Toury. It is well-known now there is a child coming, so we are on high alert for Emerald supporters or leftover enemies the draca did not wipe out. The draca have returned to the Firelands, except they often patrol the lands, never causing damage or hurting anyone. They served as a reminder—this is the reign of the Draca King.

It feels too peaceful, the kingdom too satisfied. Even though the flames do not show me anything of concern, I am anxiously waiting for something bad to happen. I have become accustomed to it. No rumors reach us about any necromancer or rebels still around. Some might've slunk into the shadows, but I expect most died, hid in fear, or had some change of heart.

I pray to the god and goddess that this peaceful time lasts as long as I think it will—at least my lifetime. That is as far as I can see, and I do not die young.

I'm trying to think of what else I have not written in you, Wundor. I so would like this to be a reminder when I'm older of times I overcame.

Let's see, my brother Craig and his family live in their estate, but he comes often to dine. Toury's sister transported to Earth, and her little brother has become a family member fully now, Lady Edwina like a mother to him. Aunt Anne has been acting more stable, but she is quiet, preferring sitting in the orchard reading for hours. Although that little forager of Toury's, Duric, has pestered her until she started talking to him. I think she will be okay now that she is home again and free of the Emeralds. She does well with Mother too as they reminisce on the old days and talk of suitors who could've been. Oh, and Wundor, of course the brilliant Tobias figured out how Toury became the Bladesung, but it is so baffling, I had to have Alex explain it to me several times. The short of it was, Toury never knew she was a powermender. She inadvertently fused her magic to her unborn child's but before that, the stone had fused Ruby's magic to her own. There is now excitement about what powers her and Alex's heir will have. The Cobalt family might move to the palace soon, so we can help his sisters marry. Holly Cobalt's baron fought in the war on our side but died a hero. I want to focus on finding her happiness in whatever form that will be.

I'm sure I have forgotten people. There are so many people to care about now who care about me, and when I started writing in you, I felt like there had been no one. Perhaps growing up is not so scary after all.

Last night, Cobalt came to bed and snuggled up to me with a contented sigh and a kiss.

"We need to set a date," I told him.

"You and your mother," he scoffed. "Mary, I just feel odd about how young you are."

"You're only two years older than me!"

"Exactly. Why rush? Let us just get married right before our engagement runs out, when you're seventeen, almost eighteen."

I huffed. "For a man who deflowered many young girls—"

"I did not."

"Huh?"

"God and goddess, Mary. I've had enough about talking about my past. It makes me want to marry you less. I am this sullied fool, and you are a draca goddess." He kissed my neck, likely to distract me.

"Stop it." I do admit privately to you Wundor, I enjoyed the compliment. "But now you have to explain."

"They were never innocents, and they were usually ladies a little older than me."

"How much older?"

"Not that much. I just had at least enough decency to never take something from a woman that she could not have back." So, he bedded no virgins. He had some scruples at least.

"You're right. I'm over this conversation." I fluffed my pillow and laid my head down, turning away from him.

"Mary, I'm never going to feel worthy of you. I want to marry you when I can feel that way. Your brother and Toury are equals, but—"

"I treat you equally." I rolled over, a bit annoyed at what felt like an accusation.

"It's not your problem to solve, Mary. You are perfect." He kissed my lips gently. "It is me. I must do something to truly feel as if I've atoned for all the wrong I've done, for every way I hurt you and other ladies."

"Helping win a war and bearing the scar for your efforts is not enough?" I asked it with an incredulous tone, but he responded with a shake of his head.

"Oh, Stephen," I sighed. I tucked his head under my chin, his scarred cheek against my collarbone, and I held him tightly. "It matters not. We love whom we love. I will have no one else."

Cobalt sighed contently but said no more. I took it as acquiescence.

Stephen and I went to Toury's orphanage. I thought maybe some charity work would help him feel "atoned." Nothing I did—including some of that forbidden book's seduction techniques of flirting persuaded him he was ready to marry me. I know not what else he needed to feel good about himself. I hate to say that I almost begged him to marry me on the morrow when I caught him being a horsey for the little ones in the orphanage. A prince-to-be crawling around on all fours to get children to squeal with delight. My heart melted as I envisioned him with our first son like this—yes, we will have a son first too, like Toury and Alex, but we'll not have to wait as long to get girls as Alex and Toury will.

I long to see him holding one of our children, a proud smile on his face, the kind I see every time my brother runs his hand over Toury's belly. I am young, yes, and I should want to cling onto that, but after thinking we would all die, and seeing my brother so happy now—no, there is more to it than that. I hadn't looked forward to the future until now. I had hated who Cobalt had been; I hated myself, drowning my self-loathing in firewhiskey. I now love him and more importantly, I love myself. I am ready to forge my future, experience everything in life that would extend this happiness and self-worth. With that admittance, I know I cannot push Cobalt. He has to learn, as I have, to love himself before he can truly love another.

Stephen and I have volunteered at the orphanage daily for two weeks, just the two hours we can spare when Alex doesn't need him, and I am not listening to grievances. Honestly, the grievances are thinning out each time Alex enacts a new law. It is great to see the progress and the people embrace the changes. A few sticklers in the sorcerer sector regularly show up to make grievances, but I enjoy putting them in their place.

Back to Stephen. He was folding laundry with Lady Edith Tanzanite and me. I went to fetch another load from the laundress down the hall. When I came back, I heard murmuring coming from the laundry room. My stomach dropped from her flirtatious tone. I longed to race in and put a stop to it, but I froze, mostly from fear of how he would respond. Fear crept up my spine. Things were going so well. He could not mess "us" up now!

"What did you just say?" Stephen's voice was full of shock. I had missed exactly what she had said, being out of ear range.

"I said it must be difficult, being engaged so long and not having a mistress," she repeated.

"That's not your business."

"I was just asking if there was an opening for that *position* in the near future." The way she said position made me gag.

I held my breath awaiting Cobalt's answer. Did he find that uncouth flirting appealing? She was a pretty girl, but throwing yourself at someone in such a way was pathetic.

I swallowed the lump in my throat. *Please don't mess up, Cobalt!*

"No. I will not have a mistress, never will."

"Oh, but it must be so *hard* for someone like you, who has such an insatiable appetite, to starve so." She purred. I heard a rustle of her skirt and worried her tone was making her act on some of her insinuations.

"My relationship with the princess is not your concern. I no longer entertain any other woman's attention. My princess is all I need. If you would let go of my arm and back away, I would appreciate it."

I rushed into the room with the laundry cart as Stephen yanked his arm away. His eyes were wide in worry that I would misconstrue the situation.

I kept my voice steady and light, although I wanted to throttle her. "Take care, Lady Edith, you might not want to get caught clinging onto him in that manner. You might get *burned*."

She gave me a haughty look as if I were a pest who had no right to interrupt her.

"It could be seen as assault upon a royal-to-be, which is still treason punishable by stake," I added.

Her idle brain caught up with her massive ego, and her jaw dropped. She went pale.

"She was just leaving. We no longer need her assistance at this establishment," Stephen ground out.

"Oh no, Stephen," I used his intimate name on purpose. You might've noticed, Wundor, that he is "Stephen" now, *my* Stephen. "That is not punishment enough, because the children suffer for it. Repurpose her help as far away from you as you see fit." I allowed him to dole out the punishment, learning equality well from the best couple I know, the king and queen.

"No one wants to help in the wash rooms. Go help down there."

Her eyes were horrified. I really did feel sorry for her. She went from hoping to ensnare a mistress position with one of the highest-ranking gentlemen in Fyr, only to have to scrub toilets and scrap the diaper linen before it got washed. Ah well, it hopefully taught her a lesson.

"Look, Mary," Stephen rushed out.

I covered his mouth with my hand and shook my head. His eyes were confused. I uncovered his mouth and kissed him instead when he tried to speak again. Stunned, he froze before he wrapped his arms around me and returned my heated kisses.

We heard someone coming down the hall. Stephen yanked himself from me, the look in his eyes full of fiery lust. He shook his head as if to shake away the desire. I can't lie that I enjoy knowing I evoke that feeling from him. Perhaps he is guarded in our quarters, but in public, I had disarmed him. That could be a fun challenge for me to unnerve him with.

One of the workers came in and grabbed a stack of towels, politely bowing her head before leaving.

Stephen's eyes had never left me. "I'm so confused."

"I overheard most of it, I think."

He was even cuter now that one side of his wrinkled brow dipped down from the scar. "Why didn't you stop her?" Then his face went slack in realization. "You wanted to see what I would say. You don't trust me."

"Of course, I trust you. You're the one who needed to test yourself. Prove to yourself you are worthy of me. I think this proves it."

He cracked a smile, his scarred cheek doing its cute two-dimpled thing. "The old me would've flirted and thought about it. But now, all I could think about was you, wanting you that way, and then the way you kissed me." He growled softly and pulled me to him by my rear, kissing my lips.

I pushed him away. "Stop!" I teased, throwing a sheet at him. "Someone could walk by again."

"Let them." He pulled me back to him roughly, making me squeal in surprise as he kissed me soundly. My inhibition melted away with his lips on mine.

Wundor, he loves me, and I love him. He is believing himself worthy enough to steal as many kisses as he can. I think we will finally set a date soon. If we stop kissing for a minute that is.

Cobalt is out of his silly "I don't deserve you" mood. Anyway, I write to say it is happening. Toury started having the pains of childbirth. It is a little early, healers say, but not in a worrisome way. I will write more when the child is here.

May

WELCOME PRINCE ROWLAND ALEXANDER SAPPHIRIAN,

the headline read, but I could not bother reading. I had witnessed it firsthand. Well, kind of.

Wundor, just like your name, he's a little miracle! I didn't actually watch the birth because Alex, yet again, threw tradition away. Instead of Mother and I being in the birthing room, he and Toury broke custom and decided she'd give birth in their bedroom of all places, and Mother and I were not to be there. Alex would be in there with her! We women were forced to wait in the Sapphirian tea room.

"A man witnessing a birth? I never heard of it!" I paced, annoyed at being left out.

"It's probably nothing you'd want to see," Cobalt murmured.

We were in the Sapphirian tea room, away from all the action.

"How would you know?" I countered.

"We all studied anatomy, Mary. I'd never understand what a woman goes through, but it sounds horrific. I would not think the ordeal worth it if a new life was not the result."

When I thought about it, and our lessons about childbirth, Cobalt was probably right. I always thought about a baby crying with life and then being swaddled in a blanket. Thanks to Cobalt, I was now imagining the worst bits. How in Fyr does a woman actually get something that big out of her body?

"It is well worth it," Mother said. "I assure you. Let me add that your brother and Toury should have the birth private, if that is their wish."

"I want to see him." When it came out, it sounded like a childish whine, but I had put so many of my emotions in this child. I was excited to see my best friend and brother—the two I love most outside of Stephen and Mother—bring something into the world that was both of them. My nephew. I could not wait to be his Auntie. Rowland will mark the beginning of a new age for us. He represented so much.

Cobalt gave me a side hug and smiled. "I want to as well. I can't wait to teach him to spar and go over war strategies with him, and horseback riding, and—"

"You can't do that for years, Stephen. He'll be a baby."

Cobalt's face fell. I wanted to smack him, but he was deep in thought. "Toy soldiers to start then."

"What if you and I have a princess first? Will you show the same exuberance?"

He sputtered and turned the deepest shade of pink I had ever seen. He seemed ready for marriage in every way possible, except for setting the date, but he was still shocked when I talked so flippantly about the future.

He schooled his expression and cleared his throat. "Mary, I would teach her all the same if you'd let me."

I leaned into him, letting him hold me. It was the perfect answer, not because he was letting me win, but because he supported the changes that were being made. We now had a full-swing women's reform: women's pants, bathing costumes that allowed men and women to swim together—my idea of course. Women were learning to defend themselves, and a woman was recently allowed to join in a sporting match.

"It's a boy!" An ecstatic out-of-breath David burst into the room. Alex appeared in flames, holding a bundle in his arms, staring as if afraid the

196

transport would hurt the baby. Likely, he was too afraid to walk through the castle carrying the little prince.

Breathlessly, Alex said, "Rowland Alexander Sapphirian." We all hurried over to admire the new addition to the family and the new heir. I saw his little Sapphire eyes blink a few times at me until they closed into a nap. Poor little nipper had been through a lot coming into the world. This auntie fell in love instantly.

I got to hold him as Alex transported back to Toury. I stared down at that little swollen face. It was too difficult to tell who he looks more like, but Mother insisted he is a replica of Alex.

Stephen smiled down at me. "You look so happy holding him." Sometimes Cobalt, sometimes Stephen to me—he is both eternally.

"I am." I grinned, peering up at him.

"Let's do it."

"Huh?" I was shocked because I thought he was talking about making babies in front of my mother.

"Get married."

My heart started hammering in my chest. "Truly?"

He shrugged. "This looks magnificent." He touched the little toes that poked out of the blanket with his finger. "I want to marry you soon, Mary, truly. I'm ready for it all. Even these little buggers."

As if Rowland knew in his dreamy sleep, he gave a little kick at Cobalt's hand, the tickling sensation instinctually annoying him.

"He's going to be a handful," Cobalt said.

"Not one his grandmother cannot handle," Mother cut in, opening her arms. I carefully handed the baby over. Mother's face spread into utter joy. All the hardships Mother had been through in her life were gone in that moment. She has found her happily-ever-after: caring for the grandkids and smothering them with love she is now allowed to freely show.

"Tomorrow," he said.

Mother gasped, tearing her eyes away from her first grandchild. "The planning! It has to be big. We must wipe out the memory of Alex and Toury's first disastrous attempt, and the people weren't happy they eloped. It has to be a grand affair."

I felt my face beam. I wanted tomorrow, and yet I wanted Mother to shine with her love for event planning. She'd make it a day to remember. Plus, as always, there is me always being in Alex's shadow—this time through baby Rowland's birth. That needs to be celebrated first.

"Mother, I know you have it all planned, but Stephen, I refuse to steal our nephew Rowland's attention. Let the kingdom celebrate him, and we'll then shine on our own, make the kingdom excited for the prospect of another baby Sapphirian before Alex and Toury will manage another."

Stephen's eyes lit up, and he leaned in to kiss my chastely, although my mother was too besotted with my nephew to pay attention to what he was doing. He pulled me up into his arms and whispered. "I hope that is a challenge, my darling, wicked princess."

"It is," I whispered back. "The flames tell me so."

He pulled away and gazed at me before he kissed me hard. This will be a fun few weeks, torturing him with discussions about things he can't yet have.

June

It is only days until my wedding. Toury is over childbirth and about, but of course, she was transporting places a couple days before the healers approved her leaving her rooms. We walk the baby in the orchards often, even though Alex worries about the roots and the pram dislodging the baby somehow. It is cute to see him worry, but I knew he'd be a great father because he has been more like one to me than our own was. Today, Toury went in early from our walk because Prince Rowland fussed, hungry. As you can guess, Toury also does the Earth-girl thing of nursing rather than using a wet nurse. It seems taxing, but the thought of someone else feeding one's child seems odder to me when I think about it.

Since it was so pleasant outside, I decided to pick some fruit, and Toury's little forager was excited for someone more spry than my aunt. Duric was annoyingly chatty in an adorable way. At least it prepared me in a way for motherhood I'd face one day, much like the fussy prince did.

I climbed up a ladder as far as I dared, but still unable to reach a branch that had huge, fully ripened dracaberries. I stretched out my foot and stepped on a thick limb, leaning to grab the branch to pull it toward me to get to the fruit. Cobalt had wanted a picnic alone after he had finished with his meetings. He said he'd procure the food, but I was sure it was almost all unhealthy with the way he thought. Fruit would be a fine addition.

A whistle blew behind me, making me almost lose my footing.

"I don't see beetles, and I don't see ants, but I definitely see Princess Mary's underpants." Cobalt sang, echoing that day so long ago when I first was called a lady.

So much has happened in the last three years that I was surprised he could recall that moment. He wows me about everything he remembers about me, which makes me realize the affection has never been one-sided as I had thought. He has loved me my entire life, in various ways as I have him.

This time, when he approached, the cad actually attempted to look up my dress.

"A little help here?" I mimicked what I had said then.

He steadied the ladder. I plucked the fruit and placed them in the basket on my arm. I climbed down, and he remained at the bottom, his body close. He wrapped an arm around my waist, my back to his front, and kissed my neck.

"It's going to cost you," he said, his voice thick.

I turned in his arms. "Cake?"

He laughed. "No, I have that in our picnic basket."

"Of course, you do." I shook my head at him.

He gazed into my eyes, his look a combination of adoration and desire that I loved to see. "It *will* cost you."

"What?" I slinked away from him, heading up the path where he had come from in search of the picnic spot. He walked behind me, likely enjoying his view, before he caught my hand in his to prompt me to stop.

"The rest of your life."

I wrapped my arms around his neck and stared right at him. "Gladly given."

Then I kissed him, looking forward to many more.

COURTLY CUCKOLDS & CADS

A CONVERTED CAD

One of our most beloved cads who graced our pages quite a few times in the past has at last settled down. More than a year of dedication to Princess Mary after his many blunders and escapades has warmed our hearts to their slow-building romance.

From childhood friends to at odds over his indiscretions, we have watched them grow and be torn apart. From a hated cad to a war hero, this sphere has witnessed his transition into a mature man worthy of our princess.

Today, Princess Mary Elizabeth Sapphirian has wed Lord Stephen Thomas Cobalt. It was a fine affair and much needed after the public missed the king and queen's second wedding, the first not being an affair anyone wanted to remember. The Sapphirians went all out in a splash. The front of the castle had an arbor, every inch covered in the loveliest array of blue and white flowers. Displays of flowers permeated the air. Rich blue drapes hung down from the windows. The crowd in front of the castle was massive, reaching the streets and beyond. All of Celestia was trying to sneak a peek.

The king and queen stood on one side of the arbor, in muted colors but looking splendid. It was the queen's first public appearance since the birth of Prince Rowland. The tot did not make the anticipated appearance, but such a gesture likely would take the sphere's eyes off the honored couple about to be wed. With our monarchs were the queen dowager and Princess Anne, both looking regal, despite shedding a few happy tears. It was only the second public appearance of Princess Anne, who reports say is reserved but healed from her madness, one created by the now extinct Emerald line.

The Cobalt family stood on the other side of the arbor, watching with pride as their son was elevated beyond any parents' dream.

The prince-to-be stood under the arbor, looking dapper in his deep blue military uniform, his stance ever the soldier, and that scar making young ladies swoon. Those blue eyes were trained down the walkway as the carriage appeared.

The princess floated from the carriage in a gorgeous white corset-dress, which flowed out at the waist slightly;

the detailing when she moved, appeared to shine and glisten, making her sparkle. The discernible eye caught the off-shoulder neckline, with a delicate flower-chiffon-lace trim, which showed off more of the princess than Fyr was accustomed to. It was a statement: I am a woman. And yes, my readers, she walked to the stunned lord waiting for her with the confidence and poise of a woman. Her hair shone in the sun, flowers and hair weaved into her circlet, allowing a full view of her beautiful face, but the back flowed down in the now-fashionable style.

The princess rendered the crowd speechless, particularly Lord Cobalt, who stood stunned until she was close. Only then did he snap back into reality, and his face transformed into bliss.

The ceremony was short and to the point. The two simply stared at each other with shared smirks of knowingness and adoration. After Lord Cobalt became a prince of Fyr, they sealed the deal with a not-so chaste kiss.

The royals quickly retreated into the castle for their celebrations, which is where, alas, we must end this tale. It was said to be a small affair among select courtiers, none of whom have spilled the details to us yet. All the inns and restaurants of Celestia were sent food and drink from the palace, and the celebrations went on all day into the night. This generosity proves again that the Sapphirian reign is one that sticks to its word: all Fyrians are equal.

We rejoice in their happiness. Let our new prince stay as true as the worth he has proven through the scar he bears for Fyr, and bless them by the god of fire and goddess of light to have many children.

Dear Wundor,

I cannot express to you how happy I am at this moment. I have married my Cobalt, my dear Stephen; although I know he is a man with faults in his past, he has proven himself to me, to the kingdom. Unlike my brother's sad little elopement and a belated party, Stephen and I were married in front of the kingdom to nothing but jubilation. No signs of past disgruntled enemies. The flames assure me that we are now entering a golden age that will last past where I can see.

It was surreal. I was nervous suddenly, even though I knew it was the right course. My brother Craig rode with me. Normally legitimate family would have, but Stephen and I wanted them with us up there at the arbor, and Mother didn't want to miss a second. I also wanted to honor a brother I could not in the actual ceremony.

Nerves in jumbles, I think I chided Craig that with me married, attention would move onto him next. That made him quiet, but his company was a balm that calmed my nerves. He reminds me of Alex and the good parts of Father. I have come to terms with Father's death and of who he was and was not to me. It would have been nice for him to see me settled, but I did not feel a sting from his absence on such an important occasion.

Then we were there. It felt like a mile to the arbor. I tried to walk slow and elegantly, but part of me wanted to run to Stephen. So far away, he was just a swath of hues: blue and golden-haired. As tradition demanded, Craig would wait an ample amount of time, then follow and sit in the front row.

I took in the beautiful scene but could not etch the details in my mind. What was clear to me was the people. My brother and Toury, both grinning; Mother and Aunt Anne, both on the verge of happy tears; the Cobalt family gazing at me with smiles and warmth. Then there was my soon-to-be lifemate.

Stephen was stunned. So much so, I had to stifle a giggle. His eyes poured over me with every step I took, drinking me in. When I was close enough to see the glimmer in his eyes, he gave a little jerk as if someone doused him with water. That's when his eyes met mine, and his face beamed with the same nervous bliss I was feeling. I could not take my eyes off him.

I don't recall words, barely able to hear what to repeat over the beating of my heart, highly distracted with Stephen's massive grin and the pride and excitement in his eyes.

Soon, the words were said. We were lifemates.

He waited only a beat after the last word left the authority's lips before Stephen took me in his arms and kissed me soundly. I pressed my lips back, which made him deepen the kiss. Someone cleared their throat, and there was some soft laughter in the crowd.

Stephen let me go, grabbing my hand in his, squeezing it. The people erupted with applause, whistles, and cheers. I only had eyes for my Stephen, and he for me.

202

We had a lovely luncheon with the family. My face was beginning to ache from all the smiling. I could hardly eat from all the excitement of the day. I grew weary quickly, making me glad Mother thought a close-private luncheon would be best. Toury met my gaze toward the end of the meal and gave me a sympathetic smile. Then she whispered something to Alex. He looked over to me and then to Toury and nodded. Next, he was standing up, clinking a glass to demand silence. People quieted down. Here we go. My brother and his long-winded inspiration talks.

"I know you are expecting one of my fine long speeches." He paused, and everyone laughed lightly. "But today is not my day. It belongs to my sister and my best friend. I cannot imagine anyone better suited for the other. To the Princess and Prince of Fyr."

He raised his glass, and there was a cheer in response. Then everyone drank. I took an obligatory sip of my very watered-down firespice whiskey, finding I could without any urge for more. I need no escape from this life of bliss and peace, but I know I am strong enough now, confident enough that in hard times I won't need it either.

The speech concluded the celebration, so after many goodbyes, we escaped to the king's room for just my family and the Cobalts to enjoy one another's company.

Stephen's mother started crying, so he joined her and my mother, throwing me a rolled-eye glance. I stood by the fire, enjoying the warmth of the flames.

"You look genuinely happy, Mary," Alex said. "I am pleased for you both." He pulled me in for a hug, and I squeezed him back hard. Alex is king and so grown up.

And now I feel that way too. "I am."

"I should've never questioned your choice."

"You are my brother, and Father was not around to. It was a just reaction back then, even if it ended up being wrong."

"I acknowledge that. He'd never enter into this marriage and muck it up. He knows I would torch him."

"Did he *know* know?" I hedged. Trust Alex to throw out a death threat condition upon his blessing of marriage.

"You damn well know it. I had to make sure he knew he had to leave his old lifestyle behind. This will be no court of mistresses."

I could not be mad at my protective brother. I wonder if he received any threats as he and I bestowed upon Stephen. "Toury wouldn't allow it."

"She and I are partners in everything. Infidelity shall be snubbed for both men and women."

I squeezed Alex's hands.

Not that I think Stephen would ever stray. I trust him. I married him; for life, he is mine. No one can change that. I gazed over at him to see him staring at me. He blushed. My, what thoughts was he having?

Toury bustled in, holding Rowland. Alex rushed away to take up the baby from his queen. The ever-exasperated nanny followed uselessly behind, trying to take the child, but Toury is used to earthly customs of raising children in almost every moment outside of duties. Alex has fallen into that pattern too. He has even brought the baby to guild meetings, much to the men's dismay. But soon another lord came with his child, and then another, and Alex had to call for the nanny to deal with all three in the meeting room. Times are changing. It feels right.

Seeing my brother doting over his son makes me want a child of my own. Our entire childhood was full of restraint, duty, and stripped of emotion. The curse made Alex solemn. These days, he has to hide a smile at official events. Every day is like those stolen moments with Mother again, but without being hidden.

After Alex cooed at Rowland like he had lost his mind, he handed the infant over to the nanny.

This "nightcap" tradition Alex carried over from our father has changed into something extraordinary. No politics, no reprimanding, no drinking—just family time. How he changed an entire kingdom so quickly is astounding. It makes me want to be a part of it, his dream. Alex immediately went to Toury, kissing her too passionately for our eyes. I turned away to see Stephen's heated stare on me.

I walked over to him, and while I walked, his eyes drank me in. What a heady feeling to know that the person looking at you loves you, even when they aren't saying it. When I reached him, he placed his hands on my hips and kissed me chastely. Ugh! Would it always be this way because my brother was around?

When his lips left mine, he pulled me closer to whisper, "I know what you're thinking, and it is true to a point, but in our quarters, Mary, I will not worry about courtly etiquette. Not in any way. I've seen you've done some reading. That will prepare you for tonight."

I couldn't breathe for a moment. He pulled away and chuckled at me. Tonight was the night: our wedding night.

He gave me a wry grin. "Under the couch is not a novel hiding spot for forbidden books."

My cheeks burned red, and he rubbed them with his thumbs. Of course, I had called Toury out once for that hiding spot, so now I got caught. I should've known better.

"Mary," he chided. "Never be embarrassed by anything we discuss. I'm glad you educated yourself."

"About that?"

He nodded and kissed me. "I'm reforming. Education for women is the key to equality." He was serious, losing our mood.

I wanted to leave him reeling. "Let me educate you about something, my darling."

He held me in his arms, gazing into my eyes. "What?"

"Tonight will begin a roughly two-decade challenge."

His brow wrinkled. "What kind of challenge?"

"Which royal couple will have the most children."

He was shocked for a moment, likely due to my candor. Then his lips quirked into a wicked grin. "I've told you a million times before, my lifemate, I'm up for a challenge."

"I know." I barely got the words out before he claimed my lips.

I write these lines as Lucy prepares me for bed. I am nervous about starting a marriage and life so young, but sometimes it is the fate that happens. Some wait longer for love, like Stephen's sister, whom I'm determined to help find her lifemate. I happened to meet mine and know he would be the one at six. A decade is hardly rushing into anything.

As I prepare to embark upon this journey, I've decided I also have to say that this is goodbye to you. My dear Wundor. I don't feel like I'll have anything else to write to you. I'm afraid I've outgrown journal writing. I will have far more responsibilities in the upcoming years, as part of my brother's kingdom, as a lifemate, a confidante of the queen, a daughter to my mother, and a mother myself—of many children according to the flames.

I want to thank you for being there for me all these years and will reread you down the years to see how much I've grown. You were my first friend. I'm finally getting better at that, making friends.

I named you Wundor because my brother handed me a mere journal, but you ended up being exactly what I had needed, the very definition of the old language word: a miracle. You helped me find myself, my confidence, and my happily ever after. True, you are just paper, but you are a reflection of my soul, a mirror into myself that helped me understand myself. Who knew writing was the path to figure oneself out? Funny thing that.

Thank you with all my heart,

Mary Elizabeth Sapphirian,
Her Royal Highness, Princess of Fyr,
Fulfiller of Her Dreams, Former Princess on the
Periphery Now Basking in Her Happily-Ever-After with
His Highness Prince Cobalt

❧ LYFT ❧

A CELESTIAL SPHERES NOVEL

COMING 2025

Bonus Material

Beyond exhausted, dripping in sweat, her body in agony, Toury lay back on the sheets in relief. She heard the cawing cries of her child and looked upon the healer holding up her first baby girl, Tourmaline. It was no surprise. Alex had spoiled the surprise of daughters for her; he had foreseen the gender of all their previous children and had insisted on the name. The second baby, who was still in her womb, would be Alexandra as she had insisted. During the ten years of peace after the Bladesung War, Alex's firebranding abilities had improved sans the curse and after Tobias Firebrand tutored him afresh. Alex could see enough of the future to assure her the rest of their lives would have few hardships and be long. In this moment of pain and exhaustion, she found comfort in knowing that.

The man in her thoughts was by her side, kissing her forehead and murmuring how well she was doing. These being babies number six and seven, she had foolishly thought it would get easier—it went quicker, but easy was not the word to describe having a child, let alone for her first time birthing twins.

The healer urged her to push.

There was no way she could do it again. "I'm too tired." Was the old woman insane? Toury wanted to shock her with the electrical-fire power that had never left her. She couldn't push.

"Give her a minute," Alex commanded the healer, then turned back to Toury. "This is what you need." Alex brought over a bundle, where a quiet baby blinked the gorgeous Sapphirians eyes at the harsh light of the world. Baby Tourmaline was small, not nearly robust as their boys had been, but then again, they hadn't had to share a womb. Instantly, like every time prior, she fell in love. A daughter.

She nodded to Alex that she was ready, not that her body would let her wait any longer anyway.

Alex handed their daughter to a healer as Toury's growled in preparation to bring Alexandra into the world.

The second birth was much quicker, and the child much louder. As soon as her mouth was cleared, she screamed as if insulted they'd taken her from her comfy home. Toury didn't even look; exhausted, she just lay there. Alex brought the baby over to her. Despite trying to swaddle her, Alexandra freed her arm and was flailing and screaming. Something in Alex's gaze was guarded. The healer glanced over his shoulder at the baby, and her eyes went wide. She could not withhold her gasp. Toury tried to push up using her hands, for her stomach muscles were incapable of working. Another healer pushed her shoulders back down. Ugh, afterbirth ensued.

Alex came to her side, shushing Alexandra, who was starting to calm.

"Alex?" Toury gripped his hand.

His eyes were steady on her. An older healer gave Alex a contemptuous glower as she passed by with soiled towels. They did not approve of his being in the birthing room, another old-fashioned custom Alex had destroyed for their first child and each one that followed.

"What is wrong with my baby?"

Alex cringed. "Don't say 'wrong,' my love, please. She's just...different."

"How?" Toury asked, exasperated. Why hadn't he warned her? Surely, he would've foreseen something going wrong. Was Alexandra missing a limb? A cleft palate? Something a scan on Earth would've seen to prepare her?

Alex gazed upon the baby girl with such admiration, he had to tear his eyes away from his daughter's face to place her into Toury's arms.

Toury stared down at her daughter and smiled. As the baby's unfocused eyes met hers for a brief second, she saw what was amiss right away. Alexandra's eyes were gray. A steely Hematite gray and nothing that could pass for the deep, sparkling Sapphirian blue. She didn't need to check the baby over for any other "imperfections." Eye color in Fyr was everything.

Alex picked up Tourmaline and sat in a chair by the bed, switching his gaze between his daughters, eyes full of pride. Toury felt betrayed. He had always known but did not care. He should have warned her.

"Her eyes, people will..." Toury couldn't say it aloud. In Fyr, eyes were the path to parentage. Sapphirians had dominant eye colors throughout most of history when it came to most children, particularly those born in royal marriages.

"The people will accept her. She cannot be...baseborn..." Alex said the word hesitantly, "with a twin that is clearly Sapphirian. When her fire powers develop and her features take after me, they will drop it—for the most part."

"For the most part?" Toury was growing concerned. To be accused of adultery, her child ostracized for having the "wrong" eye color.

"Yes and no."

Toury glared at him, but a squawk from her daughter made her turn back to the innocence in her arms. Those gray eyes were unexpected and meant a hard future for Alexandra would ensue, but they were beautiful eyes; they were Toury's. Five strapping sons who looked in various ways like their parents—all had Alex's eyes. This girl had hers, a blessing and a curse. Their first child, Rowland, was identical to Alex at that age, according to his doting dowager grandmother. Aschen, named after Toury's father, was Toury's little clone with Sapphirian eyes, while the next, David, was like a perfect blend of Toury and Alex. Alastair, named after Captain Agate, who had fallen in the Battle of Bladesung, took more after Mary and the queen dowager, with lighter coloring. While the youngest, Toby, after Alex's father-figure Tobias, was too young to determine yet. With still light hair, the toddler blended in well with his fair-haired cousins—four cousins so far with a fifth on the way.

But this girl in Toury's arms was special. "What will happen to her?"

Alex sighed. "The flames can only tell me what will happen on Fyr, and our little princess here will make her own mark on another sphere—like her Bladesung mother—but I'm not sure which one."

Toury clutched the baby closer. "You'll send her away?"

"No, my love, never." His face was pained for her even suggesting it. "I will allow her to create her own destiny away from a world that won't accept her, away from a kingdom with edicts that demand I leave her out of the line of succession. Toury," he rushed out for he saw she had been about to interrupt him. "She will be loved by her family, ever so loved and doted upon."

WUNDOR

He touched the baby's head, and Toury realized he was right. Things might be different for her, and the paths of some of their children might lead them away from home, but they would all be loved. Her daughter would be the heroine of her own tale one day, just like her mother, and Alexandra would save the hero to boot.

NOTE FROM MARY

Anyone suffering from addiction, such as ones portrayed
in my journal, please seek help. Talk to someone.

If no one is available, call the SAMHSA Helpline at
1-800-662-HELP (4357)

or

text the SAMHSA at
435748 (HELP4U).

Never give up hope.

Acknowledgments

Foremost, I want to thank my readers and Celestial Spheres fans. You loving my trilogy and asking for more is why I was determined to tell Mary's side of the story, and ideas sprouted to continue the series two more books with Sapphirian descendants and to share with you the other spheres. I never knew how much I would love that part of the author process: meeting or hearing from you.

Thank you Authors 4 Authors Publishing for taking a chance on *Fyr*'s pitch and trusting me to come on board as a member. Particularly, thanks to Becky and Brandi for the edits; I'm always amazed at how much you find.

Most of all, thanks to my friends and family for their unyielding support. Major shout out to my Mom—the best Alpha reader out there—and Graves for doing so much for us so I can live a dual-career life and still be a good mom and wife. Without you, this household would be in tatters. Thanks to my son "brah" who has overcome so many obstacles to be self-sufficient and for having your own hyperfocus sessions that let us simultaneously hang out together and yet slay a ton of our tasks.

ABOUT THE AUTHOR

LISA BORNE GRAVES

Lisa Borne Graves is a YA author, English Lecturer, wife, and supermom of one wild child. Originally from the Philadelphia area, she relocated to the Deep South and found her true place of inspiration. Her love for all literature led her to branch out from the academic arena to spin her own tales. Lisa has a voracious appetite for books, British television, and pizza. Her inability to sit still makes her enjoy life to its fullest, and she can be found at the beach, pool, or on some crazy adventure.

Follow her online:

lisabornegraves.com
Twitter: @lisabornegraves
Facebook: @lisabornegravesauthor
Instagram: @lisabornegraves

AUTHORS 4 AUTHORS PUBLISHING

A publishing company for authors, run by authors, blending the best of traditional and independent publishing

We specialize in speculative fiction: science fiction, fantasy, paranormal, and romance. Get lost in another world!

Check out our collection at https://books2read.com/rl/a4a or visit Authors4AuthorsPublishing.com/books

For updates, scan the QR code or visit our website to join our semi-monthly newsletter!

Want more romantic fantasy? We recommend:

KISS OF TREASON
by Brandi Spencer

Two forbidden lovers share the rare gift to heal others with a kiss—but at a cost. Odelia's life has been a lie. When the queen tries to remove her from the palace, Odelia uncovers the truth. Now she must decide whether to forsake her people or embrace a destiny that would pit her against the current heir to the throne...her best friend. Though her only hope of avoiding a civil war lies in winning his heart, revealing her secrets too soon could cost both their lives. And a kiss might not be strong enough to save them...

books2read.com/kisstreason

www.ingramcontent.com/pod-product-compliance
Lightning Source LLC
Chambersburg PA
CBHW010516100726
47903CB00009B/2771